THE
WAY YOU
BURN

THE
WAY YOU
BURN

A NOVEL

CHRISTINE MEADE

She Writes Press, a BookSparks imprint
A Division of SparkPointStudio, LLC.

Published 2020
Printed in the United States of America

ISBN: 978-1-63152-691-6 pbk
ISBN: 978-1-63152-692-3 ebk
Library of Congress Control Number: 2019913582

For information, address:
She Writes Press
1569 Solano Ave #546
Berkeley, CA 94707

She Writes Press is a division of SparkPoint Studio, LLC.

CHAPTER 1

E rratic orange light licked across the black pond. That was the first thing I noticed. Flickering water striders moving over the surface of the water. But if I care about remembering that night accurately, which is my intention here, the first thing had to have been the smell. The unmistakable scent of wood burn in the air differed from a summer bonfire. This burn went deeper. It cut through centuries-old framework and foundations. It tore through the beams and rot of the long-buried secrets my family tried to keep protected between the four walls of my cabin.

When I approached the land, driving the truck slow through the dark, the red wine from my twenty-fifth birthday dinner dulling my thoughts, the windows rolled down even though the night air lay heavy and sharp with the pull toward winter, I must have been able to hear the devastation. The steady hiss punctuated by pops of wood splintering. And wasn't it strange that Vincent, the dog *you* got me, who should have been asleep in the cabin, paced at the end of the drive, circling and whimpering, watching our home succumb to the heat?

In a sudden burst of effort, flames bit a hole through the roof of my cabin and shot up toward the night sky, reaching like a tentative hand testing the direction of the wind. The voices of the ghosts inside the cabin screamed as something buckled. The wood-burning stove's black smokestack remained gallant and sturdy as the compromised exterior simmered around it. It seemed like hours before my senses collected and rearranged themselves in an order that made sense.

My cabin was burning.

I left the truck door hanging open, ran to the pond, and grabbed the bucket out of the canoe. I filled it with the cold water and sloshed its contents toward the flames rising from the corners of the porch. Up close, the hot rage of the fire was shocking. I tripped, backing away from it with a gasp. Thick smoke choked me. *David, do something*, I imagined my grandfather's voice demanding. I yelled something—maybe for help, maybe for the fire to stop. But who could hear me out in those New Hampshire woods? Fire is an unwavering thing. But you already know this.

I remembered the hose just as the back window shattered. A siren whined in the distance. I cranked on the water full blast and aimed the stream at the flames, hoping I could save something. That despite everything that had happened that year, there was something worth saving. But the fire told me otherwise.

This was your way of cleansing the palate of what once was. That much I understood. This was your good-bye.

Before I met you, I was twenty-three, sure of the world and my place in it, and bored. You were this mystery, a question, an unmarked box I had to open because whatever was inside, I had to see for myself. And so began the year of opening and uncovering the things I didn't know about myself, you, or my family.

I wanted to blame you for all of it—but I couldn't, could I? Because too much was owed. So, instead, I wrote this in an attempt to understand.

Hope, this is my good-bye.

CHAPTER 2

You ran by me with your red hair waving like a fire drill. It was the summer before I turned twenty-four—August, and hot. You wore a dusty pink dress with white polka dots. A thrift-store something. It would be one of the few times in the two falls I loved you through that I would see you without a scarf.

I stared after you for almost two blocks. You appeared so unselfconscious—a rarity for women in their twenties—despite those scars.

I was still at my old job at the local Boston news station. I wrote copy for small news stories, got paid a low hourly salary, and rode around the city in a sweltering van with the camera guy who smelled like salami and the broadcast journalist who went through cans of hairspray by the day. We were covering the opening of a new restaurant on Newbury Street by some big, famous chef.

The camera guy saw you, too, but not in the way I had.

Women with shiny, straight hair and large purses teetered past us in high heels. Small groups in business-casual attire huddled around outdoor metal tables, sipping lemon water and dipping forks into their Nicoise salads. It was the first nice day of the week after a relentless string of heavy thunderstorms, so everyone in the city with legs was out walking. The red Duck Tour buses quacked down Boston's narrow streets as tourists peered over the edge at the cobblestone sidewalks below.

I spent another thirty minutes talking to diners and the manager at this new restaurant, all the while scanning for that shock of red hair. The crowds started streaming in for that night's game at Fenway. Red Sox hats dotted the sidewalk and a line snaked out the doors at J.P. Licks's ice cream shop. Customers emerged smiling, slurping from cones wrapped in soggy napkins.

"What are you guys filming?"

When I looked up, my mouth opened to speak but only air filled the space where words might have been. The skin on your left cheek and down your neck wrung itself out into twisted pink scars. It would be months before I ever got up the courage to ask you about them. It will be a lifetime before I'll be able to forget your answer.

Even that first day, you surprised me in a million ways. That you came back. That you must have noticed me, too, despite the truth that I was so average back then, before you . . . or maybe that was it: maybe I looked reliable even from a distant glimpse. Like someone you could lean on for balance.

"It's a news thing about this restaurant opening," I finally said. You never seemed to mind silence.

"Can we get a shot of you going by again?" asked our cameraman.

"Sure, I guess so. What do I have to do?"

"How about what you were doing before?" I asked.

"What do you mean?"

"Running down the sidewalk, around everyone, with your dress flaring out behind you."

You shrugged. "I suppose. I was late for this engagement party thing and then as soon as they made the announcement, I skipped out of there. *So* stuffy." You rolled your eyes and I laughed, overwhelmed by what I then mistook as an enviable, carefree spontaneity.

After we got the shot, emboldened by the fact you were still there, still watching me, your body twisting slightly side to side as you smiled like a much younger girl, waiting for something more, I asked for your number.

You bent at the waist and leaned in toward me. For a shocked moment, I thought you might kiss me then, right there on the sidewalk, with the cameraman pretending not to be watching us over his shoulder. Instead, you whispered your number into my ear. "Better not forget," you said.

I still haven't.

Later, we watched that footage of you back in the studio—something I did a lot, long after the restaurant and its famous chef were old news—and everyone in the room's eyes softened and narrowed with focus as they tried to remember a time when they had been like that. Been that light.

CHAPTER 3

punched the numbers into my cell phone and waited for something else to happen, something beyond me to push the call into motion. The ceiling fan I kept going year-round whirred overhead. I decided to call because it was a bolder, more direct approach than texting. Fitting for this type of girl, I thought, back when I thought you might fit into a *type*.

I'd planned to call you the night we met, but I'd decided to wait. I didn't want to appear too eager. So I'd waited two days, and then three. Now I was a week out, and this was my last chance. A day longer, and the window would be closed. I would be forgotten, relegated in your mind as just some guy you'd met once. I could be any other twenty-three-year-old, five-foot-eleven male with brown hair and a general interest in outdoor activities.

"Bro, you coming with us? Get off your ass!" Mark's loud holler carried up the stairs.

Mark and I grew up together. We met our other two roommates freshman year of college at the outdoors group's first meeting. I was the only one to continue beyond that first meeting and attend the events they organized—ski trips at the school's chalet in Maine, group day hikes through New Hampshire's White Mountains. Mark complained that the girls in the outdoors group didn't shave their armpits, and the other guys were too lazy to wake up before noon on Saturday mornings to ski.

That morning, my roommates were going to brunch—the usual boozy Saturday-morning ritual in Allston, consisting of bloodies and burnt home fries and making plans for later that night.

I pressed call without pausing to think.

"Hello?"

You had to repeat yourself a few times. That red hair. That pink dress.

"Hi, um, it's me. David. I got your number from you. We met last week. Well, I was just calling to say hey and to see if you wanted to hang out sometime."

I hated myself for the slight tremor clinging to the end of my sentences. For sounding like a middle-school student. For Christ's sake, I had called girls before. Met them at bars or on dating apps and brought them to dinner or noisy parties or home to my bed. But the pull of this felt different.

There was something like a sigh on the other end of the line.

"Hello?" I tried again, a little softer.

"I'm here!" You laughed. "David with the sweet eyes. And yes, I want to hang out sometime. I was wondering if you would call."

"Oh, really? Okay. Great. Let me think of someplace—"

"What place?"

"I thought we could go to that new Thai restaurant that just opened up on—"

"Oh, no, that's not the deal."

"What deal?" I kicked the rumpled sheets at the end of my bed to the floor and propped another pillow behind my head.

Mark appeared in the doorway. *You coming?* he mouthed. I shook my head no, pointing to the phone in my hand. He picked up a flip-flop from the floor and hurled it in my direction. I dodged it, tossed it off the bed, and turned my attention back to you.

"The deal! The deal that says you invited me to hang out, so I get to pick the spot."

"Where do you live?"

"In Cambridge. But I've got a thing for first dates. So I'm going to open the phone book, flip to a page, point to an address, and that's where we'll go on our first date."

"You own a phone book? I didn't know they even still made those."

"I keep them on hand for this very reason. Besides, you can bring me to any Thai restaurant in the entire state any day of the year, but, David, let me ask you something: Have you ever been to"—I heard a shuffling of pages—"185 Oakdale Street in Cambridge, Massachusetts? Because I sure haven't. And I think it'd probably make a fabulous location for our first date."

"And what then? We just show up at this person's house?"

"Just pick me up tomorrow night at six. I'll text you my address. We'll take it from there."

After we said good-bye I stared at the cell phone in my hand. I shouldn't have called. I didn't know anything about you. Your last name. Your age. Even now, I still wonder if I ever really knew you. There was so much history that lived below the surface that I was too naïve back then to prod.

Regardless, I had to see you again. There was a hook hanging up inside me somewhere, waiting to carry your coat.

CHAPTER 4

We sat in my truck outside of 185 Oakdale Street in Cambridge, Massachusetts. Black shutters hung against dingy green vinyl siding. The house was dark. Early evening sun shone down on one of those chipped bathtub Mary statues—the Virgin Mary shadowed by a ceramic concave of blue—in the front yard, a relic from the droves of Irish Catholics who flooded the nearby towns a few generations back.

Beside me, you radiated heat, although we didn't touch. Not yet. Do you remember that? The feeling of sitting so close for the first time? I was very conscious of my hand placement—limp on the gearshift, waiting for you to say or do something. You wore your red hair piled on top of your head and that yellow scarf high around your neck, covering the scars that had been so flagrantly visible the first time we met.

Your green eyes, light and shiny, focused on something out the windshield. I glanced up at the house once more. Anxiety nipped at my ribs. I waited for someone to ask us what we were doing, to demand I move the truck before they called the police, but the street remained quiet except for our breathing. I wished we were in a dim dive bar, a beer in my hand, where I could relax a little and things wouldn't be so exposed.

You wore tiny silver rings on your fingers—one with a waning moon, another with a small oval of turquoise. I thought about reaching out and touching them, but I didn't.

"Now what?" I asked.

A small smile lifted the corners of your mouth and you turned to face me. "My mom and I used to play this free-association game all the time when I was little. So, what does the number 185 make you think of?"

"Um, let's see . . . Just past half the number of days in a year?"

"So, what were you doing about six months ago?"

I tried to think back. I couldn't remember anything before this moment. The warmth of the truck's interior, your faint vanilla smell, the pressing vibrancy of your red hair. And then I remembered. "Actually, my grandfather passed away about six months ago," I said, and amended, "Sorry, that was kind of depressing." I fidgeted, shifting on the cracked leather seat. This couldn't be where you meant to take this.

"No, that's honest. I'd rather we be real, David, than just *nice*. I'm sorry to hear about your grandfather."

"What were you doing six months ago?"

"I started my new job at the hospital."

"That's awesome. What do you do there?"

"Nursing assistant. Were you close with your grandfather?"

"Um . . . not by choice. My parents sort of forced my brother and me into these monthly visits with him in New Hampshire."

You laughed and the tension eased through my jaw. Your cheeks were pink and you wore a glossy lipstick. You reached up to touch my hair and—surprised by the intimacy of the gesture, almost maternal—I sat perfectly still.

"There's just something so innocent about you," you said, "so clean. I like it."

"Thanks?" I said. "I do try to shower regularly."

A dumb joke. You smiled, watching my eyes.

"Okay, next question: If you could have any superpower, what would it be?"

I closed my eyes to think, allowing myself to relax into the moment a bit more. "Well, if you had asked me at seven, it probably would have been Spiderman-related, but now . . . maybe my superpower would be great knowing. I could touch a tree and see everything that tree had experienced."

"That's a good one. I was going to judge you if you said x-ray vision."

"Give me a little more credit," I said. "And you?"

You turned to face me and smiled a little. "To be a maker. To be able to make anything in the world. Including people."

I stared at you for a beat. "Isn't that something you can technically already do?"

"Exactly. I think the superpowers we really want are actually the ones we already have, making their way up from inside."

"Interesting," I said, but I hoped that wasn't your way of saying you wanted kids soon. I was too young for that kind of commitment.

"I read that you can tell if someone is right for you after answering twenty specific questions."

"What number are we on?"

"I can't remember. But I have another one. What do you want most from your life?"

I paused. This was more difficult than any job interview I had ever been on. I wasn't sure how specific to be. I had a good family and a job and I was sitting in my truck with this interesting, beautiful girl. "I don't know. To be happy?"

You didn't smile this time; you pressed your lips together and nodded, as if seriously considering my response.

"What do you want?"

You turned to me again and smiled, but your eyes moved beyond me, out the window and to that street in Cambridge. "To be understood. To be truly seen."

I had no understanding then of how deep that longing pitted you, how much it tormented and transformed you. If only you had explained everything to me in the beginning, on that first date, in my truck on that street in Cambridge. But maybe that wouldn't have worked. Maybe if you had told me, we wouldn't have gone through anything together. I would have been too afraid to continue with whatever it was we had started.

"Do you believe in God?" I blurted to change the topic.

"Only when it suits me." You smiled and shifted slightly closer to me on the seat.

"Which is when?"

You leaned closer. "When I meet people I feel like I was meant to know. Even for a moment. Even for a single day. Even in front of a stranger's house on Oakdale Street in Cambridge, Massachusetts." You closed the space between us by pressing your small, wet mouth to mine.

CHAPTER 5

We spent the extra few dollars to rent an apple-picking arm. I would have been embarrassed to ask for one myself, but you were impossibly short in a way I found impossibly sexy. It was one of our early dates. So early I was still hyper-aware of my body in relation to yours—my leg touching yours in the grass, my arm holding your waist as you stepped on branches to reach the reddest, juiciest picks. I just wanted to be close to you. Touching. Your hair, that warm vanilla smell again.

I hadn't been apple picking since I was a kid, but with you it turned into this textured, sensory experiment. The cinnamon spice of homemade cider donuts wafted from the farm down into the orchards. Soft steam rose from the Styrofoam cups of hot cider in our hands. The early fall sun landed on the apple trees in a way that made them tempting. Parents shepherded small children through the petting zoo area, the ice cream stand, and the pumpkin patch.

"Do you see those? Up there?" You squinted, one hand shielding your eyes, as you gazed at the top of a particularly tall Macintosh tree.

"Mm-hmm," I said. "Macintosh is your favorite, right?"

"They are. My mom has some secret pie recipe she says you have to use Macintosh for. I could live off that pie."

Our bucket was nearly full. We slowed down and rubbed the dusty skins on the hems of our shirts before cracking into the bright white interior of the fruit.

"We've got a good amount already." I wanted to be lying together in the grass and brushing cinnamon off your lips.

You stepped up to the trunk and disappeared into the tree, scuttling up the branches, lithe and fearless. I figured you must be an athlete—a dancer, maybe, or a gymnast. You were good at most things you aimed your intensity on. You made it to the top and perched on a flimsy-looking branch. Your head poked above the leaves.

"Hey, careful up there," I said, frowning. "I don't think that branch is strong enough to stand on."

You angled your face to the sun and stood. Your brown loafers—so small!—balanced on the branch. You wobbled and stretched your arms out like wings. You had forgotten the apples. It was the tallest tree in the orchard.

I stepped in closer, my eyes trained, my arms ready.

"Do you ever have those flying dreams?"

"I can't remember," I said.

"Dare me to jump?" Your lips pulled back until the gums above your teeth showed. You liked this. I could tell. The making-me-nervous part. It was almost uncanny how you sniffed it out in me—my aversion to risk-taking.

"Throw me those apples and then come down."

"What a romantic way to go," you said, your eyes shut. "Taking a fall from an apple tree."

"Romantic? There's nothing romantic about a fractured tibia. Why don't you—"

But you were already in the air. A bright, airborne thing. A meteor. You landed with a thud in the matted grass and fell back on a scattering of old apples that lay in the dirt, half-eaten by worms.

I ran to you, expecting tears, a desperate clutch of an ankle. Your hair spilled over your face. I brushed it away, saying your name.

You sat up. Your face twisted in anguish. "It's not that easy to break when you're invincible." A bubble of a laugh erupted from you. Not anguish, but laughter.

My chest heaved, my adrenaline spiked. "You're not invincible. Jesus Christ."

"But your face, David," you said, running your thumb along my jawline. "It was worth it."

Later that night at my apartment, I brushed my lips against the thicker skin of your scars. I would pour myself into you. Open up and fill in the parts that had been gutted or burned away. I wanted to push my lips in between the ridges and tangles of rope that wound around your neck and chest and cheek. Your eyelids fluttered as if shooing away a fly. As if they refused to block out all the light for a moment. As if you couldn't let yourself be defenseless by feeling good. Not even for a moment.

My fingers lingered in the hair by your ears, but I couldn't shake the need to see it—all of you—as I had the first time on that summer street. I started to unravel the soft fabric of the mustard-colored scarf, but you grabbed my hand to stop me.

"Will you tell me?" I asked. "What happened?"

"It was an accident," you said, "when I was young." You stood, leaving me sitting on the living room floor. A few seconds later, I heard the tap turn on. You returned and sat on the couch, sipping from a water glass without looking at me, just staring through the window to the street.

CHAPTER 6

My mother answered the door. "Honey!" she said. "Happy birthday! You brought a friend! Wonderful!" She ushered us inside. My brother was showing my dad something on his iPad. My dad stared at the iPad as if my brother held an alien's heart. When they gazed up, their eyebrows lifted in simultaneous amusement and interest.

"It's so lovely to meet you." My mother pulled you into an embrace and you pressed against her in a slack-armed hug. "Dinner's just about ready. Go relax, and I'll have it on the table in ten."

She vanished into the kitchen and I introduced you to the rest of the family.

"Who got me the iPad?" I asked

"You're way too old for gifts," said my dad.

"Is anyone going to help your mom?" you whispered to me.

I shrugged. "She likes cooking. Don't worry about it."

The house smelled great: roasted meat and a sweetness hinting of the dessert to come. My mother cooked often, and well. *It's my meditation*, she would say, standing over the cutting board with a pile of vegetables before her. But really, it was a necessity. If she didn't cook, the rest of her family wouldn't eat. My father always worked extra hard to counteract my mother's constant motion by taking long naps in his chair and bringing home grease-stained bags of fast food when it was his turn to "cook." Mom didn't do well just sitting. Dad, however, had perfected it.

My mother always made a fuss over birthdays during our childhood. Handwritten invitations and elaborate homemade cakes with edible soccer balls. Her birthday themes were innovative, elaborate—Robinson Crusoe, Pirates of the Caribbean, Jurassic Park. There were scavenger hunts and obstacle courses. I couldn't help but feel a bit like we'd disappointed her by growing up. I liked that she liked the special occasions so much—the details, the fringe, the colors, the things that the rest of us would never have noticed.

I showed you my old bedroom, the one Taylor and I used to share before I left for college. Faded posters of athletes and some old drawings from my graphic-novel phase were still thumbtacked above my desk.

"You drew this?" you asked. "You should have gone to art school."

Taylor poked his head into the room. "Can you imagine if Dave had gone to art school? He's already too emo as it is." A smile teased his lips. "Dinner's ready."

Taylor was counting on this dinner going as awkwardly as possible. Although we'd always had friends in and out of the house growing up, we'd never brought romantic interests home. Taylor had announced he was gay during one similar such family dinner when he was in middle school, but he had yet to introduce us to anyone special. Neither had I, up until that night.

We ate pork chops with roasted vegetables and homemade applesauce around the dining room table on the leaf-covered placemats my mother had pulled out of her autumnal decorations box. My parents' house was always cold; I scooted my chair closer to yours. My family watched me to see how I acted with this woman I'd met only a month or so earlier.

"Red or white?" my mom asked, a bottle in each of her hands, ready to pour.

You shook your head. "No, thanks, I'm fine. I don't drink."

I wanted them to hear you laugh and watch the expressions on their face move to a place of charmed amusement when you spoke about the things you loved—watching people dance, collecting things from nature to turn into art, and poetry that made you cry. Instead, you kept your head down and your scarf up, speaking into the soft material in a quiet, mumbled voice. *You know them*, I wanted to whisper. If you knew me, you knew them.

"So a bit of news, David," said Dad, interrupting a long, awkward silence with a mouthful of half-masticated pork. I caught the look that passed between my parents. "Your grandfather left you the rotting cabin in New Hampshire. So, happy birthday."

I laughed with surprise, coughing around my potatoes. I glanced around to catch my family members' eyes. They had known about this for a while, clearly.

"Seriously? Grandpa's shack?"

"Hey, that 'shack' is the house I grew up in. He knew you loved the place." My father's mouth squeezed into his trademark, thin-lipped smirk. Taylor and I used to dread going up to the cabin, despite the promise of a weekend fishing on the pond, because Grandpa was scary. Six foot four with a long beard and a hard-set grimace.

I can still picture Taylor in his footie pajamas, crying, begging our parents not to make us visit Grandpa without them. He ordered us to carry rocks to build up the sides of the fire pit, collect sticks for kindling, and wash our pale, freezing bodies in icy, spitting showers. And he didn't even have television! Visiting him was a kind of hell we coddled boys felt far too young to be subjected to.

"Isn't that sweet of him?" asked my mother. She fiddled with the arrangement of her bangs, picked up the cloth napkin on her lap, and pressed it to her lips as she looked from my father to me.

"But Grandpa didn't even like me," I said. "Why would he leave me the house?" I imagined his wingtip ears and the feathery flap of hair across the dome of his head that opened like an angry mouth when a gust of wind shot across the pond. His hands of stone were never clean and he referred to my brother and me as "the lazy boys" no matter how much effort we put into casting the line, raking his lawn, or helping him work on his old truck.

"Because your brother is too young to get it," said Dad, his eyes on his plate. "And Lord knows he never liked me."

"Oh, Frank, that's not true," said my mother.

Dad cut another huge chunk of pork, shuttled it into his mouth, and, chewing loudly, pointed his fork in your direction. "I couldn't wait to get out of those woods. You wouldn't believe how stifling an open forest can be until you live in one. Turned eighteen and never looked back. But my father thought a son should stay close to help support the family."

"You're lucky you had a father," you said. Your pupils looked small and tight.

Taylor and I exchanged glances. A pause settled. My dad chewed some more.

"Don't I get anything?" asked Taylor, breaking the silence. "He made me massage his feet once when they were turning purple from the snow. I think I still have PTSD. I at least deserve some sort of cash inheritance."

"He left you his collection of tools. He always was a very talented carpenter," said Mom.

"Now you can become the handyman you always dreamed of being," I said to Taylor. "And you can start by helping me fix up my new cabin."

Taylor leaned back in his chair, crossing his arms over his chest. "Imagine you living up there, driving a tractor and raising chickens. Maybe knock out a few teeth? You do look your best in flannel."

"I do, don't I?" I asked.

"Boys," said my mother, as she had done for two decades.

Taylor still lived at home; he'd been largely unemployed since graduating the previous May with a mountain of debt. I was the responsible one: I paid for my own room in a shared apartment in Allston and had just started a new job making fairly decent money as an incredibly boring technical writer.

"It's not like David's going to live up there," said Mom. "It could be like a fun weekend-getaway cabin."

I was offended. "Why couldn't I live up there? Grandpa obviously thought I could."

"You've been saving to buy a condo in Boston since you were, like, ten. You're not moving to New Hampshire. It's not in your five-year plan," said Taylor.

Your eyebrows hitched upward. It was the first you'd heard of my five-year plan.

"Actually, I could probably save a lot more money living up there. Aside from property taxes, I wouldn't be paying rent."

"Honey, don't be ridiculous. What about your job? Or your friends?" My mother looked—a bit desperately—to you for support. "He's a writer. He needs to be near the city. Near where the jobs and newspapers are." She addressed the table as if I weren't a part of the discussion.

"Newspapers barely exist, and I'm not even working as a journalist anymore."

My mom, leaning in toward you, woman-to-woman, ignored me. "I always knew David would end up being an artist or something. Always so observant, those big brown eyes, always watching. Even as a baby. I knew he'd see things and would have stories to tell. I wanted to work for a newspaper myself, you know, even though they tried to get all us girls to be either nurses or teachers. Except I got pregnant with David, and, well, luckily Frank made enough in sales at the time that we could get by with just the one salary."

"I'm not telling stories, Mom. It's technical writing. Plus, most of the people in my office already telecommute. We can work from anywhere. I don't know," I said, working it through in my mind as I spoke. "It might be kind of cool. Something different."

"Dad also owned a few books on rabbits, I think. Taylor, you can have those too. Hunting books and a few fictionalized dramas or something," said my father, trying to pull a strand of something out from between his molars.

"Do you mean John Updike?" Your plate was empty, aside from a few light swirls of potatoes and applesauce. The rest of us had been too busy ribbing each other to have taken more than a few bites. You blushed under our gaze; the top of your cheek—the side without scarring—turned rosy as you burrowed deeper into your scarf.

"Yes, Updike," I said. But my mind had already moved on, trying to recall the sound of the wind moving through those New Hampshire trees. The young maples swaying as dusk settled. The creak of the cabin door banging shut against its frame. The tiny pricks of raindrops on the calm pond at the start of a storm. I thought of my brother and me trying to build tree houses to play

Robinson Crusoe, imagining being entirely on our own—feeding and fending for ourselves.

I would do it. Try living up there. Even if for just a year. An experiment of sorts, to experience a dialed-back way of life—slow and syrupy in its lack of distractions.

I squeezed your shoulder, excited now by the possibility of change, but you didn't meet my eyes.

CHAPTER 7

Back then you lived with your mother in an apartment in Cambridge. I wonder if you still live with her or if you share a warm, cramped apartment with roommates. Home-cooked meals followed by wine and romantic comedies in your small living room. Or maybe you're living with a new boyfriend now. The walls bare. You press against him at night underneath the rumpled sheet that covers the mattress on the floor. You don't leave room for the light to get in between the two of you.

The entire apartment you shared with your mom was painted beige or tan or eggshell. I wondered if it was your mother's attempt to make you stand out even more. Your dad left when you were little and your mom had a rotating door of boyfriends. She never wanted to marry, you said. Never wanted to be someone else's property. I wondered if you felt the same.

Your red hair and pink skin blazed against the neutrals. A single photo of you as a child sat on an end table in the living room. A purple leotard with gold sequins, your skinny arms held above your head in a triumphant and graceful finish. So I was right—you had been a gymnast. No other pictures decorated the walls, shelves, or credenza. The clean lines and furniture all gave the appearance that neither of you intended to be there long. Maybe you both knew the place was merely an intermission, a pause before you settled deeper into someone else's life.

After your skin graft surgery—another in a long line—you lay on the couch in your living room, a cup of chocolate pudding resting on a coaster on the coffee table. I positioned myself on the edge of the couch where your stomach curved in.

"Do you feel okay?" I asked the stupidest questions during critical moments.

You turned your head slowly, your green eyes soft. "This is just what it feels like."

"Do you get scared?"

"I'm used to it." You pulled the knit blanket with waves of bright greens, purples, and yellows up to your chin. This time, they had taken skin from your thigh and moved it to your left cheek by your ear. Heavy white bandages cradled your chin in a place where I would have liked to place my own hand. Without thinking, I moved to touch the gauzy badge. My fingers hovered. The pain medication coated your high child's voice in a thick syrup; your lids were weighed down by constant transformation. A face that never stayed the same.

Your mother kept the apartment cooking at a balmy eighty degrees. A burnt-toast smell lingered in the air—left over from a cooking endeavor long since abandoned—and I felt as if maybe I were burning, too.

How did you deal with it? Looking in the mirror and constantly watching the reflection change as you healed, as the skin tightened, as the scars moved? It took on a personality of its own, the one thing in the room everyone tried to but couldn't ignore. It bothered you; it had to. The stares. There was no way it couldn't.

Sometimes, later, when you were really down, you'd ask me how I could possibly love you—love a face like that. Throughout that year, especially after the accident, I never questioned my attraction, only the level to which I was losing myself to you.

Your mother shuffled out of the kitchen with a mug of tea in her hand and sat in the beige chair next to the couch. She had just returned from her night shift—two generations of nurses, living in an apartment sterile enough to be a hospital room. Despite having worked the overnight shift, she still looked beautiful. High cheekbones and a pretty mouth with painted red lips. Maybe she colored her hair dark to make herself appear younger, but it worked. She held an unlit cigarette between the manicured nails of one hand. She could have been your sister. Tall and thin, she wore a huge purple stone ring on her middle finger and an intimidating wash across her face. She didn't look like any mother I had ever known. She'd had you at twenty and wished to protect you from the world in a way that she had never been able to do.

She gave you a few pills to take and you swallowed, sipping the tea. She rested a hand on your forehead, the other around her mug as if hoping to transfer its warmth. She flicked her gaze to me but didn't say anything. I waited there for minutes, holding my breath, not moving and not sure where to look. Your breath slowed and eventually deepened with sleep.

I waited for . . . I wasn't sure what. I stood and paused for a minute, sure your mother would say something. Thank me. But she remained silent, her lips in a tight line. I backed up around the coffee table and moved toward the door. I glanced back once more at your face, obscured by blankets and gauze and warm palms.

You still hadn't told me how it happened.

CHAPTER 8

On the way to the cabin, we drove past cows at the neighboring farm. Tails eternally swishing away flies. The town consisted of a small brick schoolhouse and a white church where cars still lined up outside on Sundays. My heart raced like it did when I was a kid on the first day of school—giddy with that clear ring of new binders and beginnings.

When I took my first steps into the cabin as its owner, I imagined the familiar signs of my grandfather from when I was younger—his heavy canvas jacket hanging on the back of the door, the rifle leaning up against the window of the front porch, a few hardcover books stacked neatly on the small wooden table next to his bed. I remembered the old empty whiskey bottles huddled together in the plastic crate underneath the front porch, the smell of last night's modest campfire hanging in the air, and the squeak of the outhouse door when it slammed shut, swallowing me in total darkness. Back when the world moved on fast-forward.

The modest cabin had been built well over a hundred years earlier—an old logging shack that had served as my grandparents' home for decades. Supposedly, it had been dragged across the pond over the ice to this spot from its original location at some point. The structure stood precariously, elevated off the soft earth by cinderblocks and heavy wooden stumps. Fresh-looking fingerprints patched the dust of the small folding table on the screened-in porch. I wondered if my parents had been to the cabin before they gave me the keys. Or someone else? A hunter stumbling across what looked to be abandoned land? Kids looking for a place to drink or hook up?

We didn't touch, but your apprehension prickled my skin. "Do you think it's possible that this house knows you?" you asked.

I shrugged and flicked the lights on. As expected, nothing happened. If I was really doing this, really going to live here for a year, I would have to do the things needed to make this place a home—turn the electricity back on, get the water running, and hopefully install an internet connection. For now, it remained shut off and cold. I would have to pretend the sleeping bag in the trunk and the few candles I'd brought would be enough to keep us warm until my dad and I were able to fix things up. Bring the bits and signs of my own life within these walls.

You're going to live here.

You tasted the idea on the tip of your tongue. You liked to talk about us living in an elaborate tree house or on a ship that sailed around the world or in a bear cave tucked away on some distant mountain. When you spoke of these fantasies, you cradled your balled fist—tiny pale fingers—against your chin like they were the dreams you'd carried since childhood.

We would be an hour-and-a-half drive away from each other now. If you had said *no way*, you wouldn't visit, I probably would have left then—kicked the welcome mat my mother made me bring up away from the door and turned the key back over to my parents. But you didn't.

I took the fact that my grandfather had left me his land and cabin as a personal challenge. As his way of saying I could do this—could live on my own in these woods. Maybe some great wisdom came from such solitude and he'd trusted only me with that knowledge. It was the sort of thing I couldn't turn down.

Your face looked pale and serious in the cool air that moved quietly through the trees around us. You stepped up into the cabin, sat on the dirty plywood floor, and curled your knees into your chest. "You'll need a rug," you said, and added, "Do you think it's possible this place could be haunted?"

"By what? Or by whom?" I joined you on the ground, leaning up against the wall of the front porch—a place where I would spend so many mornings, staring out at the pond and worrying about you.

You swirled your plastic coffee cup a bit, lifting the bits of chocolate from the bottom, smiling, and staring into it like it contained future-telling tea leaves. "I'm not sure. Just this feeling that we're not alone."

"Well, if my grandfather's the ghost, he at least liked to keep to himself."

"What about your grandmother?"

The one picture of my grandmother that still sat on a shelf in the cabin was from right after she married my grandfather. She stood on a balcony with a smile, her dress being pulled to the left by some warm, distant wind. She had been beautiful. Dead before I was born. I shrugged and stood to push open one of the windows and gulp down that sharp start of October. I could live with these ghosts. They were family.

"Come with me," you said.

You stood and led me over to the couch. My breath caught when I realized what you were doing. You faced me but didn't say anything. Your fingers curled into the hem of my jeans and you tugged me closer. You rose up on the balls of your feet to kiss me. You undid my belt buckle and zipper and I threaded my fingers into your hair. We kissed and my pulse quickened, my body adjusting to meet yours.

We hadn't slept together yet, and I had yet to see all of you, pale and soft and laid out on the old couch in that dingy little cabin. I tried to slide your tight pants down over your hips, but you stepped away. "Take off your clothes," you said, but you didn't have to because I was already pulling my shirt over my head, kicking aside my jeans. I leaned in to kiss you and started to unravel your scarf, but you grabbed my wrist and shook your head *no*. You took off your pants but kept on the sweater, the scarf.

I reached underneath, running my hands over your small, warm breasts, and you let me. I lay on top of you, covering you on the couch, your skin so warm—hot, even. I couldn't wait another second. I didn't have a condom, but you said it was okay. I pushed inside you and stifled a gasp. *You're on birth control, right?* I realized I hadn't asked. I would later.

"Hit me," you said.

I stopped moving. Your forehead flushed pink and a deep red curl of bangs fell across your left eye. I took a second to catch my breath, willing myself not to think about the dust, or the mouse shit, or the countless nights my own grandfather's old heavy bones spent on this couch. My hands on either side of your head braced my weight. "Like a slap on the ass?" I asked.

You laughed, high and short, closing your eyes and turning your head away from me. "No. On the face. Really, do it. Don't worry, it won't hurt." You brushed the heavy curl away from your forehead.

I searched your face, imagining my hand reddening the scars, the pink twist in your lips. I couldn't do it.

"It won't hurt me, I promise. I won't even feel it." Desperation for something—for me?—widened your eyes.

Taking a breath, I reached out and lightly tapped your left cheek with my palm, the one with less scarring.

You laughed. "Not like that." Putting a hand on either side of my face, you pulled me down to kiss me. The cave of your mouth and the skin of your lips and cheeks against my own felt new each time. A firmness and, in spots, an artificial smoothness. A surprise that turned me on. I reached an arm around your neck and we moved together again.

The couch bumped against the back wall; the mounted deer head hanging above us shook precariously. The heat rose, and I pushed up your sweater. You pulled it back down and pressed your hands against my hairless chest. "Again," you said.

I paused and then brought my hand across your cheek, the one with the scars, harder than the first time. Your head tilted back. I took in a ragged breath. "I'm sorry," I said. "I can't do this. It just doesn't feel . . . right."

You sat up, pulling away from me with a sigh, and began to dress.

"I'm sorry," I tried once more.

"It's okay." You turned away from me, tugging your pants up and your sleeves down. "I think we should drive back tonight. It's too cold to sleep here."

You wouldn't meet my eyes, and I was left feeling like I'd done something wrong. I didn't understand then what you needed to be able to feel. That you needed me to cut through the layers you covered yourself with. I just didn't know how to do it.

CHAPTER 9

Taylor dropped a box in the middle of the kitchen floor. "What the hell are you going to do up here all day?"

"Move that into the bedroom," I said.

"The master suite?" he asked.

The cabin or shack or "shithole," as Taylor referred to it, consisted of one large main room with a dirty black potbelly stove in the corner. The musty couch and a double bed with a mattress so old it swung down like a hammock sat in opposite corners of the room. A small card table with two chairs was tucked underneath the front window. How had my dad ever lived in such a tiny space with both of his parents? No wonder he'd moved away as soon as possible.

You didn't come up for my move-in day because of work. I felt like I had forgotten something important without you there.

My mother and I swept out the mouse shit, and I set a few traps. The screens flapped free from the corners of the windows on the front porch. Something I needed to replace. I would eventually install real windows that slid up and locked. The culmination of my carpentry work as a kid had been a birdhouse made from three chunks of discarded two-by-fours, but I would become one of those guys who knew how to do things like put in windows or a new floor, which the porch also needed.

"Dad?"

I found him standing by the end of the pond, hands cupped over his eyes to block out the sun. He stared across the pond, his body rigid. I wondered if it was strange for him, being there. He'd spent hardly any time at the cabin since leaving at seventeen.

"Dad?" I repeated. "What is it?"

He turned quickly back to me, looking as if he was surprised to find anyone there beside him. "Oh, nothing. I thought . . . I just thought I saw something over there. A flash or reflection off of something. Probably an old aluminum rowboat one of the fishermen stashed in the woods."

I shrugged. My cabin was the only property on the lovely, secluded pond, save for the farm at the top of the hill. When Taylor and I were kids we used to shout our names across the water, listening for the thrill of an echo, until our grandfather told us to shut up.

"Aren't you going to be scared?" Mom asked. She sent the final roll of dirt and dust hurtling down the few front steps. "I know you guys stayed up here with Grandpa, but all by yourself?"

I sighed and pulled the hood of my green sweatshirt up and over my head. I had already explained that my boss didn't care where I was living, since I could work remotely. As long as I had an internet connection or a coffee shop nearby with one, I could pump out my boring-as-hell content, build campfires every night, and fish real early in the morning when the mist hung in the air and the cows at the top of the hill meandered down for their morning graze.

You and I could hole away for days.

It was a definite step up from my Allston apartment, where a sticky sheen of old beer coated the kitchen floor, trash piled up in the back hallway for weeks, and my roommate's video game machine-gun fire roared at all hours of the day.

"Grab that end," I said to Taylor.

We moved the old canoe from the porch to the pond's edge. A stray gray mouse scampered out from behind it and ran along the perimeter of the room. Mom shrieked, lifting her leg, and threw the broom in its direction. The broom hurtled wildly; when it landed, the end pierced the one remaining window screen, leaving it sagging against its frame.

Taylor and I broke into laughter. "Easy, Mom," we said in unison as her chest heaved with her hand clamped above her heart.

"Help me get this up," said Dad as the end of a box spring jutted through the door. I bent to help, getting a grip on the underside. I straightened and glanced behind me. Mom blocked my path with a hand still to her chest, but now her lips were screwed up and her eyes were beginning to tear.

"Mom," I said. "It's only a little mouse."

"It's not that." She pressed the heels of her hands against her eyes. "You're just going to be so alone. And so far away. You don't know what it's like to be a mother and to raise children and then to have them leave you."

"It's only an hour away. I'll be back and forth, constantly."

She straightened and shook her head with her eyes shut. "You're right, you're right. I just don't like the thought of you up here in these dark woods by yourself."

"I'll be fine. I've got the mice."

My mom wiped her eyes as I wrapped an arm around her shoulders.

If only I had known it would be the mouse who would eventually eat the rug we found at a yard sale, and nibble off the laces to my running sneakers, and, much later, take away a giant bag of dog food, piece by piece, until only the scraps of the twelve-pound bag remained.

CHAPTER 10

Years ago, Grandpa installed a small kitchen area in the cabin with a modest sink, a sponge of an indeterminate age, and a handful of pots hanging neatly from nails hammered into the cracked beams. I was unsure where the water runoff drained. There had to be a septic system of sorts. The little refrigerator was barely bigger than the mini fridge I'd had in college. The small bathroom consisted of only a toilet and a shower stall that forced you to hold your breath if you wanted to fit into it. Grandpa always preferred the outhouse. Liked the fresh air and all that.

I picked up a bunch of those frozen dinners—the kind that advertise themselves as being healthy for men who know nothing about nutrition—from the Stop & Shop a few miles down the road. I heated my meal in the small oven, the little crystals of ice clamoring over my meatloaf. The creamed spinach was welded into a square patty in the right quadrant of the meal. The chips of what I guessed to be carrots hovered together in the left side of the plastic dish. When I took the whole thing out of the oven, the plastic had melted and the spinach—now a lethal-looking green— had bubbled over and contaminated the other sections of food.

I decided to eat at the picnic table outside at the edge of the pond. I wanted to eat as many meals as I could out there, where piles of acorns, green moss, and a generous carpet of leaves covered the earth. I would soon discover that if I sat out there when it rained, the leaf cover would keep me dry as the pond's surface exploded into millions of circles.

These were the parts you didn't see—me stumbling through my attempt at adulthood, at solitude, at actually being alone with my mind for entire days. This was me trying to be better, to know more—all the things you wanted from me but didn't have the chance to actually witness. You complained about the men you knew who suffered from Peter Pan syndrome, never wanting to grow up, and I didn't want to be one of them, so I'd moved to this land for you, in a way. To prove to both of us that I could be self-reliant, independent. A real, adult man.

My land spanned three acres and was bordered on the left by a small stream that slipped through the trees unnoticed for most of the year until spring, when the thick sheet of ice covering the pond gave up its hold to warmer temperatures. I spent a day walking through the woods, refamiliarizing myself with the land. It was a cool, overcast day. I headed to the other side of the stream, past the old dam where the algae collected thickest by the end of August. Wild blueberry bushes grew heavy there by midsummer. Farther back, where an abandoned apple orchard still bore fruit, the deer congregated and ate. It was there that I found the first tree.

The bark was roughly etched with seven letters. A name. Made from sharp gashes of a blade. I ran my fingers over the lines. *Patrick.* I didn't think much of it until I continued on and found another tree with the same engraving. Something inside me tugged. This was strange, wasn't it? This name looked older—it was less legible and higher up on the trunk—but was still clearly *Patrick.* I kept walking and found there were more. At least a dozen. *Patrick. Patrick. Patrick.* Repeated through the forest as if in a chant.

The skin on the back of my neck tingled, the autumn air feeling cooler than it had moments before. I couldn't imagine why my grandfather would scratch another man's name into these trees. I spun around instinctively, feeling something in that forest, a presence. But finding nothing, I shook it off and kept walking.

On the right—halfway through the woods, before the field where the cows grazed lazily in the mornings, tails swinging and their jaws always moving, moving, moving—the property butted up against the nearby farm's land. As kids, Taylor and I had tried to make a rope swing to cross the stream, just like in *Bridge to Terabithia*. Even though we could simply step over the narrow stream, to be transported one needed a rope swing. For the apple orchard beyond the stream to become alive, we needed to adventure to get there. For the bed of pine needles to light up the kingdom floor, we needed to get the damn rope swing to work. It never did, and we never worked up the nerve to ask Grandpa for help.

At first, the weight of the silence felt too heavy. I played indie folk music loud from my portable speaker—something unfamiliar and with a banjo—just to distract myself. I downloaded podcasts and audiobooks, plugging my ears with headphones to keep my head filled with sound. If I had a TV, it would have been on. I needed something, anything, to remind me I was not the last person on earth. That this silence wasn't total.

That evening, I brushed away two daddy longlegs spiders from the picnic table as I sat down with my meal and a beer. As soon as I sat, a rustling by the tree to my right caught my attention. An upside-down squirrel stared at me with eager black eyes, its back legs splayed and clinging to the bark of the tree. He clucked a few times, hinting that he was considering leaping to my table to snatch a semi-thawed spinach cube.

"Hey!" I said. My voice sounded strange to my own ears. He clucked once more and resorted to a purring sound—calling a mate for backup, I imagined. I wished I could do the same. I had spent only a week's worth of nights in the cabin alone, and I needed to push past the barrier that stood between this feeling like some sort of test, some sort of rite of passage, to it feeling like home.

A horse whinnied in the distance—a loud, frantic type of cry. A horse farm stood somewhere out of sight on the other side of the pond. They gave horseback riding lessons, and based upon the loads of horse manure dotting the roads leading to the cabin, they must track by my land fairly often. Maybe I would learn to ride horses, I mused. Maybe I would buy a horse. Yes. Be something like a cowboy.

That morning, I'd stood on my one sturdy desk chair to peek up into the small area above the rafters, and I'd found Grandpa's old rifle there. The one he'd used for hunting deer. He had shot a thing or two in his time—the antlers now mounted to the cabin wall over the tattered couch. I hated to admit I felt ever so slightly safer knowing the gun rested up there—not that I knew how to shoot or wanted to kill anything. I didn't have it in me. I never burned ants with magnifying glasses or salted slugs or tortured the neighbor's cat as a kid. I liked animals. I got squeamish around blood. And yet . . . it seemed like something else I should be familiar with, because what if a bear wandered onto the property—a big one, hungry—and tried to attack me, or you? I'd have to do something other than hide, because you would never hide. You would walk right up to that bear, and I hated that. So I added it to the list of things to incorporate into my new life: cooking lessons, horseback riding, target practice.

The horse whinnied again, but this second time it sounded a little different—a little higher and less like a penned-in animal, more like something wild. The chill in the air smelled almost sweet. Things rotting and falling back to earth.

I rolled down the sleeves of my flannel and grabbed a few logs from the pile I kept covered by Grandpa's old blue tarp. I leaned the logs in toward each other like he taught us. The tiny teepee. I crumpled a few pieces of old newspaper under the base of the logs, and with one of those long kitchen lighters I lit an edge, two, waiting for the flames to expand. For the warmth to grow.

When Taylor was six and I was ten, Grandpa handed us each a rod. A real, shiny fishing rod, one I would be far less likely to snap in half when the fish never bit. We put the old rods Grandpa had helped us make—long sticks with a nylon line attached to a hook—to rest for good underneath the cabin. I wondered if I would find them under there, or if Grandpa had used them as kindling ages ago.

When we'd made the original poles, he'd said we had to earn real rods. Taylor hooking me through the back of my neck and me through his shoe set us back a bit. So did the time I knocked Taylor out of the old canoe and Grandpa got his new fishing vest wet trying to fish my squirming brother "out of the drink."

Grandpa slapped me hard on the side of my head for that one. Something our parents never did. Something I couldn't do for you, not even when you begged me to. The force of his open palm sent me backward over the seat of the canoe. I landed in a small pool of water with dead mosquitoes floating in it. Taylor, sopping wet, his hair matted down past his eyebrows, looked as shocked as me.

"Don't try anything like that again," Grandpa snapped. "You gotta behave when you're up here. Stop acting like a kid."

I bit my tongue to keep from blurting out the obvious fact that I *was* still a kid.

For the rest of the weekend, I did my best to act like a man. I pulled my shoulders back and puffed my chest out. I even resisted pantsing Taylor when he leaned over the fire for the perfect toast on his marshmallow. Grandpa didn't seem to notice all the work I put in. He didn't talk to us much when we stayed with him, and he talked even less that weekend. He tried to teach us that men were quiet, severe. I tried to mimic the strict lines of his forehead and the grim movement of his lips as he smoked thick-scented cigars by the fire.

We only saw my grandfather and my father in the same room together for the occasional Christmas. My father held a palm out the window of the car when he dropped us off at the cabin, never making eye contact with his father, never getting out to chat or stay the night. I never knew what had happened between them to push them to such opposite poles, to a place where anything more than a vague wave was too much of a connection to make. Grandpa tolerated us, it seemed, because he sensed he had some responsibility to teach us something he'd failed to teach his own son. "Biting off only what you can chew," he'd tell us, "is bird shit. You better be man enough to eat the whole goddamned thing."

These memories of my grandfather inspired me to seek out something he would have approved of: a thick, earthy cigar. I drove my dad's old F-150 truck with the four-wheel drive (something else I'd inherited) down to the local liquor store that night. I felt that completing my first week alone in the shack—or no, I had to refer to my home now as a "cabin" to lend it some legitimacy—deserved some sort of celebration or ceremony.

The man behind the counter pointed to a dozen I shook my head at, until I said, "I don't know. You pick one for me."

The deep brown interior of the cigar reminded me of the fresh soil my mother patted down around the tomatoes in her garden. Once my fire caught that night, I cut the end of the cigar and lit it. I took a strong inhale and coughed on the stale earth-and-coffee-grounds taste. Once my lungs quieted, I tried it again. Sitting in the red L.L.Bean camping chair by the only fire reflecting over the pond, I realized why Grandpa liked his time alone up here so much. The pond remained smooth except for the slight blips of bouncing bugs. An occasional circle stirred the water—a fish reaching up from the dark below. They stocked the pond each year with trout. Catfish; large, croaking bullfrogs; and backward-skirting crayfish darted underwater over the rocks by the shore.

I took another long inhale on the cigar just as my stomach began to turn. I leaned over the edge of my chair and vomited next to the fire.

It was my first and last cigar.

CHAPTER 11

I n the early days of living in the cabin, it only felt right, like
some kind of foraged home, when you were with me. I didn't
want to rely on you to be happy. I tried to fight the thought
from entering my mind—the one that wormed its way in during
the nights I was alone—*this would be better with you.* The start of
any relationship was like this, I knew; then it faded, or something
changed. Usually, I was the first to let go. But maybe nothing
changed—not even our wiser, future selves, braced with armfuls
of knowledge and experience—our need for companionship. My
need for you back then.

We saw each other less than when I lived in Allston, but it
made our time together that much better. We would spend the
day in bed, naked, curling around one another underneath the
down blanket. You talked of buying me a puppy. I talked about you
staying with me for longer bouts of time. Maybe, I suggested, you
could find a job up here and we could live in the cabin together.

The last graft had left your cheek looking a bit stretched and
waxy, like you were close to tearing free from yourself and floating
up like a bubble toward the sky. I would run my hand along the
slick skin, and you would try to turn away. Sometimes I would

force you to keep still. You'd struggle for a while, but eventually you'd lie still beneath my fingers.

On the days without you, I would wake early, go for a trail run through the woods, pull myself together a bit of breakfast, and then head down to the local Starbucks in the nearby outlet plaza to work. Two Fridays a month I had to head back to our office in the city for company-wide meetings, but the rest of the time, I worked alone. Writing up documentation content, pumping myself with caffeine, pretending to know and care about the intricacies of a new computer software that boasted an expanded database.

Living alone had turned me into a creature of habit. A man of ritual. I had a nice system in the cabin. I used the same mug every morning for coffee. The same bowl for breakfast cereal. You liked messing with this system. I would notice you smiling, waiting for the booby trap you set to be triggered—drinking from my mug or moving my toothbrush to a place I would never keep it. I'd try to point out your habits, like your scarves, and you'd give me the look that said, *You're comparing covering scars to the placement of soap in the shower?* You were good at making me feel like I should put my foot in my mouth, not having thought things through. I called you sensitive. You called me a jerk. I kissed you hard, pressing my hands into your shoulders, opening your chest. You leaned, back and back, until I was sure we would both fall, but we never did. You were surprisingly strong in ways like that, balanced when I least expected it. But you relied on me for the counterbalance. Stability. That was something I could give to you.

Taylor was coming up to join us one night, so I spent the day doing chores around the cabin: raking the leaves around the picnic table and starting to repaint the trim on the cabin a hunter green. I had found a grill on the side of the road outside of an aging white colonial house with a *FREE!* sign taped to it. I loaded it into the truck bed with pride—I was building something here. Although the chill in the air warned that frost would harden the ground come morning, I insisted we have an old-fashioned barbecue that night. Hamburgers, hot dogs, Cape Cod chips, marshmallows toasted over the fire. I wanted the two of you to be friends.

I went outside to start to build the campfire, and I found my heavy, flannel-lined canvas jacket—formerly belonging to my grandfather—splayed across the picnic table, arms outstretched as if his ghost waited for my embrace. I assumed it was one of your pranks, but something in the careful arrangement of the coat in the center of the picnic stable, as if on display, gave me a hitch in my nerves. A prickle on the back of my neck, like I might spot him lumbering out from behind the cabin at any minute.

"Hope, come on," I said, brushing the pine needles from the sleeves.

"What?" Your head appeared in the shadow of the cabin's screen.

"Very funny," I said. "My grandfather's jacket. On the picnic table."

"I didn't touch anything," you said.

I opened my mouth to argue but knew there was no point.

You were curled in the armchair on the porch, knees pulled into your chest. A slim hardback of Mary Oliver poems rested against your knees. Your eyes scanned the lines with an intense focus. I enjoyed how thoroughly absorbed you became when reading poetry or painting. Poetry always seemed like a foreign language to me, but you reread the same books over and over, writing your own bits in the margins.

That was when we heard it. A loud crash in the woods to the left of the cabin. We both froze. It was too loud to be a squirrel. A falling tree branch? We held our breaths until we heard it again.

"David," you whispered.

I nodded and held up a hand for you to stay put. I tiptoed up the steps into the cabin. The rifle. I had read an article about bears wandering into yards this time of year, looking for some last scraps of food before winter hibernation.

I pulled the milk crate I had been using as an end table over to stand on, and I felt around in the rafter for the gun. My fingertips pushed through dust. I stood on tiptoe and reached in farther until they brushed something heavy. I tried to wrap my hands around it, but it was too large. This wasn't the rifle. I strained my arm against the rafter until my fingertips caught an edge of a box and I was able to slide it closer to me and lower it down.

I held an old wooden chest with a small lock on it.

"David?" you asked from behind me, and I jumped. "What were you planning on doing? Throwing that box at the animal?"

"Sorry, I was looking for my grandfather's old rifle."

"It's okay. Whatever it was, left. It was definitely a good-sized animal. Maybe a deer. Or a moose."

"Look at this," I said, stepping off the milk crate.

The rectangular cedar chest looked handmade and old; its carved edges were lined with heavy dust. Something was carved into the bottom. A name. A word. But I couldn't make out the letters.

"Was that your grandfather's?"

"I don't know. I've never seen it before. My parents must have missed it when they cleared out a lot of his old stuff."

You pulled at the lock, but it held firm. I tried jimmying it with a screwdriver, but it was too big.

"Here, let me see it." You reached into your hair and began poking at the hole. "Bobby pin," you said. "I used to be good at breaking into my mom's room when she locked her door."

"Why would she lock her door?"

You shrugged just as the lock popped apart.

I lifted the latch and threw back the top, the hinges whining. Inside, the cedar box looked almost new, the wood still fragrant. The bottom was lined with a delicate red velvet, but it held no gold, no grand treasure. Instead, what lay inside appeared to be the personal effects of a woman. A small pair of lacy gloves, a delicate and ornate gold band with a single pearl, a square of folded cloth with the initials A. R. stitched onto it, and a bound stack of letters.

We sat to inspect the contents. You reached into the box and slid the ring onto your hand. "God! This vintage ring is amazing." It had looked so tiny, alone there in this keepsake box; I wouldn't have thought it would have fit anyone other than a small child. "Can I keep the ring? I love it!"

"No," I reached out, touching your wrist. "This must have been my grandmother's or something. I think you should put it back."

You pulled the ring off and read the inscription inside the gold band.

"Well, for one, your grandmother's dead. And two, your grandmother's initials weren't A. R., were they? Your grandfather's last name was Maloney."

She was right, but I still didn't want the items disturbed. These things needed to stay together until I knew what or whose they were.

I picked up the small folded handkerchief. Who owned the property before my grandfather? I wondered. Could that have been A. R.? I shook out the square of cloth, and something fell into my lap. I felt around under my leg until my fingers found it, and I held it up to the light. It was a lock of blond hair, tied off with a single red ribbon.

We decided to wait until Taylor arrived to open the letters. Or, more specifically, I insisted. We had never known our grandmother.

We had always been told she died of a broken heart. So if these keepsakes were hers from a world ago, I wanted Taylor to share in the discovery.

The bonfire's flames lit the contours of your cheeks. Overhead branches rustled in the wind as sparks caught on the current of air and twisted skyward. I jerked my head toward the trees, straining to hear a sign of the animal from earlier. You leaned in close to the fire, a small stick with a marshmallow on one end in your hand. "Back up or your sneakers will melt," I warned you. Your little white Chucks stayed put, but you glanced over your shoulder at me, smiling wickedly.

Taylor sat farther back from the fire, drumming his fingers on his thighs and occasionally swigging from a small bottle of Jim Beam. He was glad I'd waited for him to open the letters. He hoped they would explain some unnamed inheritance that would befall him instead of me this time. He kept fiddling with his cell phone, alternating between social-media apps, until I grabbed it from him and tossed it on top of the cooler and out of reach. "Fine," he muttered, bringing the bottle of Jim Beam back up to his lips. He was twenty-one and still really excited about drinking. I just prayed he didn't end up puking in the morning like last time.

He passed me the bottle as he wiped his lips with the back of his hand, and his glance flicked across the fire. He watched you when he thought neither of us were aware of it. You made him uncomfortable, I could tell, but I couldn't put my finger on why.

Crickets hummed and the stars hung bright. The pond was quiet, save for the distant howl of coyotes and the whinnying of that same horse. I pulled the box out from behind my chair and removed the letters. Something like nostalgia rose in me when I held them, something like missing my grandparents. I wondered if I had seen the chest as a kid or if maybe it was hidden up in the rafters decades before I ever came around.

You showed the ring to Taylor.

"This ring came from the chest?" Taylor's eyes met mine. What he really wanted to ask was, *This ring was probably our grandmother's and you gave it to her?* Taylor and I loved our grandmother as much as we could based on the stories we heard. She loved to bake. Loved to be in the tiny kitchen, hovering over the tiny stove making the most delicious pies you could imagine, all from scratch, all from the local blueberry bushes or apple orchards. "She probably wanted to keep away from your grandfather," my mother would whisper to us when my father was out of earshot.

You took the box and placed it in your lap. Taylor glanced my way again. He waited for me to stop you, to say something, but you were already pulling out the letters and holding them close to the fire, trying to read the outside of the envelopes. I grabbed them back.

"Hey." You looked hurt.

"We should probably be the ones to read them, you know?"

There was something written in neat script on the outside of the envelopes, but time and moisture had worn it unreadable. I worried all we would find was more of the same inside the envelope until I pulled out the first letter and saw that the ink had been pressed down so hard it was embedded into the paper. The letter was badly creased, as if read many times.

Theo, the letter began.

Taylor stopped me. "Didn't mom say Grandma always referred to Grandpa as Pop? Which I think is so weird; when wives refer to their husbands as *Dad* or something."

"Read it," you said, speaking over Taylor.

Theo,

    I wish you could come see me now. Until the arrangements are finalized, they won't let me leave this place. It's awful here.

All night long, I can hear them crying. I have three days with him before they take him away. Is it horrible I don't feel any guilt for what we did? For any of it? Does that mean I'm a bad person? Or as the rest of the world thinks of me—a sinner? The worst of it is over I suppose. My biggest fear—the thing that keeps me up at night with the moon—is that you'll learn to hate me, to blame me. But I never planned for this. I only wanted you. Please say you love me, Theo. Tell me again and again until my ears and my lungs and my heart fill with it. I need all that we've done to not be in vain.

I love you and I will love you when this is over and we are finally and wholly together. I will love you even when you're gone.
—A

The three of us sat there, not saying anything. I wished I could suck the words back in. To reverse the questions that spilled into the air. *Who was A?* Certainly not my grandmother, whose name was Blanch. And what had Grandpa done?

You spoke first. "Wow."

"Yes," Taylor agreed. "Wow."

"Her desperation is so intense and so sad. It's like you can tell just by reading it that things won't end well for her," you said.

"It has to be written to Grandpa, right?" asked Taylor. "I mean, it's addressed to *Theo* . . . but what the fuck did he do?"

"We don't know that he 'did' anything," I said, making air quotes with my hands.

"We need to find out who she was," you said with conviction. "A."

You reached for the pile of letters again, but Taylor got to them first. Without a second's hesitation, he tossed them into the fire.

We yelled *no!* just as the flame caught the edges of the old paper.

"Why'd you do that?" I hit Taylor on the shoulder.

His eyes were wide and he jammed his hands into the pockets of his jeans, stepping out of reach. "Maybe we don't want to know. What if what they did was bad? What if it's something they could get someone in trouble for, or . . . I don't know."

"Taylor, Grandpa is dead. I doubt that—Hope, stop!"

Your hand plunged into the blazing orange. Your eyes maintained a focused glint as you tried to retrieve the remainder of the letters. I tugged you back by the shoulders and we toppled onto Taylor's camping chair. You fell on top of me and stayed there, clutching your empty hand to your chest, your rib cage heaving.

"I have to know what happened to that woman," you whispered. A redness, an intensity rose to your lips and cheeks.

Taylor kept his head down as he poked at the edges of the fire with a long stick, a shameful slouch to his shoulders.

Later, I wondered if Taylor had done the right thing. Maybe it wasn't any of our business, digging up our grandfather's past. Maybe those letters were meant to be locked in the chest and pushed to the back of the rafters for a reason; maybe uncovering them would result in truths we couldn't yet imagine.

CHAPTER 12

When I checked my watch again—the clock on the old truck's dash was long since dead—fifteen minutes had passed. "This is fucking ridiculous," I muttered, and I jumped out of the truck. My worn hiking boots thumped down the walkway to your apartment building.

Once inside, I knocked on your door, hard and fast so you would know I was pissed.

"I told you to wait for me in the car!" you said through the closed door.

"Well, what the hell, Hope? Are you going to make me wait all day? We were supposed to get an early start."

"Don't talk to my daughter like that!"

Your mother. A lower but similar voice, so similar I got the two of you confused when I called your home phone if you didn't answer your cell. I always worried those times it went straight to voicemail that maybe something had happened. Maybe you were hurt somewhere . . . and what could I do?

I imagined both of your faces pressed up against the door to share the eyehole. I tried to appear calm. I pulled my knit cap with the brim lower over my eyes. You did this sometimes—strange things, like ignoring me or making me wait long periods of time for no good reason. Was it intentional? Sometimes when we were in public, you acted like we weren't together but merely acquaintances. I think, although I knew you'd never admit it, that you wanted to make sure you could live without me. You were afraid I'd get bored or meet someone else and leave you. So you tested me and made me wait. And usually, I did.

This time, however, something about your mother getting involved really pissed me off. I didn't like an audience.

"See you later, then. I'll hike on my own."

I imagined I heard a faint call of *Wait!* through the door. I turned quickly and retraced my steps back to the truck. I could just make out my early footprints, some of the first sets, the ones I made when I nearly skipped down the hallway at the prospect of seeing your bedroom.

As the weeks passed, my naïveté had become increasingly clear. You were not simply the effervescent fairy I'd seen on that summer street in Boston, a harbinger of light and goodwill. Glinda the Good Witch was not a real woman. You were much more complex than that.

I exited the apartment building. The cold never failed to shock on days like this. The wind violated each pore of exposed skin with an icy prick. I walked fast and with intention, ready to get back to New Hampshire. Frustrated I'd driven down here for nothing.

I had stayed at my parents' house the night before and had taken the opportunity to corner my mom as she pushed the vacuum cleaner up and down the living room carpet, making neat, light rows over and over. I had been trying to get some information about "A" from my parents, but without any luck. "Hey, Mom, do you know if Grandpa knew anyone who had the initials A. R.? Like a friend or cousin or something?"

Mom paused, resting her forearm on the handle of the vacuum. "Why do you ask?"

"Is that a yes or a no?"

"Well, as you can imagine, your grandfather didn't have many friends I knew about. He was great at building things, though, and helped a lot of the local farmers and neighbors in the area. Maybe one of your grandma's friends?"

She said this all without making eye contact. My mother was the worst liar.

"Mom," I said. I plucked a few dead leaves off the tall houseplant next to the couch. "You didn't answer my question."

"Hmm?"

"Just tell me. Who was she?"

"Who do you mean?" Still playing dumb. I considered telling her about the box and the letters and the ring, but I came out and asked the thing I really wanted to ask.

"Mom, was Grandpa involved in something? Like a crime of some sort?"

She straightened, her eyes wide, her lips parted in shock. "David! You know . . . Well, your grandfather . . . wasn't a criminal!" She was flustered. She unplugged the vacuum and rewound the cord. She was halfway to the storage closet when she paused. "David, just don't go to your father about this. Okay? It'd just upset him. You know how he gets with anything related to Grandpa."

I did know, which is why Taylor and I had collectively decided not to mention the box or the letters to him. I thought back to all those chilly mornings with Dad pulling up the long drive to the cabin, never leaving the warmth of his car, never even saying hello as he dropped us off. Grandpa would stand looking back at him, hands on hips, as if considering something. Sometimes he would ask Taylor and me about Dad, about how he was doing, but I never thought too much about it back then.

"Is that why they weren't close?" I pushed. "Dad and Grandpa? Because of something Grandpa did?"

"David," my mother said in a stern tone she almost never used, "just drop it."

When I was almost at the truck, gloved hands pushed against my back. Your scarf slipped, and the shock of seeing your exposed neck, the burns worse there than on your face, stilled my movement. Your chest heaved from the effort of trying to catch up with me. Your wild hair blew in blustery paths around your head. "Don't leave."

You told me you woke up early to run by yourself, even in the winter. A couple of times, I tried to catch you with your small sneakers snapping against the bare pavement. I would leave my parents' house before the sun rose and roll the truck quietly down the streets of your neighborhood, but I never found you.

"What are you trying to do? I don't get it. What's the point?" My voice, nearly gentle now, had lost its edge.

"I don't know. I was just finishing a few things. I'm sorry."

You stared down at your feet. You wore only slippers—the kind with a rubber bottom—and I imagined the cold seeping through and tracing the arch of your foot. I wondered then if your trust in me had faltered after reading the letter. Was I from some sort of tainted bloodline? A family of bad seeds?

I knew I couldn't possibly stay mad.

"Just let me get my things," you said quietly.

I placed a hand on top of your head for a moment and nodded.

"Are you sure we're not lost?" You paused for the forty-third time and leaned against the nearest boulder. "We haven't seen anyone in like an hour. This can't be the right trail. Look up there. Sheer cliffs. We have totally gone off course."

We drove an hour and a half north that morning to Mount

Monadnock for a hike. Temps were low but the trails weren't yet icy. I brought a thermos full of hot chocolate for us to share, and boot and glove warmers for you. You wore a heavy white cowl scarf that day.

The view from the top would be spectacular with the leaves now gone, the landscape dry and open. I imagined you having romantic notions of us being the last two humans on earth. I didn't know then that you can't plant romantic notions into others' heads. They simply grow there or don't. The reality was that we'd had a weird start to the day and you were cold and whiny and wanted to be anywhere but with me on that mountain. I wished I knew what was really going through your head.

I had wanted to see you outdoors and active. I'd wanted to get out of the cabin and breathe in the air of the empty, dying, autumn forest together, our brights brighter than anything around. Sure, we were good lying around, sharing meals and our bodies, but I wanted to see you in different environments, in different countries. I wanted to see you tired from physical exertion, and I wanted to see what your hair looked like at the top of a mountain. I wanted to see you uncomfortable and out of your element. I wanted to know you in impossible ways.

You breathed heavily, not looking up at me with love as I expected. Instead, you shoved your hands into enormous mittens that slipped over the smooth surface of the rocks as you tried to find balance and traction. You glared up at me with a wild, furious sheen. Like I was *doing* this to you.

Maybe, in a way, I was. We had at least an hour to go. We both fell silent. You pouted, moving at an intentionally glacial pace.

"Is something wrong?" Caution edged my voice.

"It's just I think you think I'm someone I'm not. You have these expectations of people that they are supposed to live up to, to be as good as you. And sometimes that is just exhausting."

Mud was smudged across your left knee from when you'd slipped earlier in the hike.

"You're going to love it at the top," I said. "I swear. I know it's a little cloudy, but we should still be able to see for, like, hundreds of miles."

You picked up the pace as the trail leveled out. We were getting closer to the summit, to the open expanse I had begun to dread. Maybe we were better in a box, with four walls, a roof, and a wood-burning stove. Maybe openness and expansion were not things we did well together. There was too much room, too much oxygen for you to ignite.

We passed the tree line and the landscape opened to a rocky expanse peppered with miniature pines. Another couple stood at the summit in the distance. It was a Tuesday. Still fairly early. It wouldn't be crowded.

I had no idea how a simple walk through the woods could turn your thoughts into darts headed my way. I should have taken your delay that morning as a sign. I didn't want to admit the clouds overhead were darkening—the same ones you'd pointed out on the drive up. A sharp, biting wind picked up, and your hair became a frenzied funnel of red.

"We're almost there," I said weakly, although the actual summit looked farther away than I had expected once we got to the clearing. The granite smoothed and stretched at the top, the boulders looming. You fell silent again. Your small hands, pink and out of their gloves, clawed into stone for leverage. You refused my hand. You could be so stubborn. Did you want me to soften, to pick you up and carry you the rest of the way? Or did you want me to stiffen and plod through this thing alongside you, for us to be silent and determined in our unflinching annoyance and love? I never knew who I was supposed to be with you.

Just then, the snow began. I didn't notice it until you stopped.

You held out your hands, cupping them, looking into that empty space and back up toward the sky. "It's snowing." You looked shocked and almost happy.

I smiled because maybe I'd done something not so terrible after all. Those dark clouds opened up more and the snow spun downward, the wind pulling the crystals so they never accumulated, just showed up for a brief moment and then were whisked away. We leaned against a high rock, out of the wind, our shoulders touching, our backs pressed against the granite. I stared into the miles and miles of space—the openness, the trees, the mountains in the distance, the lack of anything truly existing, except for us. You stared into your palms, waiting to catch one of those brief, shimmering moments before it was gone.

CHAPTER 13

Christmas is a holiday designed for children who still believe in Santa, people who really like pie, or those in relationships. That year, you and I drank gingerbread lattes while walking arm in arm, the warm sweetness filling our stomachs as we poked through stores decked in colored lights. The snow was not a messy nuisance to be salted and shoveled away but a thing that forced us to stay huddled close, warm, and indoors. Baking cookies was a wonderful mess of spices in the kitchen. Fires in the wood stove, homemade ornaments from your craft nights, wrapping gifts over bottles of wine, and watching childhood holiday movies—these became the evenings I craved.

I'd spent the past few nights on my own in bed, the lights out, curled over my laptop searching the historical records of Sanbornton. I looked at obituaries and photos. I scanned through old news articles. I read internet archives and historical data. There were 223 family names in the town back in the late 1800s. Those family names were shared with the local church, streets, and farms. In the online archives, I found a book that listed the extensive genealogies of all the original families in the town. I turned straight to the *R*'s in the glossary: the Randalls, the Roberts, the Robinsons, the Rogers, the Rollins, the Rowens—but where and who was

A. R.? There was a very good chance she wasn't from this town. Or this state. Maybe my grandfather met her in Boston or when she was just passing through, visiting a cousin or aunt.

I knew I could ask my dad, but I resisted, at least for now. My dad liked to keep his private life private. Taylor and I often joked that our parents, especially our father, didn't exist before we came along. He never shared stories or jokes or misadventures from his past. He kept those details tucked away somewhere—or maybe locked up in a box, hidden out of reach, like his father had.

Your mom was away with her new boyfriend again, so I'd driven to Cambridge for the night to keep you company. At your apartment, my cell rang and Mark's name flashed across the small screen.

"Are you coming to Fenway tonight?" he demanded when I answered. "It's Timmy's birthday, and I'm ready to get fucked up."

"Shit, I totally forgot. What time are you guys heading out? I'm in Cambridge right now." A long red sweater covered the tops of your bare thighs. You rubbed my leg with your foot as you took a hit from a joint. I had never seen you smoke before. Or drink, for that matter. I wasn't going out to some stale-beer bar in Fenway with ten guys to stare at the twenty-one-year-old girls in short dresses while you were here, looking like this.

"Don't tell me you are still holed up with that girl. You are coming out tonight, no excuses!"

"I was planning on it, but, shit, my mom has this thing that she's been nagging me to do, and tonight's like the only time—"

"A thing? That your mom wanted you to do? Damn, Dave. You are whipped." I flinched. "Let me know when you get bored of all that and we'll go out."

Mark hung up and I exhaled a sigh of relief. He had been dating his girlfriend, Clara, since they were in middle school and didn't let the whole "attached" thing stop him from picking up one-night stands when the mood was right. Holiday pussy, according to Mark, was the best kind, because girls were desperate to land a date for their New Year's Eve party. I was more than happy to miss out, and in fact I pitied my friends in their matching striped button-downs, laughing too loud and feeding reusable lines to the nearest blonde with a shot in her hand.

"You can go if you want," you said in that way that I knew you knew I wasn't going anywhere. You leaned back against the pillow, your eyes lightly closed. Of course I wasn't going out.

"No. I want to be with you. We're getting a tree."

You sat up and pulled at my arm. "You're right. We better go before it gets too late or we get too lazy." You and I had taken it upon ourselves to shop for a tree for your apartment. You insisted we go to this place within walking distance that played only Charlie Brown Christmas music.

When we were kids we used to drive up to New Hampshire, near Grandpa's cabin, to cut down a tree ourselves. Taylor and I would pick the largest, burliest tree in the lot and my father would sigh as mom hugged us. *Oh, Frank, but that's the one they want!* She would smile like you were now. My father would hold on to the half-rusted saw, swearing and puffing out cold gusts of air as he hacked away, and Taylor and I zigzagged between the trees, trying to nail one another with snowballs.

You were right about the Charlie Brown music. You skipped ahead of me, the pom-pom on your knit hat bopping from left to right. The tree stand bustled with shoppers, each inspecting the lot like it mattered which tree they chose. As if the perfection of the tree was a predictor of the impending holiday's success.

"David! Over here!"

You held up a six-foot tree, its gangly branches enveloping your torso in a piney hug.

"God, it is you," said a wiry female voice from somewhere behind you. "I thought I recognized that hair."

I tried to peek around the tree to locate the source of the voice, but you did this weird deer-in-headlights thing. Frozen, eyes wide. You didn't turn toward the voice; instead, after a pause, with a forced smile on your face, you said to me, "It's perfect, isn't it? I think we have to get this one. Let's go pay up front." You marched ahead, dragging the enormous tree in your arms.

But then that girl appeared in front of us. She stood a few inches taller than you but was so thin I could make out the shape of her bones through her bulky, oversized sweater. Her upper body rounded in on itself, and oily brown hair limped over her shoulders. She bit her stubby fingernails through fingerless gloves. "What? Did you forget me already? We only shared a room for two years."

"Excuse me," you said. You tried to push past her, but the girl, although timid-looking in posture, stood resolute, her eyes strong and daring. "You're blocking my way," you said. "Would you mind moving to the left?"

"Oh, so you're one of those," said the girl, her voice oilier than her hair. "You leave and pretend nothing ever happened. Pretend you're just like everyone else. Go ahead. Ignore me. But you and I both know you'll never be normal."

The girl stepped out of your way then, her grin set in a smug line. I took one last look at her before following after you, but she never noticed me. Her eyes were locked on you. She laughed a little and turned away down a different aisle of trees, her gnawed finger returning to her mouth.

"Hope, who was that?"

"I have no idea! Pretty weird though."

"Um, yeah. Like, crazy weird. She seemed so sure she knew you."

"Knew me? She looked homeless or something."

I took out my wallet to hand over money for the tree, but you stopped me. "I've got this." You reached into your homemade purse—something crocheted and orange. You smiled at me, sap sticking to your gloves, but your hand shook, ever so slightly, as you handed over payment for the Christmas tree.

CHAPTER 14

The holidays ended in a red and green blur. You disappeared for a few days surrounding Christmas to visit family in Michigan. We got together earlier in the day on New Year's Eve to exchange gifts. We sat in my parent's basement, ensconced in the glow of icicle lights. You kept your mouth closed and your eyes down. I asked you what was wrong, I asked you about Michigan, the relatives you visited, but you only shrugged. The holidays had caused something to come a bit loose in you—a slight, indeterminable unraveling was happening. Something I could sense but couldn't name.

You unwrapped your gift first. One of those overpriced candles with a wood wick you liked so much and a painting kit in a box with brushes and a mini easel and small palette of paint. I liked when you painted and made things and wrote poems. We'd promised each other small gifts this year. Things that would inspire us to do more, to be better people. I wasn't entirely sure what that meant since, obviously, it was your idea, but I was proud of myself, and I'd thrown in the candle just to make the whole thing seem a little more substantial.

You handed me my gift. The wrapping job appeared dainty and intricate, almost hand-painted, so I took my time, unfolding the paper carefully. Underneath lay a flat brown box, and inside that was a beautiful knife with a carved wooden handle and a sleek blade that slipped in and out. My initials were engraved into the handle, and I wondered if this was some sort of nod to the engraved items belonging to A. R. You were still wearing the ring.

This was an awesome gift. It was really well made. Something my grandfather would have admired. I had expected an online class or poetry book, some approximation of your thoughts on how I could be most improved.

"Do you like it? I thought you could use it for fishing or whatever."

"This is awesome, Hope. Thank you, really. It looks expensive. I didn't know we were doing gifts like this. I would have . . ."

You shrugged. "Just a little gift." You smiled without meeting my eyes.

That night we headed to Mark's annual "Ugly Sweaters on New Year's Eve" party at my old Allston apartment. Taking a spin on the classic ugly sweater party, rather than limiting guests to only ugly holiday sweaters, he opened it up to ugly sweaters for all occasions. I borrowed something my mom actively wore—this bulky thing littered with knitted barn animals that grazed on various parts of my torso. It felt like my core body temperature hovered close to 105 degrees in that thing. You wore a thick rainbow turtleneck you said you'd worn daily in middle school.

You hung in the doorway when we entered. Certainly not your scene.

"Is this okay?" I asked, because there was something still beneath your surface. Simmering. Something had changed that you weren't telling me about. Before you could answer, Mark, Tim, and their new roommate, Brad, were clapping me on the back and shoving cups into our hands and shuffling us deeper into the house. We said our hellos and gave our introductions. We were initiated with shots called NYE Kisses that had a Hershey Kiss tucked at the bottom of the glass to cut the burn of the alcohol. "Hope doesn't drink," I started to explain, handing them back one of the shots, but you took it and threw it back into your mouth before I could finish. And then you had another.

"Tonight, I do," you said.

I put my hand on your arm to ask you what that was about, but you pulled away and moved deeper into the room.

The party was crowded. The same crowd of people who had been congregating in the kitchen and hallways of that apartment since college. A tub of Mark's famous punch took up a corner of the kitchen floor. The dining room table had been transformed into a beer pong tournament, with brackets and a scoreboard. Champagne bottles lined the entire bottom shelf of the fridge for midnight, and Mark's girlfriend, Clara, who worked as a baker in some fancy chocolate shop, weaved through the party with platters of artisanal chocolates all night long when all anyone really wanted were slices of pizza to soak up the booze.

As I laughed and toasted and played drinking games, I watched you out of the corner of my eye. Were you realizing how much better you were than this? Than me? I tried to see my friends through your eyes. Were they all so average? Twenty-something-year-old drunks without any spark?

You twisted the cap off the bottle of red wine I'd brought and started drinking it yourself. You pulled the bottle away from your mouth, your teeth a faint purple.

"Hope, are you okay?" I asked. "You might want to go easy on that bottle of wine . . ."

Before you could respond, Clara approached us. "Hey, girl-friend! How are you?" she asked, air kissing your cheek. You had met once or twice at some other similar party. Clara asked you another question, trying to be friendly. You tended to close up in crowds, but tonight—maybe it had something to do with the liquor and the grandiosity of your turtleneck—you started to talk.

"Do you ever feel like you have an out-of-body experience at end-of-the-year parties?" you asked. "Like you're looking down and wondering if this moment is reflective of your year to come? Is this some catalyst, some starting point, for the next twelve months of your life?"

Clara smiled and sort of shook her soft bob of curls, not sure how to answer.

"What would July look like if it reflected off of this moment right now?" you asked.

"God, if this were July, I would never allow myself to eat this much chocolate," Clara said. "Not during bathing suit season!"

You stared at her with something like disgust. Before you could say anything more, I interjected, grabbing you by the arm, "I'm sweating. Want to join me on the balcony for a bit?"

Fireworks cracked in the distance. We caught the sparkling tops over the peaks of apartment buildings. We shared the small balcony with three other partygoers who were smoking and huddled together for warmth. You turned to face the night street; it was empty and quiet, except for the muffled sounds of indoor voices floating above the neighborhood. A car drove by playing some song with a fast dance beat. The streetlamp below us sputtered out and went still. We breathed in the quiet together.

"I love you," I whispered into your hair. You leaned back against the railing, your eyes shiny. You smiled, sort of sad, and leaned back more, your head and hair and arms dangling over the night street. I held you by the waist. You righted yourself, placed your hands on my shoulders, your wobbly eyes focused on my own.

"Do you ever wish you still lived here? In this apartment? That you never met me or moved to the cabin or changed anything in your life at all?"

"Of course not. I'm really glad all those things happened."

"But in the end, it won't really matter, will it? You'll end up leaving. You won't stay in the woods alone forever. Everybody changes in the end."

"Hope, I don't want to leave you. Is that what you're asking?"

Light snow had fallen earlier in the evening, but it had stopped for the moment.

"That letter, David, to your grandfather. I can't stop thinking about it. Why don't you care enough to really find out who that woman was or what they did together? I just have this feeling that something bad happened to her. Something horrible."

"I do want to know. I just don't know how to go about finding out. I've done some searching, but I don't have much to go off of. It was all a long time ago, and it's something that was obviously kept very quiet."

"And that's it? You just give up? You have to work a little harder for the truth. Blind ignorance doesn't look good on you."

"I'm curious, but I'm not going to lose sleep over it. I asked my mom, but she didn't know anyone with those initials."

"But that's not enough, David. Don't you see? You're handed this piece of land and you don't have to pay for anything and aren't accountable to anyone because you can work from home and make good money, but you don't consider putting in effort on somebody else's behalf. Things aren't as easy for the rest of us as they are for you. And what's it all for? Do you even care about the work you're doing? Does it even benefit anyone at all?"

I got defensive. "It benefits the clients when they like my work. It benefits the product users. Isn't that enough?"

"No!" Your voice shot up and the three cigarette-smoking partygoers turned to look in our direction. "That's exactly not enough!"

I tried to pull you to me, my arm around your back. I whispered, "*You don't need to yell.*"

"Stop trying to silence me. I don't want to be quiet. You know, you're just like my last boyfriend."

"Who was your last boyfriend?" I pulled back slightly. You had never mentioned any exes before this point, and I selfishly hoped I was your first serious boyfriend.

"He tried to keep me quiet and squashed so I fit exactly the mold he wanted me to fit. He never wanted to know the truth. If you haven't noticed yet, there's no mold for me."

"Baby, what are you even talking about?"

"I'm talking about you! And don't call me baby."

The bottle of wine slipped from your hand and shattered on the balcony. The others outside jumped back in surprise, exchanged glances with one another, and stubbed out their cigarettes. As they headed back into the party, I bent down, picked up the biggest pieces of glass, and deposited them in the small ashtray on the café table next to us.

"Is everything all right? Can I get you guys another drink?" Clara poked her head outside, her eyes instantly watering from the cold, her cheeks a bright pink.

"More wine!" you nearly shouted.

I tried to send Clara a tiny imperceptible shake of my head, but she only called over her shoulder, "I'll find something!" as she headed back into the party.

"Do you ever feel that you're just not enough? Not doing enough for the world? For me? Jesus Christ, David, do you even understand what I'm trying to say? Sometimes you have to leave a *mark*." With each word, a thing seemed to grow inside of you—a thing like hate—looking for a way out, looking for me.

This must be why you didn't drink. That night, drunk descended on you grandly in a way I didn't see coming.

"Is that what would really make you happy, Hope? For me to leave a mark?"

You pulled away from me and leaned against the café table as if mulling this one over. Your eyes welled but never spilled. "Feeling something. That would make me happy." You let out a long, slow breath. "I need to get out of here. Let's go."

"Hope, it's not even midnight. We're supposed to crash here. Mark has a blow-up mattress for us."

Clara opened the sliding door just as you plowed past her, knocking red wine down the front of her fuzzy snowflake sweater. Her mouth locked open in silent surprise.

"I'm sorry!" I said to Clara as I rushed past, chasing after you through the apartment and out the door.

"Hope!" I called as you marched down the dark street, marking a path in the light snow. Our jackets were still inside. The shouts and music from the surrounding parties were more obvious out there.

You didn't turn to face me until you reached my truck a couple of blocks away.

"Give me the keys," you said, not meeting my eyes.

"Hope, what are you doing? We've both been drinking. Let's go back to the party. We can grab some water, sober up . . ."

"Either give me the keys, drive me home, or I'll start walking."

"What's the matter with you? You're being crazy!"

"Do not call me crazy," you hissed, and you extended your palm for the keys.

I swore under my breath and unlocked the truck. I would

certainly not be giving you the keys. You slid onto the passenger seat, your hands soft in your lap. I turned over the ignition and started off down the road.

Only a few minutes into the drive, you said, "Actually, we can't go to my house. My mom and her boyfriend are there and I don't want to see them. We have to go to the cabin."

"Hope, I can't drive all the way up to New Hampshire now. Let's just go back to the party, enjoy the night, and drive up in the morning."

"Then let me out of the truck," you said. You pulled at the locked door handle and then at the ends of your sweater sleeves and scratched at your neck like you wanted to crawl out of your skin. I didn't understand what was happening.

"Stop, Hope! Okay, fine. I'll go up north."

You turned the heat on full blast and tucked your arms tightly around your waist when you weren't trying to eject yourself from the moving vehicle. I headed toward 93 North. I knew I shouldn't be driving, but I didn't know what was happening to you. We didn't turn on the music or speak. I was so caught off guard by this different side to you I'd never seen before; I was too freaked out to speak. I felt like I had a stranger sitting beside me. You simply stared out the window for the remainder of the drive while I shook my head in little violent turns to keep myself awake, my eyes focused.

Finally, an hour and a half later, holding on to my last threads of consciousness before sleep, I veered off the exit and the metronome of my blinker set you off again.

"Why would you take me there? To a party like that? So I can just be a total embarrassment? A freak to show off? How good of you to love the disfigured girl."

Shut up. Just please shut up. I was so tired. The words pressed against the back of my tongue, but I feared I would have to scrape you off the pavement if I said as much.

It was so hot I tried to tug off my stupid ugly sweater, struggling against the confines of the driver's seatbelt as the truck swerved. I worked to wiggle my right arm free. My snowboard in the back shifted and banged against your shoulder.

"God!" you cried. "Are you trying to kill us? This is the worst night of my life."

My white-knuckled grasp on the steering wheel intensified as I picked up speed. I didn't have the energy to coddle or convince you to calm down. I'd just wanted to have a good time with my friends for a night. To relax. To drink champagne and kiss drunkenly at midnight. I didn't need all of this.

I pulled out my phone from my back pocket expecting a *WTF—where'd you go?* text from Mark, but nothing. They were probably too drunk to notice much of anything.

You let out a dramatic, disgusted sigh. "You're always on your phone. Have you noticed that? Who are you waiting for to call you? At dinner, you spent the whole time texting or trolling through Facebook. You've got a real problem."

"Hope."

"Don't *Hope* me like you're my parent with that tone of voice. I'm not being quiet. In fact, I want to get out of this truck right now!"

"Would you put on your seat belt? Please. We're almost at the cabin." Sweat droplets gathered at my hairline. The roads were dusted with snow, but the snow tires my dad had insisted I put on handled the winter roads well. So I sped up to wait at the red light. When the light blinked green, I slammed my foot on the gas and took a hard left. I felt so heated—whether from frustration or the rocketing temperature inside the truck—I began to wonder if I had a fever.

"Seriously, pull over! I'm getting out."

Trust me when I say I wanted you out of the truck as much

as you wanted to get out that night. "Hope! We are five minutes from the cabin! Would you just calm down?"

I pulled up fast to the next intersection. The roads were darker here as we left the commercial area and entered the rural, quiet roads leading to the cabin. I barely breathed. The truck engine hissed. The blinker flashed. It shouldn't have to be this hard, right? To love someone? We'd only been dating five months.

I gazed left, ready to jerk the truck right.

"David! Look out!"

The only thing I registered once my foot touched the gas pedal was the sound of your voice. *David. Look out.* Such a simple directive, and yet the weight it carried was life-changing.

The rest of the scene caught up with my brain in a slow procession of senses firing, one after the other, until I could piece together what had just happened.

A thump against my bumper. The clang of metal on snow-covered pavement. The blurred white paint of the crosswalk. The dark, quiet night sky, empty of stars. An eerily silent pause before my slow-motioned moment of clarity allowed me to look up into the steady beam of headlights to see an old woman standing by the bumper. She yelled something unintelligible and slapped the hood with her mitted fist. And then I saw him. The collapsed form of an old man lying in front of my truck, his oxygen tank rolling away from him.

"Oh my God. Oh my God." My breath tore in sharp bites out of my lungs. I undid my seatbelt and started to crank open the door, but your grasp—I can still conjure the phantom pressure of your hand squeezing my arm—stopped me. I couldn't explain why. I pulled my door shut and yanked the gearshift into reverse.

I glanced up into the stream of my headlights once more, the old woman leaning over her husband in the crosswalk. His head lolled to the left. They were the type of couple who had shrunk over time together, merging to look more and more alike, almost like twins. Same tan winter coats and white hats. The same curved backs and squat frames. A light snow still filtered down from the sky. Had it been snowing this whole time? The commotion of their two bodies messed the smooth white sheet covering the earth, and dark swirls of pavement showed through.

The crosswalk. The oxygen tank. Your hand still squeezing my arm.

I sped into reverse, banged a sharp U-turn, and jumped back on the main road, speeding down to the cabin the back way.

Turn back turn back turn back.

I shut the heat off, and you didn't try to stop me. My breath came out in short puffs. A panicky darkness sat between us. My arms shook as I gripped the wheel. Saliva pooled behind my teeth, and I wondered if I would throw up. I was a horrible person. I was going to hell. Or maybe even jail.

I had just committed a hit-and-run.

I wanted to scream, but I couldn't say the words circling in my head because there were too many. *What if he never gets up what if he freezes there what if he dies what if they find me what if I go to prison what if the rest of my life is ruined because of this one tiny moment what if this is the end what if I never see you again?*

I slammed my hand against the steering wheel. "Fuck! I can't believe I listened to you. We should have never left that party. I should have never gotten in the truck."

"Listened to me? You're the one who just drove away. Don't alleviate your conscience by putting this all on me."

A sick putrescence poured through my veins. I pressed down the gas pedal and sped down the deserted road. Fifty miles per hour. Sixty. Sixty-five.

"Slow down! What are you doing?" Panic clogged your throat. "He'll be fine. It was only a tap."

"He had an oxygen tank!"

You changed tactics. Your voice becoming soft, as if you were speaking to a child. "That woman was helping him. If you stayed and the police got your information, they could have sued for all kinds of bogus medical reasons or you would have been charged with something. David, the situation seems bad, but your punishment, if you stayed, would have been far worse than deserved."

"Shut up, Hope!" This time I did say it. "Maybe, if I stayed, I could have just helped the man up and then felt entirely better about myself as a human being and a citizen worthy of carrying a license and existing in this world."

You sat back in your seat, crossing your arms back over your chest. "Well, God, David. I was just trying to help."

CHAPTER 15

The cold, snowy night. The slide through the intersection. The quick turn of the wheel. No streetlights.

It had been so very dark. I couldn't have seen them. Why had they been out there, at that hour, walking? Not near anything. I played it over and over again in my head: The hollow clang of the oxygen tank as it went down. His crumpled mass, prone in front of the grill of my truck, and the dark splashes of pavement exposed underneath the snow cover. Had there been blood? A black pool creeping out from underneath that poor old man like it does in movies? Somebody's grandfather. The long, tan, matching winter coats. The look of alarm, panic, anger, in the old woman's eyes. Maybe the truck had stopped, the moment frozen, before the man fell over. Maybe it was just the tank I'd hit. And *hit* was too strong, wasn't it? A tap. It had to have been a tap.

I sat up the entire night watching you sleep, your body buried under a mass of blankets. I will never forget the way you sleep. Curled so tightly around yourself, impenetrable, that childlike flush to your face, your mouth always moving—over the words of your poems, your stories, I imagined. The words assigned to this night and the accident and the fire that melted your cheek and the other weighty images that keep us pinned to dreams at night.

It was freezing. I didn't bother to light a fire. I hugged a scratchy wool blanket around my shoulders and sat on the couch in the dim night air of the cabin, watching my breath, replaying the scene over and over in my mind. Each time I did, I came to the same conclusion. *This was your fault.* I needed to blame you. I had to. It was you who'd made me get into that truck when I knew I shouldn't. It had to be you who'd turned me into someone I didn't want to be—the kind of person who left.

Something locked and hardened inside me that night, something deep and cold and solid. Each time I looked at you, anger and disgust and shame roiled together inside me.

We didn't speak for the rest of that achingly long night, or during the drive the next morning back to your house. When I dropped you off, you stared at me for a moment and I looked away. I wondered if this was it. If this would be the thing that would end us. I could tell you knew I had decided something already, and right then, at least, you didn't try to fight it.

When I returned to the cabin alone, I researched accidents and hit-and-runs reported in the area. I obsessively clicked through New Hampshire news sites and police blogs, but nothing came up.

I spent the rest of the day scrubbing the truck. The water froze as it hit the metal. My hands shook as I moved the icy sponge in tight circles. I was washing away evidence. This was a crime scene. I was a criminal. But so far, no one had reported anything about the accident, as far as I could tell. No one was looking for me. And that felt worse. I would never know what happened to that man. I would never make up for what I did.

I kept having this dream where it's winter and I'm running through the forest. Running for my life. Branches scratch at me as I crash through and the farther I go, the darker it gets. An animal is chasing me. Something huge and dark, with teeth. Finally, I see the pond, my pond, and I turn once more to look behind me, but it's not an animal chasing me. It's my grandfather. And instead of looking like he's going to kill me like I expected, he looks stupendously disappointed in me. Disgusted, in fact. And this is worse than anything else I can imagine.

Turn back turn back turn back.

I felt desperate in my need to repent, desperate to make my fantasy of going back in time a reality. To do things differently. I could almost see it. My hand on the man's arm as I bent beside him, my fingers furiously dialing 911.

This loop in my brain kept bringing me back to a memory from middle school when a group of my friends decided to break into the house at the end of my street—a crumbling yellow house, previously inhabited by an older couple and their mentally handicapped adult daughter. In my childhood mind, all three of them were bloated, horrific, deformed. One night, ambulances showed up outside their house, the reflection of the red spinning lights casting creepy shadows through our living room window. Someone left on a stretcher, or they all did, but we never saw them again.

After that night, we dared each other to ring the doorbell, but no one ever had the courage to go through with it. I never developed that fearlessness that drove boys that age to do daring things. I was the idea man but lacked the guts to go through with my crazy schemes. I despised my practicality, my love for coloring inside the lines, my guilt-laden Catholic upbringing. But there were certain things you didn't risk not doing at twelve out of the fear of being a social outcast forever.

One night, we planned to sneak out to the yellow house. We stood side by side on its front porch, staring up at the sulking frame. The paint had chipped and the porch sagged underneath our feet. The second one of my friends mentioned he thought he saw a hand in the window, I made up some excuse and sprinted home.

My hand shook as I turned the knob quietly to let myself into my house. I wasn't supposed to be out that late. My breath heaved in my chest. Taylor sat across from me on the steps when I opened the door.

"Why aren't you in bed?" I asked.

His face looked grim and he didn't say anything. The cordless phone lay on the step by his side. "Taylor, what were you doing?"

A distant wail sounded. The boys had to be in the house by now. Maybe they'd found something.

"I was afraid the people who live in the yellow house would attack you. I heard you talking."

The wail sounded louder. The stirring cry seemed to be following me. Mom and Dad must have been up in their room. Hopefully asleep.

"I called the police," he said to his knees. "So they could protect you."

As soon as the words left his mouth, I recognized the wail. Blue and white lights flooded our street. Taylor and I ran to the window, pressed our faces against the glass. A deep roll of dread replaced any excitement I might have otherwise felt.

I wondered if I stayed that night how my life could have been propelled on a different trajectory. I could have ended up a career criminal like Jimmy. Or grounded until high school like Nick. The only difference in the equation this time was you. You clouded my vision, my ability to reason and make rational decisions for myself. You'd held my hand and walked me straight into this sea of guilt and regret where even my reflection appeared skewed, unfamiliar. Just like your own.

CHAPTER 16

We went a few days without talking at all. When you did start to call, I hit decline. *Sorry. Can't talk right now. Huge deadline*, I texted back. You must have known it was a lie—I barely opened a work email that entire week—but I could have committed vehicular manslaughter and I wanted to put you at the center of it all. I would never drive drunk and leave an old man to die in the snow with his poor wife huddled over him. You had to be at the root of this mistake because I knew myself, right? I was responsible David. David who did the right thing. David who even volunteered at a few of the charities his mother was involved in each year, face-painting the cheeks of toddlers and ladling out globs of mashed potatoes at a homeless shelter. I wasn't the type of person to run from a mistake. An accident. I would face it. I would take care of it. I would stop and call 911. I would make sure the man was okay, apologize, and apologize some more. I would check his pulse, his breathing. I would . . . what? What would I do?

The fact was, I hadn't done what I thought—no, what I *knew*—to be right. And that didn't make you evil; it made me a coward. A coward without the strength to trust his own judgment when his inner voice screamed, *Turn back. Put the truck in park and get out. Get out and see if that man is okay.*

One cold morning a week and a half after the accident, a knock sounded on the wooden door of the shack, and the realization that other human life forms were in my proximity sent such a rush of disorientation to my head and a bolt of fear to my stomach that I dropped the book I was reading and paced the length of the room a few times before moving to the door.

I was wearing gray sweatpants and a hoodie and had a scarf wrapped around my neck—the one you'd knitted for me. I staggered to the door. When had I last showered?

At first, I thought it was you looking to smooth things out between us. Or my mom or Taylor checking in on me because I hadn't talked to either of them since the accident. I unhooked the latch and pulled back the heavy wooden door to see a uniformed police officer peering at me through the screen that sagged against its wooden frame.

I stopped breathing.

This.

This is what I had been waiting for. Tire tracks in the snow. His squad car parked in the drive, waiting, like a shark, for its prey. I hadn't heard him approach—I'd been too wrapped up in the splendor of my own solitary misery. All the guilt and grief and worry was all for this moment. When they would find me. When the cold lick of metal would click over my wrists and his gloved hand on my head would guide me into the back of his vehicle.

"Good afternoon, sir," he said as I pulled open the screen door to face him. I stood there in awkward silence, my lips parted slightly and the pounding of my heart feeling so exaggerated in the quiet winter morning that I was sure he could hear each *thump thump thump* as I waited, steeling myself for the inevitable. For the reading of my rights. For the phrase *hit-and-run*, those words that circled like a carousel around my subconscious during my waking hours.

His gaze wandered behind me to the unwashed dishes, the pile of clothes, the books tossed open and askew as if prepared for a ceremonial burning. "Are you the homeowner?"

I tried to speak, my lips smacking together dryly. The horse—always that horse—whinnied its sharp cry, sounding closer than ever. "Yes," I managed in a high, gasping voice.

His eyebrow twitched and he pulled the brim of his hat down lower against the cold. And suddenly I thought of my grandfather. Of that letter. Of *what they had done*. Had my grandfather stood on this porch and felt the same thing I did right now? The burning shame and stunning fear of what was to come?

"I'm just here to inform you that they are going to be doing some work on the main road out here"—he nodded his head back in the direction he'd come from—"for the next week. A couple of serious frost heaves they want to get ahead of. I'm giving the residents in the area a heads-up to keep an eye out for construction when you're pulling out. Especially with the low visibility in this weather."

A pause. The coffee machine ticked behind us. I swallowed. "And that's all?"

His eyebrows parted and finally, a smile. "You're a little young to be living all the way out here by yourself, aren't you?"

I nodded stupidly, my jaw slack. I suddenly felt twelve years old again.

"Well, that's it. Have a good one." He tugged at his brim again. His heavy boots imprinted the snow with tracks as he walked back toward his car.

The white cover that weighed down the pines and the birches and the maples pressed in on my lungs. Nothing moved; nothing called. Snow covered the frozen ice of the pond that periodically let out deep, melancholy gurgles, air trapped beneath feet of frozen water. A wheezy sigh hissed its way out of my lungs.

That was it. The moment I had anticipated, waited for, dreaded, and depended on. It had snuck up on me and fizzled dead without so much as a spark. Not even a slap on the wrist.

I stood there in the doorway for a while, the air so cold and sharp it pierced my nostrils with each inhale. I was the only living thing. The only thing in color. The farm on the top of the hill across the pond remained still; the cows and tractors were tucked away somewhere, watching the snow, the quiet.

It was only then that I made out a set of footprints in the snow on top of the frozen pond that led to the edge of my property. They seemed to disappear halfway across the pond, into the sharp, dry winter air. I tucked my arms tightly around my chest against the bone-chilling cold. That feeling that someone, something was watching me, was with me in those woods, returned with a swift, humbling weight.

Later, I would become more aware of what existed around me under that wintry blanket of total silence. I would know that if I peered closely through the snow, I could find the tracks of deer or the piles of their pellet droppings or the hawk waiting on a tall branch for something furred and small to make itself known. Sometimes an owl would alert me to its snowy presence or the high shadow of a moose would move from the corner of my eye. When I took the time to look, the quiet and white were never all-encompassing. Underneath the surface, there was always something shifting or rustling. The world wasn't completely dead. With everything stripped down until only white remained, a serenity persisted. It was perfect, in a colorless, miserable way.

CHAPTER 17

You said once that these woods held the whispers of my ghosts, and when I first heard the sound, my mind went to you. I reached for the space next to me in bed, but of course you weren't there. A shard of silver light blinked on the old wood floor of the cabin. The moon shone like a half-broken spotlight through the dusty windows. But the sound hadn't been a whisper. It had sounded like a woman's scream.

A surge of panic thickened in my chest. Just a dream, I convinced myself. But then I heard it again. A wild, guttural echo carried across the pond.

Aside from my first week alone in the cabin, when I was still getting used to the sounds of the woods, this was the only other time real fear had spread from my joints to raise the hair on my arms since I'd moved there. *David, it's your intuition giving you an ice bath*, you would have said.

But whatever was out there wasn't my intuition. What or who was calling me to listen?

The scream sounded a third time. I held my breath and listened. Something twittered, maybe a mouse. The energy in the air changed.

The scream echoed through the screens of my modest cabin

once more before I fell back to sleep. I considered going to look for the source, but the New Hampshire forest stretched on for acres around my small cabin. It could be a coyote, a calf, for all I knew, and I'd be laughed back to the city if I called someone to come out to investigate a lost farm animal on my behalf. Sound carried for miles across that open cavern of stars above the ice cover of the pond. So I held my breath, waiting for something more, until there was only dark and the still air and the sound of my own breath.

CHAPTER 18

Years after the yellow-house incident, when I was in high school, I walked into our family's television room and my mother came up behind me and swept me into a violent, impromptu hug. "Honey, are you depressed?" She cocked her head and smoothed the space around her eyes to express concern. "Because if you are, that's okay, you know. It's okay to feel like that once in a while."

At the time, I was stunned. I don't remember having had an answer for her. If I did, it was in the negative. Depressed? That was for other people, wasn't it? People who dreamt of death. But now? I was sure I felt it: paid-in-full depression. I couldn't describe it any better than as feeling like I'd taken a bite of a poison apple. I fought the urge to walk around bent at the middle, my arms cradling my waist.

The infection spread. I didn't want to work, calls from my family or friends annoyed me, everything was stupid. I just wanted to sleep. My fingers and feet froze as snow piled up outside, over the steps to the cabin. It was all my doing, I realized. I was the one who needed the space. I was the one who stopped answering your calls. I was the one who drove away. I was the one who left.

- - -

I knew I had to drag myself out of the house for a change of scenery and to get the bare minimum of work done. I made it as far as the Starbucks in the outlet mall fifteen minutes from the cabin. I was there only ten minutes when I proceeded to knock my double-shot soy latte directly onto my laptop's keyboard.

"Shit!" I jumped up to grab a stack of napkins. I shook the computer upside down, desperately mopping up the drops of overpriced espresso. I had just about finished writing this long and incredibly boring project for another fitness app that counted calories and breaths and steps and heartbeats and basically told you when you were hungry and when you might have to shit—all the things a normally functioning human body should tell you on its own. It had taken me ages to finish, and if my computer crashed now . . .

A finger tapped my shoulder and I turned to face this small, rounded man who held out his hanky. I wasn't sure what to do with it at first. When we were young, my father used to carry one around with him in his pants pocket, sitting on a magnificent collection of boogers all day. When I hesitated, the man reached out and dabbed his hanky against my arm, soaking up the coffee stain spreading down my shirt.

"Oh," I said, "thank you." I took the hanky from him to finish the job. I placed it back in his shaking hand when I was done.

Thick glasses covered his eyes. His brown coat was buttoned up high, and he wore one of those wool scally caps over his spotted head. "Any time, son," he said, laying his hand on my shoulder. As the warmth from his hand met my arm, I took a closer look at him and nearly dropped my laptop.

It was him.

The man from the accident. I was sure of it. Same slumped frame, same glasses, same coat. It had to be. We were less than a mile from the spot. That crosswalk.

He's okay. He's okay.

At my frozen, shocked expression, the man asked, "You all right?"

"Me? Oh, I'm fine. How, um, are you? Do you want to join me? This seat is free," I said. My words jumped over each other. This was my chance. I would make it up to him. I moved out of the way to clear space for him in the chair across from me. No more oxygen tank. The image of his crumpled form in the snow-dusted crosswalk flashed in my mind, and I winced. But this is what the universe did sometimes, right? Gave you a second chance. A do-over to make things right again. I would clear my moral debts and digest the terrible weight that had lingered in my stomach ever since that night and finally, I thought, be free from this feeling within me.

Holding on to the side of the chair across from me, his hips lowered until he was close enough to plop onto the cushion with a *humph*. Meeting this man's watery eyes—Harold, I learned his name was—made my stomach toss. Maybe the police were still looking for me, or worse, maybe he recognized me, knew me for what I had done, for who I was, and was waiting for my confession.

As I was about to ask Harold if he came to this Starbucks often—the best I could come up with as I sweated through my long underwear—he volunteered the information.

"My teapot sprung a leak. And they've got all these fancy flavors here; I'm trying something new each week. Toasted caramel and spiced what-have-you. When you get to be my age, it's hard to find the newness in things. But then again, there's always spring." His voice wavered in a way my grandfather's never had.

91

"What I don't understand is what you young people are doing spending all this time here on those tiny computers? It's a wonder they make them so thin."

"I'm a writer. Well, sort of. I work for a tech company writing up manuals and such. Nothing too exciting."

"You know, it's funny—you carry around these machines that store all your information. But people like me . . . we keep it all up here." He tapped the side of his head where his wispy gray hairs were the longest. He coughed loudly, couldn't shake it, thumped his chest with his fist. Maybe he did still need the oxygen tank. His collared shirt was neatly buttoned; suspenders looped over his shoulders. He appeared dressed up for an event. Too nice for a coffee shop full of puffy jackets and UGG boots.

"You're right about that," I said. I wanted to ask him if he was okay. If he had any injuries from the night of the accident. If he was breathing any better. Where was his wife? Had she put a mortal curse on my soul? I wanted this off my chest. To confess. But it wouldn't help this man feel any better. It would probably just make him think less of the younger generation of this world. *No ability to accept the consequences of their actions.* That was something my own grandfather would have said.

"How long have you lived around here?"

"Oh, lifetimes," said Harold.

I liked the idea that if you lived someplace long enough you would find your way back there in the next life. Maybe it was the same with you and me. Maybe we would always end up meeting again on a street in Boston, you in your polka-dotted pink dress—or maybe not. The thought pulled at the knot inside me that twisted for you.

"How about yourself?" He brought his tall Starbucks tea up to his lips, carefully testing the temperature before sipping more liberally.

"I just moved into my grandfather's cabin down the road a few months back. He's gone—well, he passed away—so I'm living there now. On a pond."

"Is that so? Which pond, if you don't mind me asking? I do love to fish."

"Mountain Pond," I said, "by the farm. It's just a small little pond, but—"

"Of course, of course. They stock it with trout, right? You can get some catfish in there, too. You know, back when I was more nimble, I had this great little hunting cabin in the woods, a bit farther north. And those weekends away alone in the cabin were probably the best times in my life."

I smiled. This was going okay.

"You hunt?" he asked.

"No . . . well, not yet anyways."

"Gosh, I couldn't hit a moose standing in front of me now with these eyes. But you should get while the getting's good, if you know what I'm saying. Take advantage now, do the things you always wanted, try new activities. While you're still young and able. Take it from an old person like me."

I considered touching his arm in a gesture to show I understood exactly what he was talking about. That this was just the thing I was trying to do. Live independently. Prove to myself I could be self-sufficient. I nodded, my eyes on his, as he went for another sip of tea.

"You should come by sometime," I said, "to fish with me."

"Oh, that'd be great. Really nice idea." Harold nodded as he set his tea back down on the small table in front of us. "Yeah, I'll pick some sunny day when the roads are clear. That's an easy drive from where I am. That'd be nice. I could use the fresh air."

And just like that, a wave of relief, so welcome it nearly brought tears to my eyes, flooded my body. This was one of those fated encounters you always talked about. Synchronicity. The universe lining things up. My opportunity to make things right stood before me. I would fix this mistake. I would befriend this man, help him, offer him companionship—I owed him that much. And then things would be better again. Back to normal.

CHAPTER 19

A few weeks after the accident, we still hadn't seen each other. I kept putting you off. I know. I know what you'd say. *I was being immature. Avoidant.* Canceling plans, cutting our calls short. But I didn't know how to talk to you anymore. I didn't know how to apologize. I felt too much shame for that awful night and everything that followed.

My boss called twice, and I sent those calls to voicemail, too. He asked about the latest project and when I would have the completed copy finished by. I didn't have an answer for either of you.

The crack that formed between us the night of the accident had grown into a crater and then into something so deep and black I wasn't sure I would know how to be with you anymore. As lonely as I was, part of me hoped you would just forget about me. It would be easier that way. If you could just let me go. If enough time passed and I never saw you, maybe I could forget about the accident and my guilt entirely.

But man, it was fucking boring up there by myself in a way I didn't want to admit. I had often proclaimed in the past that I didn't understand people who got bored—I had far too many interests to be bored! This was different. This was cabin-in-the-woods-of-New-Hampshire bored, alone with a version of myself I couldn't reconcile with my past.

I could have invited up Nick, or Mark, or my buddy Aaron from college. A guys' weekend. But alone I was so good at making things worse for myself. And I've never been one to take the easy route. I craved the hollowing isolation of hibernating in the wintery wilderness. I hadn't visited my parents' house in a few weeks. Mom wanted me for dinner. Taylor kept asking, *Why aren't we going snowboarding, bro?* I didn't want to have to explain everything to them. I'd seen Taylor a week ago, and I kept catching him glancing at me.

What? I finally asked. He shook his head. *I don't know, man. I feel like I don't recognize you like this. All somber. You're not yourself. Even your cheekbones look sunken.*

An eerie silence settled on the pond. The sun, brilliant and white, seemed to be up earlier than it should be in winter. I woke with that weird feeling something was missing—something familiar I couldn't put my finger on. I sat on the old picnic table facing the water. It seemed all I could manage. The winter sun warmed my face. Close to forty degrees. I laced up my winter boots and donned the bright orange hunting jacket my mother had gotten me so hunters wouldn't mistake me for a deer while hiking in the woods.

A few inches of snow coated the heavy layer of ice on the pond. I spent thirty minutes shoveling and sliding and sweating on the ice until I cleared a large-enough area to skate on. The last time I'd skated might have been hockey practice in high school. My mom, always thinking of us, of the things we might need—even in her sleep, I imagined—had dropped off my old skates during her last visit. *It could be fun!* she'd said.

I pulled the thick laces tight around my ankles and pressed into the ice, testing it with my weight. Press. Glide. Press. Glide. The ice lifted in bumps and patches, not like the smooth rinks I grew up skating on, but it felt good to be digging into my thighs. To have my breath moving in visible puffs. My hands sweated in my gloves. I bent low, skated faster, then stopped on a dime, turned, went back toward the other end of my rink. Just like we used to do in practice. Again and again. Until I was breathing heavily.

I stopped, my hands resting on my knees.

What was it? That feeling. That thing I seemed to have lost. Something inside me. I was hollowed out as an old tree snag. But as fate would have it, I'd been given another chance with the man from New Year's Eve—a chance to make some sort of peace and build myself back up new.

Riding the first surge of energy I'd felt in weeks, I took off my skates and cut through the woods for a walk behind the cabin to the small stream, past the Patrick trees, as I'd come to call them— that lonely name etched desperately throughout the forest—and past the bare bushes that would hold blueberries come summer. I'd brought my camera with me—a Christmas gift from my parents—and I experimented with the settings as I went.

Deer tracks traced through the snow and stopped at a bed-ded-down area at the base of a wide tree. The ice never froze completely at the dam, and water slipped underneath its old boards. With a stick, I fished out an ancient beer can sunk into the mud. Sometimes I found pieces of glass or beer bottle caps from careless fishermen or sloppy hunters here. My grandfather had kept a collection of really old bottles he'd found in the pond years back; they still sat on one sill of the cabin.

At the sound of a *huff*, I froze. I searched for a deer, a moose— the blast of exhaled air had the makings of a large animal. I walked a few paces along the stream, away from the pond, and saw it. A tall brown horse stared me dead in the eyes. It looked old, its coat was patchy, and it tugged at the leather rope tying it to a nearby tree. I spun around and called out *hello*, looking for its owner or rider.

With each passing second, the horse appeared to get more and more agitated by my presence. I approached it with my palm out, a gesture of surrender, but the horse erupted into a panicked whinnying and began lashing its head back and forth, attempting to break free of its restrictive harness. Its loud, sharp cry was the same sound I'd heard from the cabin all those times.

I backed up, wondering if I should return it to the horse farm on the other side of the pond, but eventually the horse settled back down, and it watched me watching it as I slowly backed away toward my own property.

I cut through the woods and headed up the road toward the farm. Two large black labs ran down the hill to sniff me before heading back up the hill. I looked around for someone to check with about the horse, but the area was empty. The air held the sweet, decayed scent of cow manure.

I decided to continue my walk and I turned right at the small white house with the broken-down tractor in the yard and a collapsing shed in the back. I saw that a lot around here. Heaving gray barns about to give up their ribs and cave in on themselves, and others that already had, looking like a sad reminder of an abandoned past.

Silver buckets clung to the maple trees, collecting sap for the gooey, thick syrup I smelled boiling when the wind was right. In April, the farm down the road opened their pancake house and petting zoo. I thought about those future mornings a lot and how my long run or hike would end with a plate full of pancakes and hot syrup when they finally came.

Someone who didn't know the secrets of a New England

winter would only see the dead land and not realize that fresh buds lay right below the surface, ready to pop in a month or two. At which point, I would start my first garden. My mom would be proud; it would give her something to fuss about when she visited. You would have liked that idea, I knew. You would have probably wanted to plant a few things yourself. Herbs and such.

Small streams crossing the road picked up steam from the ice and snowmelt. I leaped over them, sloshing mud up to my knees. I could still see my breath. Every now and then, if I peered close enough into the woods, I might come across old rusted iron cans or the frame of a tractor part or wheel rod. Low, wandering rock walls marked the property lines that had been put down by someone generations earlier. Grandpa told us once that if you lined up all those old stone property lines, they would be long enough to reach the moon. Whenever I found myself alone, in a place I couldn't imagine other humans had been, I liked to look closely for those traces and wonder about those long-ago people. Who they were and the work they put in to collect and lay these stones and divide this land and what those trees had witnessed since. Maybe my own ancestors, my own family members, had walked these same paths decades ago. Maybe "A," the woman connected to my grandfather, had done the same.

I stopped when I spotted a stone property wall that formed a small square. I squeezed through a tiny metal gate that was stuck halfway open and kicked aside the brush and old leaves to find headstones poking up out of the earth.

The gravestones were old, simple granite squares or crosses, some with more ornate tops or bigger concrete bottoms. Most of them shared the same family name. Some dated back as far as the 1700s. I brushed away the leaves, branches, and forest debris to look at each one. Some stones were adorned with flowers, now colorless and dried; a tattered American flag sat at the base of a veteran's grave. In the back corner there were two small grave-stones—simple, with no design, and with the same birth and death dates. Twins, only a couple years old. I looked for those two letters on each and every readable marking. No A. R.

I sat on the stone wall with mud and cold oozing in through my pants. My eyes and nostrils burned.

I was getting better at not thinking about that night. The clang of the oxygen tank. Harold's eyes, his heavy glasses. Did he slap the hood of the truck as he went down? Or did she, his wife? I tried to remember it, and as soon as I realized what I was doing, I tried to forget. I was making it up to him now. I was making it right. He could have been dead now because of me, because I left. He could have been buried in one of these graves now, hidden underground with centuries' worth of ancestors. And I would have been a kind of killer.

Generations of family rested here for hundreds of years, with all their lives and all their deaths compiled into this small space of forest. Had these people stood in the same spot as me on the pond? Were they the ones who'd laid the stone walls and left the old cans to rust in the woods? Who committed unspeakable acts with married men and addressed them with love in their letters? Did their family line live on?

The word *legacy* loomed in my head. And so did your words: *Do you ever feel like you're just not doing enough?*

CHAPTER 20

I hadn't seen you in almost six weeks. We had exchanged a few texts and short calls, but nothing more. Without you in my life, it was easy to feel unoriginal. I realized that the whole thing about life was as soon as I thought I knew myself, I found a way to prove that notion completely wrong, until I was left with this container of things that had happened and space for the things that would happen in the future and no sure way to connect the lines between the two.

But I had finally settled into the New Hampshire way of life and into my new house. It no longer felt like Grandpa's place, like he perched in the rafters waiting for me to fuck up so he could call me out. Everything was set the way I wanted. A modest TV I streamed movies from my computer through. My bike, snowboard, and hiking shoes stacked up in a corner. Smelly candles you brought up that I got in the habit of lighting in the evenings rested on window sills, the thin trails of smoke following me around the porch like spirits.

My dad promised that once the God-awful stupid cold eased up he and Taylor would help me install a more legitimate kitchen. He came up a few weekends in the fall with his truck full of tools and an oversized tool belt slung around his hips, pretending to look the part of a knowledgeable carpenter. He'd waited all these years for his chance to get back on the land without his father's critical gaze following him. Waited for us to grow up and move into an underdeveloped home in the woods so he could jump in with the excuse to rebuild. But Taylor was actually the handiest of us three. He was good at looking at projects and figuring out the most logical way to approach them. If only he could find a career that allowed him to do as much and get paid for it.

When Taylor had days off from his part-time gig at a local bar, he drove up and we went snowboarding and stayed up late drinking beers and talking about how we actually loved it up there without Grandpa.

The trees were still bare and the sky, wanting to give over to the sun, remained clear and cold. That morning, the grinding of gravel on the road announced a car coming up the drive. I sat on the front porch, drinking coffee. Although the previous week's storm had left snow on the ground, the air held the unmistakable smell of things warming and softening. The birds had woken me again that morning, calling to each other in different chirping tones. I wondered if you would notice that same thing today. We used to be in sync like that. We paid attention to seasons, to the small details that change a person and a place. *It's all in the light*, you once said. The time of day and the season could be determined by the way the light hit a person's face. *We are all just sundials.*

I put down my book and stayed in my seat, listening. Nerves picked up from the base of my stomach. My body always knew things before my mind did. Sensed them. A car door opened; I heard a soft voice, a jangling of something. And a bark.

A bark? Now I had to look. I stood and put down my coffee. The screen-door hinges resisted with a screech as I peered outside and down the drive. Something moved—no, darted—toward me.

Tongue hanging, ears flopping, with each uncoordinated pounce in my direction.

The gray puppy jumped on my legs and fell over backward off the bottom step and into the snow. He squirmed until he found his footing and righted himself. His tongue licked at anything it could find—my arm, face, knee—as I bent down to pet him. His muddy paws left marks all over my shirt as he tried to gnaw on my hand. Then, just as feverishly, he lost interest, his ears perking up as he stared into the trees—something had caught his attention.

He took off into the woods.

"Vincent!" you yelled, standing a few yards away from me, car keys dangling from your hand.

I approached you shyly, like a stranger meeting a girl for the first time, as if I hadn't dated you intensely for months. Could you tell how nervous I was then—my heart racing, my body vibrating with energy?

"You got a dog?"

"I got *you* a dog."

"What? Why?" I stared into the woods, suddenly nervous that the puppy hadn't returned and that it might be my responsibility to make sure he did. A thing that size could be devoured by coyotes or picked up by a hawk. But the dog bounded back through the woods, crashing and tumbling, almost entirely covered in mud now and carrying a branch about twice his length in between his underdeveloped jaws. He looked like a mix between a Husky and a coyote.

"David, if you don't want me here anymore, fine, but you need some company. A dog will be perfect for you. It just makes sense."

I closed the space between us and squeezed your small body to mine. Instinct. When I pulled back, tears crowded the corners of your eyes.

"What's the matter?"

You swiped at your face with the back of your hand, eyes glowing beneath their watery veil. "I missed you," you said. "That's all."

You smiled, kind of sweet and sad, and I regretted any negative thought I'd ever held against you. How could I have blamed you for the accident this whole time? I had been the one to get into the driver's seat that night and the one who'd pulled the truck into reverse and sped off into the night. You seemed to be, once again, the Hope I first met. The Hope with the yellow scarf, pilly and faded in this light, the material stretched in places from overuse. I pressed a kiss to your temple and to your cheek and to your lips.

You wore those tight black leggings you know I like with tall brown riding boots and a cream-colored sweater topped with a puffy jacket. I reached out to touch the scarf before I could stop myself. That same smell of vanilla and lavender and your sweat all mixed together there. You stood as still as a statue, ready for anything. We were only inches apart, and that heat, more heat than I could imagine, emanated from your small body.

"Whose car?" I asked, nodding toward the shiny Beamer in the drive.

"My mom's boyfriend. He let me borrow it." You smiled. "I'm a little nervous driving it. I don't want to scratch it or anything." You brushed your bangs back away from your face. They were cut heavier, hiding more. "Listen, David, about that night . . . I'm sorry I . . ."

I held up my hand. I didn't want you to dredge it all back up, to shatter this moment of easy peace between us, especially when I was handling it. When I planned to make things up to Harold. It wasn't about you anymore.

You nodded. "Okay." So we wouldn't talk about it. After a pause, you added, "You know, I had this dream last night. I was in a raft on this muddy river, trying to get to you, but there were these huge black snakes rippling through the water."

I watched your eyes move over my face.

"I think those snakes are the dark parts of myself I am afraid to face. But I realized I can't do that without you."

"Face the snakes?"

Your laugh sounded perfect, happy, and I would have done anything you said or wanted. I was right back there again. Anything. Putty.

"You should probably feed your dog. I think he's hungry," you said as Vincent attempted to bite the tire on my truck.

I hadn't expected you to stay the night, but maybe you had. You'd bought me a puppy and driven all the way up to the cabin, after all. You had intentions of reuniting us, bridging the gap that had opened between us with the drop of that oxygen tank and the slap of that glove against my hood.

That night, you told me your stories—the ones I'd never heard before. Those black snakes. You knew I had to be able to understand you more if we hoped to continue.

These stories were the ones your lips worked over as you slept. The poems of your past that moved through your subconscious.

You told me the story about the years your mom would throw camping trips in the living room and drag out the sleeping bags and candles whenever the electric bills went unpaid. You told me about your mom's ex-boyfriend, the one you nicknamed Jekyll because in the morning he would smile and make you both pancakes and then by night he'd have transformed, grown dark wings and angry red eyes, and would bellow and squeeze your little arms until his marks of hatred ringed your biceps in blue and black stepping stones.

You told me the other story, too. The one I will never forget. The one that turns my stomach still, to this day. The one when you were too young to be at that particular New Year's Eve party. It made sense now. This past New Year's Eve. How you reacted. How you came loose. When you were only fourteen, too young to be drinking, your mom was working the night shift and the downstairs neighbor in your old apartment building was a senior in high school and having some friends over for a party. They thought you were cute. You had one drink. That was all. All you remember, anyway. But you woke up in a room in that apartment downstairs that you'd never been in before. Your underwear was gone and so was one of your shoes. There was blood on your leg. When you came out, a few of the guys were in the living room, still drinking. When they saw you, they laughed. You ran.

You never told your mom. Or anyone, back then. But you didn't like the way it felt to be inside your body after that. *Like a poison*, you said, *that you can never flush out*. Your body became not your own anymore. Or maybe it never had been to begin with.

I thought of finding those guys and the worst things I could do to them, but still it wouldn't have been enough.

And finally, you told me about the fire. An accident. A candle left burning when the curtain caught. And the smoke. And you not really remembering much more of that night either. You woke up in the hospital and once again, you were transformed. Your body was not your own. But you were glad to be rid of that apartment, of having to pass that senior boy in the hallway. Of that rip cord of terror that shot through your feet whenever you heard his laughter floating up through the floorboards.

There was nothing that could be done or remedied for any of your stories, but that night I didn't sleep because they moved through my mind in ways I knew would change my ability to harden against you. To lock you out as I had that winter.

For once your lips remained still as you slept, your stories already spoken.

- - -

In the morning, you lay resting against my arm. We stared at the ceiling, marking the spider webs in the corners of the farthest beams, listening to Vincent's quick breath from the foot of the bed. We were quiet in the warm air, and it felt as if the whole world thawed with us. I considered apologizing—for the whole stupid fight, for blaming you for that night, for leaving that man, for leaving myself somewhere behind on that dark turn of road, and for everything that had ever happened to you at the hands of a man. But the words got stuck below the hollow of my throat, and I let them stay there, absorbing into the soft tissue, the blood-stream, the bones. They would be my sorries to keep, because playing this game of ours—pretending nothing, ever, had gone wrong between us—felt better. Or, at the very least, easier than the alternative. Easier than the truth.

You drew your hand lightly back and forth across my bare stomach. I let out a deep sigh. Contentment: a simple feeling I had missed since you left. Something I hadn't felt since the last time we lay here, in this bed, with the quilt my grandmother made and the old sheets my mother brought up from Boston, with the mattress that sank so low it hugged us as we slept, and with the wood-burning stove hissing slightly as the remnants of last night's fire smoldered behind the smudged glass-plated door. I came back to you this time, the time before things between us ended in a way where they could never, not even for a warm, quiet morning in my cabin, go back to what they had been.

The local farm's pancake house had opened for the season the previous week, so we drove down for breakfast. The borrowed

BMW's heated leather seats were a far cry from those of your mother's Buick LeSabre, which smelled of old cigarettes—a habit she promised she'd given up decades earlier. The smell just liked her, she said.

I rolled down the window and inhaled because even though the thermometer only read forty-something, the air tasted new.

The pancake house had animals in the back, and we stopped to see them first. Two pigs rooted their muddy snouts around in a trough of something foul smelling, their hooves trampling the brown snow. A yellow-eyed goat pressed his nose between the links of the fence and stared intently at me. A group of chickens pecked at what would eventually be grass.

"I forgive you, you know," you said. You put a quarter into the small red machine, and a handful of chicken feed poured into your palm. You tossed a bit in the direction of the scrambling chickens and held it out to the goat, whose pale tongue roved around the creases of your hand until the last of the feed disappeared.

"For what?" I asked, because I couldn't resist.

"For everything that you've done and will do," you said.

"Good," I said, kissing your hair, because I had already done the same for you.

CHAPTER 21

Harold was coming to the pond to fish for the first time since our chance meeting, although we'd run into each other at Starbucks a few times since then. We'd had to wait for the temperatures to warm, the ice to melt, and the pond to be stocked.

I picked up a bunch of different flavored teas from Stop & Shop, remembering our conversation at Starbucks about his broken teapot. I also bought a container of worms and a few new lures. I cleaned the cabin and set the canoe up by the edge of the pond. I played fetch with Vincent for nearly half an hour, wearing him out to ensure he wasn't a total nutcase when Harold came by. My heart pounded in my chest as if I were prepping for a first date. I wanted to make a good impression on Harold. To show him I was—or could be—a good person.

He was supposed to be there at 3:00 p.m., but I still hadn't heard from him by 4:30, so I decided to give him a call. I picked up my phone and dialed, and I looked up just in time to see Vincent lifting his leg over a stack of books I'd promised myself I would start reading any day now. Kerouac. Vonnegut. Bret Easton Ellis. The kinds of authors guys my age all claimed to be into.

"Shit! Vincent, no!" I ran toward the dog, his tail already between his legs, as I shooed him out the door. The third time this week.

"Hello?" Harold's groggy voice sounded unsteady, like I'd woken him from a nap. I grabbed an old rag from the edge of the sink and started to mop up the yellow puddle.

"Harold? How's it going, buddy? It's me, David." I picked up the books and brought them to the picnic table outside, splaying the pages out to dry.

"David?"

"Uh, yes. David from Starbucks? We were supposed to go fishing." I felt ridiculous. It was worse than the first time I called you.

"Oh, yes, David. How is everything?" I wasn't entirely convinced he remembered me.

"Ah, things are great, thanks. I was just checking in to see if you were still planning on coming down to fish."

The local men with their trucks had already kicked off the season, driving down through the path in the cow pasture on the other side of the hill, dragging tire lines through the mud, as predicted. They fished from the shore or from small rowboats. Some brought sons; others brought fancy tackle boxes and coolers of cold beer. It was the perfect time of early evening—the bugs flitting over the water, the concentric circles rippling. The fish were biting.

"Coming for what dish?"

"I said *coming to fish*. On Mountain Pond? You wouldn't believe the size of this turtle I saw kayaking earlier." I let Vincent back inside.

Ricki, my neighbor who made her own jam and ran a farm stand up the street, had told me about Oscar. "Is he a farmer?" I had asked. But no, Oscar was a turtle, a legendary beast who patrolled the waters of the pond and had only been seen by a lucky few. Bigger than a tractor tire, they said. Older than dirt. I could have sworn a dark shadow had moved under my kayak that morning when I'd sat bobbing in the shallows of the northwest side of the pond—by the lily pads the frogs would soon be frequenting, once they outgrew their tadpole selves.

"Fish. Were we supposed to fish?"

"We planned it when we talked on Wednesday. Remember?"

"Oh, sure. Sure. Well, it might be a little late now for me. It's hard to drive in the dark with these eyes. Practically useless. Could we reschedule, David?"

"Of course," I said, sitting back into a deep pocket of the old sofa. Vincent sat by my feet again, his brown eyes heavy. He licked my hand once, then twice in apology. I tried to give him my sternest *don't pee in the house* look, but I soon caved and scratched at the place in between the ears that he liked. A small cloud of fur lifted and hovered above him for a moment before falling to the floor.

Harold's breath wheezed into the phone.

"Hey, Harold, is everything okay? Do you need anything?"

"Of course not, son. Just caught me out of sorts. Let's say Friday, then? For fishing. Let's make it a sunrise. I'm more likely to remember if it's first thing."

I agreed and ended the call. Vincent took this as an open invitation: he leaped into my lap and licked me right on the lips, as he always managed to do. The horse in the distance whinnied again, that same high, agitated call. Vincent froze for a moment, growling, but let it pass. We sat there together, watching the sun hit lower over the water, until I stood. Tonight, I would fish alone.

The first time Harold and I actually did go fishing—just a few days after that phone call—we didn't catch anything. Just floated for nearly two hours. He told me about the history of the farm at the top of the hill, run by generations of the same family, until more recently, when they'd been forced to sell most of the cows and cull the forests for the lumber, all to make enough to keep the wood stoves burning through the winter.

It was true. Heavy machinery lumbered up the roads all winter long, the trees dropping, the splitters emitting their high whine. More wildlife came down from the woods across the road through my property—deer and coyotes, displaced from the deeper woods and looking for new shelter. Vincent's ears lifted and his barks howled into the night from the protection of the porch.

At intervals throughout our conversation, Harold would pause midsentence to look out over the water, blink, and turn back to me. *Where was I?* he asked each time, and I was happy to jog his memory, eager for him to fill in the color of this land from the time when my dad and his family lived here. Those stories disintegrated with my grandfather, who had never been willing to share, to divulge, to elaborate on what life had been like in the 1900s in small-town New Hampshire. With Harold, it was like diving into a history book.

I was grateful—more than grateful—that during those two hours, he didn't ask the question. Didn't ask why I was out there on the water with him. Didn't wonder about my motives for spending my morning with an elderly gentleman I'd picked up at Starbucks. Maybe, I thought, it was because that's what you do in a small town. You get to know your neighbors. You share gardening tips and eggs and space in a canoe.

At first, my time with Harold did feel like a sort of necessary penance. I remembered the time spent with my own grandfather, after all, as a bitter pill I'd had to swallow. But I found myself really enjoying Harold's company. Conversation was easy. I could relax with him. I didn't have to worry about saying the right thing. He liked to talk, and he was a good storyteller.

"You know," he said, "when I was a kid, you weren't able to see this pond at all from the road; it was completely hidden by pines. That is, until Dynamite Jim came in and blasted the space for the stream, and the loggers cut down the trees on the hillside for cash. As kids, we loved going down to watch the blasts."

"Really?" I looked up at the red barn at the top of the sloping field where the cows liked to graze. The other three-quarters of the pond's perimeter were still tree-covered. "My grandfather never mentioned that."

"What was his name again?" Harold took off his glasses and slowly rubbed one wrinkled eye.

"Theo. Theodore Maloney."

"Theo. Theo. Theo," repeated Harold.

"Yeah, tall with white hair," I began, but I couldn't think how to describe him to distinguish him from any other grumpy old man. "Always wore a red flannel shirt no matter the season," I finally said.

"Of course!" said Harold. He peered back at the small opening in the trees where my picnic table sat bordered by two wooden tiki torches for when the mayflies and mosquitoes were in full force. "It's funny. I didn't recognize it when I first came down your drive. Looked different before. But sure, I knew Theo. And I've been here before, too, on his property. Just didn't recognize it! A small town like this, it's hard not to know everyone. Theo was a serious fella, but always willing to help out a neighbor."

"I always assumed he was a hermit. He never talked to anyone else when we were around."

"Your grandfather kept to himself, but he had a handyman business on the side. Whenever something broke or us less handy folks could no longer use something, Theo would come over and fix and modify and hammer what he could. Never said much doing it, but he was a good man."

"Huh," I said, trying to reconcile this version of my grandfather with the man I knew. I could imagine the grumblings coming out of his mouth about the *cheap bastards*.

"You must take after him." Harold smiled. "He was always outside. Loved these woods. This pond."

A scoffing sound caught in my throat. If Taylor ever heard that comparison, I would never hear the end of it. "I do like the outdoors, but I think that's where the similarities between the two of us end."

"Well, you never know," said Harold. "Sometimes the things we pass on take decades to make themselves known."

I tried to think of what internal things had been passed down from my family to me. My dad's practicality and responsibility. My mom's nervous energy and love of social gatherings. I thought of A. R. and the thing she and my grandfather had done. Maybe it was something like the accident. A dark, snowy road. A small misstep. Maybe eventually it was a choice each of us had—to decide if we wanted to let those genetic properties rise to the surface, like fat in chicken soup, or force them to lie dormant within us until they died off entirely.

CHAPTER 22

"David, something's wrong."

"Hope, what is it? Are you okay? Where are you?" The red, oversized numbers on my alarm clock blinked 3:42 a.m. I pressed my fingers into my eyes, trying to bring myself back to consciousness.

"It's not me. It's the house."

"What's wrong with the house?" I rubbed my head, surprised the call woke me up. I usually kept my phone on silent. Vincent was still sleeping soundly in a pile on my feet, just as he had every night since you first dropped him off.

"The house . . . it's moving. Shifting."

"Hope. I don't understand. Your house is moving? Like an earthquake?"

"No, David. Not like an earthquake. It's the house. It's shifting. It's an old house."

You and your mom had moved into her new boyfriend's house over the winter. I know you weren't crazy about the idea to begin with—moving in with an almost-stranger. But it meant saving a lot of money for your mother, who was happier than she had been in years, according to you. I suggested you could move to New Hampshire with me, but it was too far away from the hospital. And the guy was nice, you guessed. He always wore denim—denim shirt, denim pants—and he wore his hair in a stubby ponytail you thought was gross. For a nursing assistant, you tended to find a lot of banal things to be gross. Other people's toothbrushes, hair gel, chipped nail polish on toes, and the way grease from the bacon I made every Saturday morning hardened to a solid in the coffee mug I kept by my little sink. It made me wonder what about me you found gross.

"So, it's probably just what you said. An old house shifting. You're just trying to freak yourself out. You know how you do that sometimes."

"David, don't patronize me. I'm serious. Just now, I got up to go to the bathroom, and I couldn't get out of my room. The door was jammed shut. I tugged using my full body weight, and just when I was sure someone had locked me in there and I was going to scream, it popped open. No problem. But it always worked fine before. It's like the house is trying to seal me away."

"Hope, it's just an old house. Go to sleep."

"David, listen to me! If you just come here, you'll see it, too. Yesterday, I noticed the windows don't shut right anymore either. They close on a slant."

I propped myself up against one of the pillows you complained was too flat with the pillowcase you deemed too nubby. Sometimes, it was amusing to play along with your fantasies—the ghosts in the attic, houses having memories, and such—but I was tired and it was late.

"And that's the house trying to trap you again? It sounds like this guy needs to have the foundation looked at, not a Ghostbuster."

"It's not a ghost! It's the house itself. It wants to keep me here. Even the floor in my room, around the corners, is starting to curl back on itself, and I'm too scared to look to see what's underneath."

"What kind of floor do you have in your room?"

"David! You don't understand what I'm trying to say, do you?"

I dropped my head back against the headboard and closed my eyes. "Apparently not. Why don't you talk to—what's his name again? Jack? Show him what you noticed and ask him what he thinks. It's an old farmhouse, right?"

"Yeah, but could you just come here?" You used that little-girl voice, that sad one I found so hard to turn down.

"When?"

"Tomorrow, like when you wake up."

"Seriously, Hope? I need to finish up this project I was supposed to get done last week for work. If I don't do it, I swear my boss is going to kill me . . ."

"Please?"

I tried to imagine the way you looked on the phone, sitting in the dark on the edge of your bed, your knees pulled up into your chest. You were trying to tell me something then. This was a hint at the thing lurking between those walls, but I couldn't see it and wouldn't for some time.

I let out a sigh. "Okay, I'll see you for breakfast."

The ranch-style home sat squat with an attached barn that had been converted into this great, open family room. An awesome house that my dad would describe as *having character*. An antique spinning wheel sat in one corner and the high, open shelves in the kitchen housed a collection of colorful, dainty china, probably centuries old. A little alcove with a small vanity mirror and sink sat kitty-corner in your bedroom. The ceilings were low, and a fluffy white duvet covered your bed. Fireplaces lay vacant like gaping mouths in the bedrooms and living room.

When I arrived, you sat on your bed with a collapsed posture, your hands resting in your lap, palms up. You looked drained. Defeated. The wind kicked up outside, and things creaked and hissed. You didn't seem to want to make eye contact. I could see why you had been spooked. "I'm now convinced there are dead bodies hidden under the floorboards," you said.

I had dropped Vincent at my parents' house and already wished I had stayed there, eating my mom's food, joking with Taylor. I rolled my eyes. "Hope, you are acting totally crazy. It's just an old house."

"I am *not* crazy." The intensity of your stern gaze silenced me from saying anything more.

A rug the color of a faded sky covered much of the floor. An antique crystal chandelier hung from the center of the ceiling, and a huge white bureau and mirror took up much of the wall. A whole lot more character than the sterile apartment you'd just moved out of. A few photos were tucked into the seam of the mirror. One was of us from that day on top of the mountain—the day of the first snow. In it, your eyes were wide and your mouth, while not necessarily smiling, seemed at peace. My hair was twisting in ten different directions.

When I lifted the photo for closer inspection, a second photo, tucked behind it, fell to the bureau. Two girls with sharp cheekbones and shadowy hollows beneath them. I had seen this girl before. In the photo, the two of you smiled with your faces pressed together, a dulled expression in your eyes. It was taken outside somewhere. A brick building loomed in the background in what looked like early spring: stark tree branches poked out from behind your shoulder, but the light looked warm. I turned to you as you rummaged in the back of your closet for something, hangers pinging to the floor. I wondered if that dress with the polka dots hung forgotten in the back somewhere.

"Hope, who is this girl?"

You glanced up and did a double take, launching to grab the photo from my hands. "She's no one. An old friend."

"But she looks familiar. Where do you know her from?"

"Why are you being so nosy?" You stuffed the photo into your back pocket and returned to the closet.

"Didn't we run into her once? At the Christmas tree place. I remember—"

"Finally," you said. You emerged holding a necklace with a cross hanging from the end of a dull gold chain. I'd never known you to be religious. You noticed my gaze as you tugged the cross over your neck. "To keep away the spirits," you said, shrugging.

"Oh, that's right," I said. "The spirits of the dead bodies. So they keep them under here, huh?" I stomped my foot a few times on the hardwood floor.

"Stop teasing," you said. "I hate it when you don't take me seriously."

"Who says I'm not taking you seriously?"

"Your face does. I know you, David. Was Jack downstairs when you came in?" you whispered.

"No, why, would he care that I'm here?"

You looked flustered. You pushed your hair away from your face, but it just stuck there. You were sweating.

"Hope, are you all right? You seem really freaked out."

"That's because I am freaked out. And I need Jack to tell you what he told me."

"What'd he tell you?"

Without answering, you grabbed me by the arm and tugged me downstairs.

- - -

"Jack, this is David."

Jack removed his head out from underneath the kitchen sink and—true to Hope's description—he wore denim from top to bottom, intersected in the middle by a brown leather belt. He stood in the kitchen barefoot, his chubby white toes tapping against the floor as he walked over to greet me.

"Buddy." He slapped me on the back, and I half expected him to offer me a beer or something, even though it was before 10:00 a.m. Jack stood a good number of inches taller than me—a big guy, with irises almost as dark as his pupils. "Nice to meet you, pal." He smelled of cigarettes and unwashed clothes.

You shifted from foot to foot, chewing on the side of your index finger. I remembered I was supposed to ask him something.

"Hey, nice to meet you. So, Hope was wondering if you could relay the information about this house being haunted? She thinks I might believe it more hearing it from you."

Jack laughed, a hairy hand on his stomach, as he leaned in toward me. "Women, right? Always worrying about ghosts when it's the Peeping Tom next door that's the real problem!" He slapped me on the back again, harder than I expected, and I lurched forward.

You giggled, a hand covering your mouth. This was a new thing of yours: a hand up to your face almost always, whether you were biting on the nail or tucking it by your chin or curling it over your cheek.

You ducked inside the fridge for something, and Jack angled himself to eye your ass in those tight jeans. He punched me in the arm with an approving wink as he began talking. "I never said anything about a ghost, but if you ever get scared, honey baby, you just let Jack know." He directed this to you.

You hated it when I called you baby. I considered punching him back in the arm, a little harder than friendly. How could your mom be dating this prick?

"Anyways, so the story I was told when I bought the house was that right where we are standing"—he tapped his right foot a few times for dramatic effect—"a murder was committed."

"See?" you said, as if this somehow explained your increasing paranoia. "Tell the rest, Jack."

Jack smiled proudly. "So, this used to be a working farm, obviously. Back in the day. And this is, like, in the 1800s or some shit-crazy time. And anyway, the farmer—Farmer John, we'll call him—hires this farmhand. This local kid does a decent-enough job around the farm, until he starts to pick up extra responsibilities where Farmer John's wife is concerned."

Jack winked and nudged me in the side with his elbow, still smiling, and to be an asshole I shook my head like I didn't understand.

"The kid was sleeping with Farmer John's wife," said Jack a bit louder. "So, one morning, Farmer John comes into the kitchen, sees the kid leaning into his own wife for a kiss, and he blows the kid's head off right there in the kitchen." Jack cocked his imaginary rifle at me. "BLAM!"

You and I both jumped.

"So, that's your ghost?" I directed my question to you. "The farmhand?"

Jack leaned forward, inspecting the wood floor of the kitchen. "I wonder if you can still make out the blood stains . . ."

You leaned in to get a look, too, and he jumped up with a yell and grabbed your shoulders and you let out a scream. Jack laughed as he pulled you into a hug, a hug you seemed okay with. Again, I wanted to punch the guy, but instead I turned to head back upstairs to your room, muttering, "Well, I guess it all makes sense now."

You joined me upstairs, your eyes down, a small smile playing on your lips.

"I found him, you know," I said. My voice held an edge I hadn't intended.

This caught your attention. Good. I wanted to shock you, because I'd felt this uncomfortable feeling in my stomach ever since getting that call from you the previous night. It felt like you were slipping out from under me to a place I couldn't reach.

Your smile disappeared, and you met my eyes. "Found who?"

"The man. From the accident. Harold."

Your eyes widened, and you sat down on the bed. It was the first time I'd spoken of the accident since that night. "Harold? That's his name? Jesus, David. How did you . . . where did you find him?"

I knew what you were really asking—*Did you find him in a morgue, in a hospital, in a police report?*

You stood suddenly. "You didn't tell him, did you? About that night? That you were the one who . . ."

I let you trail off, then shook my head. "Don't worry about it. I'm handling it."

"But, David, listen. If you get caught, if the police find out . . ." You started to pace the room.

"I have it under control," I said, all the while wondering if I did. Wondering if there was a way you could make up for a mistake of that caliber without ever actually uttering the words *I'm sorry.*

CHAPTER 23

Vincent ran around me, indulging in intermittent, feverish bursts of digging in a desperate search for chipmunks. I had bought him a runner and strung him a wide breadth of space between two trees, but I'd quickly learned that Vincent wasn't a "runner" type of dog. He needed to tear through the woods and leap into the water. The vet guessed he was part Husky, as I suspected, but he was the clumsiest dog I'd ever met. Often, when he came crashing into the cabin, he slid into the little card table I used for my meals, sending cups and plates flying to the floor, where they shattered to pieces.

At first I thought you were crazy for getting me a dog, but after that winter I realized a person couldn't exist without connecting regularly to another living being. And Vincent did help close the terrible space between the night of the accident and those weeks we stopped talking. I'd learned the hard way that having you, even with our challenges, was infinitely better than not having you.

I brought Vincent to explore the surrounding woods with me regularly. He would zigzag through the forest, chasing the smells of day-old deer shit as I snapped photos. So much of the local ecology I knew nothing about, so I began collecting. Picking leaves and pocketing stones and snapping digital photos of the herd of thick black tadpoles I spotted lazing in the sunny, shallow water and the dark, leafy fern shoots that curled at the end like a come-hither finger. There are forty-eight 4,000-foot summits in the White Mountains, and I vowed to conquer them all within the year. More and more, I turned down invitations to birthday bus parties in Boston and camping trips with friends. I liked being alone, outdoors, with the dog. My mind opened, and I was getting better at learning new things, like how to fix a leaking roof without asking my dad. How to make you happy. How to cook poached eggs without the whites spreading out into a filmy ghost in the bottom of my pan. I was growing. Exploring.

The rain had been relentless for the past two weeks and had kept Vincent and me inside more than I liked. The previous evening, a sharp sound had cut through the steady patter on the roof. An animal? A fallen branch? A hunter choosing the rainy evening for target practice? Something was off. This had been happening a lot the past three weeks. I strained my ears for the sound of a yowl, a scream, anything like that other night.

Just then, the screen door creaked open and banged shut, as if someone had come onto the porch. I put down the book I was reading and considered the rifle tucked away in the rafters. I had left the heavy wooden door open so air could circulate. I crept over to the window that faced the front porch, trying to make as little noise as possible. My breath came out quick, and the room felt muggy—steamy, even.

The porch was empty except for Vincent, who stood at the door to the cabin, growling. The screen door swung open on its old hinges again. I usually slipped the small hook-and-eye lock into place before heading to bed—more out of habit than for protection from anything. My mother used to lock the windows even on an eighty-degree day in July so as not to "send an open invitation" to local burglars.

The wind swung the screen door open again and it thumped twice, bouncing against the wooden frame. I looked at Vincent. "Do you need to go out?" He cocked his head to look back at me. I decided to join him for a short walk.

I liked the way the rain sounded on the new leaves, and the cool light of evening fell lightly over my shoulders as I followed Vincent into the woods. He kept his nose to the ground, sniffing and pausing, running up ahead and back to me. The longer daylight hours were a welcome relief from the knife cuts of brief sun during the winter. But no matter the season, nights in these woods were busy and more populated than I liked to believe in the daylight. Small, glowing eyes—green, red, orange—shone in the dark. Owls hooted from out-of-sight branches. Things rustled and cracked.

We took the path behind the shack toward the stream. Sometimes I found Vincent there, digging wildly, up to his ears in dirt by the dam. One time, he emerged with a bleeding chipmunk. He trotted over to the front steps of the cabin and dropped it proudly, sounding his single bark to announce the arrival of his gift. The poor thing's back legs still kicked, his middle crushed. The blood in the fur around Vincent's mouth bothered me more than the half-dead chipmunk. I squeezed my eyes shut when I lowered my shovel down hard and fast over the small rodent.

You wanted to give the animal a proper burial. I didn't tell you about the part with the shovel in case you saw some violence in me you hadn't noticed there before.

I made it to the stream just as the rain changed from a light mist to a steady patter. Vincent ran ahead of me and out of sight. I called his name and whistled for him, pausing to listen. I thought I made out the sound of his bark, so I continued on, pulling up the hood of my raincoat, feeling secure and secret as I moved through the trees.

Still no sign of him. "Vincent! You pain-in-the-ass dog." I stumbled almost a quarter of the way around the pond when another bark sounded. It was higher, alarmed, like maybe he was hurt, so I started to run.

Vincent, who loved swimming after my kayak on the pond and scaring away all the fish, didn't like the rain. When the drops hit him, he looked up with surprise, even indignation, at getting wet against his will. It wasn't like him to run this far out of sight. I prayed I didn't find him circled by a pack of hungry coyotes.

"Vincent!"

Another stream ran fast down on my right. I wasn't familiar with this side of the pond. He barked again, and I ran up the embankment along the stream, stumbling and grabbing branches to get myself up the slippery slope.

Finally, I reached a clearing. The ground leveled, and for a moment the rain slowed. I spotted something at the far end of the clearing. A modest structure that looked like a round, domed teepee. A yurt, maybe.

"Vincent?" I called with less confidence now. I stopped moving and spun around at the sound of branches cracking. I whistled. "Vincent? Come here, boy!" I started walking toward the strange house. Living grass covered the roof. A dirty canvas flapped against the sidewalls. A modest fire pit sat a few yards away from the structure. A tattered blue tarp covered a long stretch of firewood. Rope that could be clotheslines crisscrossed in between trees. Rusted lawn tools leaned against the thick base of an old oak.

Thunder cracked in the distance. I scanned the area for Vincent. There was no clear access to the road. No sign of a driveway or car.

Vincent barked again, and I finally saw him. He stood at the far end of the clearing by a fence—soggy planks hammered together haphazardly—with a horse on the other side. It was the same horse I'd found in the woods those months back. The two animals stared at one another. Something like a whisper crawled up the back of my neck, and my hair stood on end. *Maybe lightning is about to strike*, I tried to convince myself as I ordered Vincent back to my side, but I knew it was the chill of clarity that someone else lived on this pond. My mirror opposite, sitting across from me all this time. I wasn't as alone in these woods as I had imagined.

CHAPTER 24

The door opened easily—Harold never locked it—and I found him sitting on his back porch, yesterday's newspaper sprawled across his lap. A carton of recently washed strawberries sat on the side table next to him, bleeding pink into the paper towel below.

"David!" he said. Pressing his hands into the sides of his armchair, he heaved himself up and down a handful of times before gaining enough momentum to stand. It was hard to watch.

Harold had invited me over to dinner after two successful fishing outings. I worried about meeting his wife. There was a good chance she would recognize me even if Harold didn't, but I took his invitation as a sure sign of our friendship progressing. Spending time with Harold was a salve on my ruined conscience after this winter, and I enjoyed his company more than I cared to admit. After our first day of fishing, I'd started calling to check in on him every few days to see if he needed anything—groceries, a Starbucks tea, a walk outside.

"Let me give you a hand with that," I said, joining Harold at his stove as he began to stir a pot of limp spaghetti noodles. I was relieved to see the house seemed empty except for Harold. He moved out of the way and collapsed into one of the straight-backed kitchen chairs. He got tired easily. It may have been his leg. His hip. Some trouble I'd caused with the accident, which I now doubted I would ever bring up. I had gone too far down this road with him as my friend to ruin it by alleviating my guilt.

"Thanks, son. You know, you're pretty good around the kitchen."

I laughed. All I had done for him thus far was boil water. "So, this Saturday, we'll get out on the pond again?"

"Oh yes, absolutely. You've got to get out there before all those poachers with their big-wheel trucks drag up all the good ones. That's what they do. Dig up the pastures with their big tires, use their fancy lures to catch every fish in the pond within the first week of spring, before they even have a chance to grow. It's a shame."

I nodded, remembering some of the jackasses in canoes who tossed Bud cans into their wake. I clicked off the burner to Harold's gas stove. Steam rose from the pot of boiled, murky water. The colander on the counter looked dirty, so I gave it a quick rinse before letting the hot, wilted noodles slide to its bottom. The steam hit my face in a hot rush. I rolled up my sleeves.

"Speaking of Hopkins Farm, do you know if they own all the land on the other side of the pond from me?"

Harold looked out the window, his face crinkled in concentration. On the far sill sat a collection of ocean remnants: brain coral, bleached driftwood, a conch shell. A little old fishing net hung below it with a fake plastic fish and sea life superglued to the net—a faded rubber shark, his eyes rubbed out, opened his flimsy jaws toward a chipped sunfish. Harold followed my gaze. "Carol loves the ocean. Always wanted to live near it, but we could never afford it." He sighed and coughed into his fist. "That was the best I could do."

"About that farm," I tried again. "Do you know if anyone lives out there on that property across from me? Maybe a relative of the Hopkins family?"

Harold smiled a little. "Well, there have always been stories. A hermit. People living off the grid out there. Living off the land. Not paying taxes. Not really a part of society as you and I know it. But this was all ages ago. I haven't heard anything like that in a long time. Did I ever tell you about how my wife and I used to run a maple sugar house right down by your pond there?" Harold tucked his hands up under his arms as he leaned back in his chair.

"Really? I didn't know that. That's awesome. Do you still know how to make it? The syrup?"

"Of course. Of course," said Harold. He leaned forward to pull his black socks higher up his waxy calves. "We would make big batches of it. Had an evaporator, and you had to toss all kinds of wood in to keep it going. And that steam would rise. *Mmm.* I miss that smell. My wife swore it kept her skin looking young. Did I mention my wife was a nurse?"

"I don't think you did. Was she one of those nurses who traveled to people's homes to take care of them?" I tried to imagine her at my own cabin, leaning over my grandfather, a palm on his forehead to check for fever. But I couldn't imagine him coming down with anything—or, even if he had, seeking medical help. He wouldn't let it get to him. Couldn't show that kind of weakness. Not until the heart attack got him for good, of course.

"Oh, sure, they had that back then. But she worked at a hospital in Laconia for the feebleminded." He chuckled. "They used to call them *nut houses.* Not a particularly nice term."

"She must have been a pretty tough lady," I said. I imagined Nurse Ratched in heavy white shoes and a grimace that could scare a patient of any size into submission.

"She had to make jokes about it, I think. To keep sane herself.

Saw things, people, that would make your skin crawl. Even worse so, a lot of her patients were just young women."

"What was the matter with them?"

"Sadly, nothing at all. They just happened to get pregnant before marriage. Met a nice-looking guy, home from the service. It was really not all that uncommon. And then the girls would be sent away, institutionalized, and some never really left the system."

"So they didn't have a mental illness? They were just pregnant?"

"That's right, according to my wife. It broke her heart to see those poor girls, totally alone, abandoned by their fellas and their families. Surrounded by folks who were actually insane. They would cry for weeks after giving up their babies, and it was assumed they were broken anyway, so they just stayed."

"That's crazy!" A clock with an alarming rooster face ticked away above the table.

"In more ways than one." Harold smiled at the unintentional pun. "My wife was the progressive one. Invited those women over for dinner some nights. Those poor, sad girls. She did what she could to help."

"And you? Did you mind the extra company?"

"The more the merrier, I always say!" Harold's voice rose louder than needed. "Especially, when it comes to pretty young ladies." He winked at me in a way that made it clear he'd never been the type to wink at these pretty ladies. He'd been a loyal husband, no doubt.

"Where is your wife now, if you don't mind me asking?" I tried not to look nervous as I asked this, turning away from Harold and pulling two large plates down from the cabinet, one of which was missing a triangular chip of porcelain on its edge. I scooped a huge helping of spaghetti onto each of our plates, my heartbeat thumping, remembering the old woman's steely gaze through my windshield.

"Oh, she's gone, son. Got sick, bless her heart. Cancer. It was over quick. It's just me now."

Gone? I could still hear the strong, gravelly sound of her voice as she yelled something to me through the window of my truck. Her mittened hand whacking the hood. That was only about four months ago. But I supposed that was how it went when you became his age. People just slipped away. You couldn't count on anything from one season to the next.

"I'm so . . . I'm so sorry to hear that." This news somehow felt like my fault. It all felt like my fault with Harold. The fact this guy was old and sore and tired and I wasn't somehow felt like my fault. I upturned the jar of pasta sauce Harold had left out on the counter over each plate and finished them off with a couple shakes of grated Parmesan, the kind from the green container that sits in the back of a fridge for years. I handed the plate of spaghetti to him, along with a glass of water.

"Just how I like it," he said, smiling. Within seconds, sauce formed a halo around his mouth. "She painted all those rock animals, you know."

Doe-eyed creatures painted on stones of every size were propped up in the corners of Harold's home. A gray rock with a jutting beak had been transformed into a duck. A kitten curled up by the fire on a smooth, mica-flecked stone. A rabbit posed by the back door as a doorstop, ready to make a quick exit. The collection of brightly painted pets must be his only company now.

"Well, you've got a beautiful house," I said, because I remembered this was something polite people said. The sentiment was a bit generous—sure, it had once been cottage-cozy, probably when Carol was alive, but now newspapers, books, and stacks of mail cluttered the tables, and the smell of something like old sandwiches and shoe polish hung in the air. How was it that women all seemed to know how to do those things? To keep up a home? To feed a family?

134

"Maybe I can teach you how to make maple syrup. Do you see how much in sells for in the supermarkets now?"

"Yeah, especially in stores outside of New Hampshire. I would love to. This weekend?"

He laughed with his eyes closed, a hand on his stomach. "Oh no. Forty-degree days and twenty-degree nights. That's what you need, David. Some years, your window is smaller than others. We are too far along in spring now."

His kitchen was about ninety degrees. The ornamental roosters perched, unmoving, in every inch of the room—on the tablecloth, on top of the cupboards, as salt and pepper shakers— looked about ready to drop their feathers. His heating bill must have been astronomical.

"My grandfather used to buy us those maple sugar candies," I said. "My brother and I would eat them one lick at a time to make sure they lasted as long as possible."

"That's some self-restraint. I love popping the whole thing in my mouth and then waiting for that moment when it all goes to liquid. Kind of like solder."

"I've never soldered anything before."

Harold's gray eyebrows arched up toward his hairline in surprise. The brown-spotted skin of his forehead wrinkled like a shar-pei's. "You got a special girl?" asked Harold, changing course abruptly.

"Yes, I've got a girl."

He nodded, his gaze on his spaghetti, as if he already knew all this, and he waited for me to get it out. I waited for him to ask me something more, to urge me on to tell him about Hope, but he continued to chew with what I presumed were dentures.

"She . . . she's great. She's got red hair. She's Hope."

"*She's hope.* That's a great sentiment. I felt like that about my wife. She was wild, too. Wild and hope." Harold laughed, head back, eyes closed.

CHAPTER 25

knew this girl who could control lightning.

"I can't do this with the dog watching," you said.

Vincent sat by the door to the porch, his eyes locked on mine. He wanted to go out. He had been in front of the door like there was something out there he had to get at. His ears perked up as he stared out the window in the direction of the water. He scratched at the floor with one paw, whining. He would have to wait.

"Just ignore him," I said.

You put both your hands on my shoulders. "Seriously, David. This is creeping me out. He's just *watching* us."

"He's not watching us. He's a dog. He's waiting to go outside."

"Well, do you think you could put him outside?"

"Just let him wait."

"I'm serious." You tugged your dress back down over your waist. Your thighs were thin and hairless, like a girl's. A bird protested loudly somewhere over the pond. I tugged up my pants. I left the buckle undone, but I knew my window had slammed shut. You often found some excuse for us to stop mid-romp, especially if we were in the cabin. *I think there are ants crawling on me. Did you hear that? It sounded like someone laughing. Do you think there's someone out there? Why is this creaking so much? Do you think*

*the bed is going to break? We have to stop. I'm too hungry/cold/tired/
fill-in-the-blank.*

Did I disgust you in some way? Sometimes when I kissed
you, my mouth full on your mouth, I could feel you pulling back,
shrinking, ever so imperceptibly. Like you didn't want to be doing
this, but had to. Other times, you were entirely someone else.
Like that time after I found those letters—it was like something
untamable rose out of you. A lust inspired by those words of devotion you wished you felt for me. Or maybe you did feel that for me
at some point. I'll never know.

That night, the sky had taken on an eerie green. The trees
bent back and forth under the weight of the wind. The rain
pinned a deafening orchestra against the old roof. The lightning
brightened the pond and flashed through parts of the forest in an
unpredictable display.

You loved storms as much as I did. *I can feel the electricity*, you
once told me, the littlest hairs on your arms rising, a flame burning down the center of you.

I had just run out to the truck to grab the bags of groceries
we'd picked up. The paper bags melted in my dash through the
rain. The screen door slammed shut behind me, and as I shook off
my hood, I saw you on the porch. One graceful, pale leg draped
over the edge of my blue recliner. Hair, down and wild, looking
longer and a deeper shade of red than I ever remembered it being.
You wore a tiny, lacy pair of black underwear and a matching bra.
No scarf. It had been a long time since I'd seen you like this, so
exposed. So open. The unscarred skin of your limbs shone white
and clean against the dullness of my dirty cabin. The look in your
eyes was unreadable. The candles flickered in strange animal patterns along the walls of the cabin.

"Come here," you said. Even your voice was different, deeper,
rooted down into something I couldn't name.

Did you plan that night? The way you arranged yourself so fast, looking like this tiny, bad ballerina . . . The thought that this had to be motivated by *something* crossed my mind, but I never bothered to explore it further. Your arms stretched out on the chair, manning your throne.

I dropped the bags and stood there for a moment—not sure what to do, not wanting to ruin this image. I needed every bit of this, of you, forever. But if I got in the way too soon, I knew it'd be ruined. So instead of moving toward you, I grabbed my camera and paused. You didn't react. I moved up close, shrugged off my sodden jacket. Your chest rose with each breath, a bit ragged, unfocused, as if the air and all that came with each inhale was too much to contain.

Click. Your wild hair. A gentle, sloping ear and a side profile of your face. The small nose. Red lips. I couldn't remember if your lips were always that red. Or were you wearing makeup? You rarely did. You dropped your head back. Click. The strong line of your chin and the delicate throat and then thick scars pulsing with your heartbeat. Click. You let out a little sigh. It was hard not to touch you this close up. Click. Your stomach, smooth and white. Click. You writhed a bit on the chair, your hips twisting. You were enjoying it—were electrified, even. By being seen.

Your fingers, with nails also painted red, arched on the armrests as you turned away from me. Click. The sharp angles of your knees and ankles led to small, delicate feet. Click. Your breath quickened. Click. You let out a moan. I dropped the camera, scooped you up, and covered you, those red nails clinging to my back.

Thunder sounded. You were fierce and fiery, ripping off my shirt and climbing on top of me. Lightning flashed once and then again. The screaming of the rain on the roof drowned out any noise, as if your hands were covering my ears—and maybe they were. The thunder boomed and the trees swayed faster around us.

Another bolt of lightning flashed and you quickened, squeezing and grinding on top of me. The thunder shook the small cabin and you began to laugh. You threw your head back, your chin tilting up, your teeth bared. And then, at once, you dropped back down, your hands on either side of my chest, smiling, your chest heaving.

"I can control it, you know." You moved your hips in slow circles. You were killing me.

"Control what?" I asked.

"The storm." The room lit with another flash. "Inside this room. This is all me." You laughed again with a toss of your hair. And although I didn't understand it at the time, that the feeling of control was something you experienced so rarely in this world, so rarely even in your own body, that just a glimpse of it electrified you.

I said "I know" as you began to move again and the wind picked up.

CHAPTER 26

Vincent licked the foot I dangled over the edge of my recliner on the front porch. Late morning, still in my underwear, the coffee just beginning to drip. I didn't have the energy to make it into Starbucks that day, although I always did better work away from where the fish were biting. As I patted Vincent, I thought of that property across the pond and the eerie feeling I had finding out that someone else had lived so close to me this entire time. I planned to keep Vincent away from there, just in case.

My phone alarm trilled, reminding me that I should also worry about normal things, like working.

I was assigned to write about this new app—another rideshare service. My deadline had come and gone a few days earlier. Again. I couldn't focus the way I usually could. I missed the creative writing I'd played with in college, the way it had pushed my mind. Back then, I would squeeze my eyes and try to rephrase an idea or image in my head to enable its freedom. This work, in contrast, was rote, manual, technical, dry, free of any flare or personality. But it paid for and allowed me to live this experimental life for the year. I was so close to finishing this project, I just needed to sit with it a bit longer and get it over with.

My cell phone made an agitated vibration on the folding

table, and my heart jumped thinking it'd be you, thinking of that night with the storm, and wondering if I'd ever get to see you like that again. So exposed. So wild. Before you, I'd really only had one other girlfriend—in college, a friend of mine for a long time before anything happened between us. She hung out in my larger group of friends, and we started sleeping together when we got drunk at the same parties and continued doing so until we graduated. That went on for so long I think neither one of us was ever sure how to make it into something more, even if we wanted to. She asked me once when I was going out to a brunch with her parents what should she introduce me as, and I looked at her stupidly, blank-faced, not sure what else we would call each other aside from friends and realizing in that instant that the whole time she had been wanting us to be something more. And that I couldn't ever give her that. I was so clueless then.

I reached for the phone to answer. "David," said Harold's voice. "Is that you, son?"

"Harold! How are you doing?" Vincent cocked his head to one side as I sat up in my chair.

"Oh, I'm good, good, real good. I was just coming around the corner and was going to pull into your drive. I didn't want to give you a start, so I thought I should give you a ring first. I never care for people sneaking up on me."

"Oh, of course, Harold, drive right up. I'm just inside."

I pulled on an old T-shirt and a pair of shorts and hopped the few steps down off the porch and outside. Vincent ran up to meet the car: an old, tank-like Volvo crawled up my long, unpaved drive. It took him about twenty minutes just to reach the cabin.

I gave him a wave, still standing by my steps. The driver's side door creaked open and, after lowering one foot at a time, he hoisted himself out. He wasn't wearing his glasses. I thought how frightening it would be to encounter this man on the road.

He waved back to me and slowly ambled to his backseat to remove his rod and tackle. He wore khaki pants and a button-down shirt with suspenders, even in this weather. Even for a boat on a remote pond. His white hair whipped around his head like a halo.

He finally made it over to me. "David! How've you been?" He stuck out his hand and shook mine. I smiled at the formality of it all. "I've been looking forward to getting out there this morning. I appreciate you taking me on the boat. I've got to admit, on my own, balance can be a little tricky. I usually can only fish from the shore these days."

He said this every time we went fishing.

"Oh, no problem, Harold. It's good to see you, too." I was certain we hadn't made plans.

"What a good boy!" said Harold, running his hand along Vincent's back. Vincent was a sucker for pats and would roll over for anyone if he believed there was the chance of a belly rub. He seemed to think so now, because he flopped over and stretched out his legs.

"Yeah," I said, "he's a pretty good dog. When he isn't eating the side of the couch or chewing branches in the house. He has an eye for destruction."

"Oh, well, he's still just a pup. They all outgrow it. It's nice to have the company, though. We used to have a dog—what was its name? Big as a horse, this thing was! Would walk right up to the dinner table and steal the dinner ham right out from underneath us. My wife would be furious."

Harold held on to his stomach when he laughed, and his eyes crinkled. He must get lonely. No wife. No kids. No more pets. I was all he had, in a way. A friend. The kind that would hit him with a truck and run away like a coward.

Today was the day I would come clean, I decided. I didn't

want him to think the only reason I was friends with him was to make up for my mistake. For what I had done. For the accident. I mean, maybe it started that way, but now I considered him a genuine friend. Would I have invited him fishing in the first place if it weren't for that night? Probably not, but maybe that was the way fate worked. It made you fuck up just so you turned around another corner to find someone you needed to meet or something you needed to learn.

I dragged the canoe out from underneath the porch and down to the water. I got in the water up to my shins, pulling the boat down in with me. Vincent rooted around in the first foot or two of water, searching for crayfish or frogs. He submerged his whole head, not realizing he couldn't breathe down there, until he burst back up, eyes wide and shocked.

I loaded up the rods and tackle. It was too early for a beer and Harold didn't seem like the type to imbibe, so I threw in a few water bottles and a bag of chips. If my dad had taught me anything, it was to be prepared.

My grandfather was the opposite. He believed in scarcity. *You only need what you can carry.* And the rest you could lock away in a box, I guessed.

I held on to the edge of the canoe for Harold. I thought, as I had every time I'd taken him out in the thing, that a rowboat or something sturdier would have been far more practical for attempting such an endeavor with an eighty-year-old man. He stepped one shoe in, and the boat rocked considerably. The cool water moved around my calves as I dug down deeper into the soft bottom of the pond. "Don't worry," I said. "I've got it."

He put his hand on my shoulder and set the other foot in. The boat rocked violently, side to side. Harold grabbed the top of my head, knocking my hat into the water. Vincent pounced on the hat like it was a live duck and dragged it back to shore, shaking it between his jaws. Just as I was about to lose balance myself, Harold sat with a bit of a splash onto the back seat. I held the boat for a few more moments to settle it. I was glad I'd put the padded red cushion out for him on the canoe bench; his landing might not have been as smooth had I forgotten.

"She's a shaky bastard, isn't she?" said Harold.

I laughed, retrieved my hat, and stepped over the edge and into the boat myself. "She sure is."

Things were calmer on the water. Harold resumed normal breathing—or at least I did. The boat leveled. The water smoothed. Harold, squinting his eyes, squeezed a worm onto the end of his hook. A vibrant green surrounded the lake. The things newly sprouted stretched toward the sun. A few of the mallards honked their way into a landing across the pond. Cows grazed up on the hillside by the farm. It was a perfect day.

"I don't know how you fish with that nonsense," said Harold.

"Power bait?" I pinched a bit of the bright orange stuff onto the end of my hook.

"It looks toxic. I wouldn't want to eat it. Would you? If I were a fish, I would much rather go for a worm. You know, my wife once tried to convince me that worms were good for you and contained lots of healthy protein. She sautéed one up—a big fat earthworm—with butter and a little parsley, the works, and set it out in front of me for dinner."

"Seriously? Did you eat it?" I pulled apart the sides of the bag of potato chips and threw a few into my mouth after casting. I extended the bag to Harold, but he politely declined.

"Very seriously. Her face was stone calm." Harold started laughing. He leaned back and squeezed his eyes shut. I grabbed the end of his rod as it started to slip into the pond. "I stare at the worm for a few moments, not sure what to make of it, and then I stare back at her, and she's already busying herself in the kitchen, cleaning up pots and such. I look back at the worm and pick up my fork, and she turns"—Harold pauses to put on a fishing hat to cover his face from the warm sun—"and finally she says, after I'm sitting there a while just staring at the thing, 'I swore you would eat anything I put in front of you. Guess I was wrong.' So she picks up the plate with the worm, dumps it into the trash, and hands me spaghetti instead."

Harold doubled over laughing, and I joined in. I wasn't sure I got the joke, but I found it hard not to smile seeing Harold enjoying the memory so much.

When he sat back up, he wiped his wet eyes and shook his head. "She was always like that. Pulling pranks. She was a funny woman. I can't help but worry that each day she's gone, I lose a bit more of her. It wasn't until she was gone that I realized how much she did. I probably wouldn't have survived this long without her all those years. I took it all for granted. The cooking, the cleaning, the bills. She did so much more than I ever did in this lifetime. I wish I had been able to see that sooner."

My hands shook as I forced a smile. I had to tell him now, or else this was going to drive me crazy. "Harold, there's . . . well, there's something I have to tell you."

"What's that, son? Ooh, did you see that? I think they're biting." He started to reel in his rod quickly, yanking it back, again almost knocking himself into the water.

I had to get this out. Adrenaline surged through my stomach, and I tucked my hands in between my knees and squeezed.

"Harold, this winter, back in January . . ." I paused, wanting to form the words correctly but knowing I needed to ride the wave of momentum to get them out of my system. "I was driving and it was dark and late, and I was heading to the cabin with Hope."

As soon as I said your name, I knew I shouldn't have brought you into this. This was my mistake. My burden to carry. Not yours.

"Oh, right. Such a pretty name. My wife's name was Carol. A solid name. Just like her."

"I'm . . . I'm sorry to hear about your wife . . . passing away."

"It was very hard. I always wondered if she was happy enough with just me. I hoped so. I wanted to give her a happy life. Whether we realize it or not, women bear the brunt of the weight in this world. It's not fair, really, what they are put through that most of us men never even recognize."

I couldn't hear what he was telling me then; now I wish I had. It would have helped me understand you better. But I was too focused on getting my own message out. "Well, what I was saying . . ." I thought a fish tugged at my line, but I ignored it. The fish could wait. This couldn't. "That winter night, I was driving and, well, I think I saw you. You and your wife. You were crossing the road and it was dark—"

"This January?" Harold crinkled his nose and let out a chuckle. "You saw my wife and me walking this January? Well, that sure must have been a sight, huh! Me, hand in hand with a ghost!" He lost it again, laughing, until tears gathered and spilled down his wrinkled cheeks.

"No, Harold. I'm sure of it. It was when you were sick. You told me you were sick this winter. And you were walking across the road. The snow—"

Vincent barked a few times from the shore.

Harold placed his hand on my knee and straightened his face. "Son, my wife's been dead for eight years."

I shook my head. *No.* That couldn't be right. Maybe it hadn't been his wife, then, but someone else he had been walking with that night. I recognized him the instant I saw him that day in Starbucks. I had to make it right. "But I know it was you. I . . . I . . . I hit you."

"What do you mean?" Harold's eyebrows knitted in confusion.

"With my truck. I was with Hope, and she made me . . . well, we were . . . and suddenly you and this woman were in front of me and I pulled out too fast, and I hit you, it was more of a nudge. A tap. I can't forgive myself for leaving. I'm so sorry, but I just had to tell you."

Harold looked down at the bottom of the boat. He despised me. I was a low form of human. And I stooped so low as to throw you under the bus with me. I'm not sure why I cared so much, but it screwed up my insides imagining such a good soul thinking so poorly of me.

"Son, I think you've got something on your line."

"Oh, right." I began to reel it in slowly, the weight of a fish tugging against me, swimming against the hook, against his fate that would always, always be pulling him forward.

"The thing is," Harold said, "sometimes we do things and we're not sure why. And maybe we're not proud of those things, and that's fine. But the only way to make sure we don't make those same mistakes again is to stop fooling ourselves. Sometimes bad things—or in your case, old men who look like me"—Harold smiled here—"pop up in the road to tell you something is not right, you're heading off course. And you have to take your head out of your ass just long enough to figure out how to set yourself straight."

And that was it. He didn't ask any questions or probe for more details. He was okay to leave it at that. I sighed with gluttonous relief and a release of the breath I'd held since that New Year's night. I expected Harold to look up at me with disgust—hatred, even—after I confessed. But I should have known better. Harold would forgive me. For anything I did or would ever do, as you liked to say. Because he was a friend. I wanted to hug him as my throat tightened with some kind of emotion—some swell of surrender—as if finally the black weight lurking in the back of my mind was lifting. It didn't matter that Harold wasn't the guy, wasn't the one who I'd wronged. It still made a difference to me that he didn't see me as a bad seed, even after my confession.

"I know, I know," he said. "That's another one I got from my wife. The mouth on that woman!" He blessed himself and gazed heavenward before pointing to my rounded rod. "Nicely done, son. I think you caught yourself the first trout of the trip."

CHAPTER 27

Harold's words kept looping in my head: *sometimes bad things pop up in the road to tell you you're heading off course.* But how was I off course? Moving into the cabin? Dating you? My job? I had been happy then, hadn't I? I tried to remember New Year's Eve, that party, but the details blurred, overridden by the memory of the accident, which was branded into my brain. And most shocking of all—it hadn't been Harold in the road. He had been home, warm and safe. Probably snoozing in his big armchair, his TV airing end-of-the-year festivities on low. This whole time it hadn't been him.

Although we'd never even really discussed our time apart, or what, in the end, brought us back to one another, I knew you knew how deep the accident had cut into me. How that kind of guilt could weigh on a person. Typically, you could recall my past transgressions or things I said months earlier, take them out of context, and seamlessly work them into a current argument with ease and skill. You must have had a whole filing system worked out for the tiny facial expressions I inadvertently made that all meant something. But never that night. That one you left alone.

After letting Vincent out, I logged into my computer to start work for the day. The bold email subject line at the top of the inbox brought all meandering thoughts about Harold and the accident to an abrupt halt. **Re: Change in Employment**. The email was from my boss. My first reaction was to not open it. To ignore it completely. I knew what it would say. Maybe if I deleted it right away, I could pretend I hadn't gotten the notice. That this wasn't happening. I'd only started this job in September. How would this look on my résumé?

We're going to have to let you go. I read the line about a hundred times once I eventually did work up the courage to open the email. They were downsizing. The startup had grown too fast, too soon. They were letting me go. I'd just turned in the work for my last project, so I was done now. Officially unemployed.

I lay down shirtless on the rug, my laptop propped open beside me. Vincent lay next to me, panting. My stomach grumbled. I hadn't eaten anything for breakfast and neither had the dog, through no fault of his own.

All that day, I lost the will to manage even basic human tasks like showering and feeding myself. Grease weighed down my hair, and my own stink seemed trapped within the four walls of the small cabin.

I was officially what some might refer to as a complete loser. And like any other loser, I immediately called my mom, the one person always willing to offer me judgment-free advice when all I needed to do was complain. She was always on our side. Even when Dad was being an asshole, she would whisper confidential reassurances to us when he left the room.

"Well, honey," she said, "maybe you should call your boss."

"And what? Ask him to un-fire me?" I hated hearing that tone in my own voice. My mom didn't deserve to be given a whiny attitude by anyone, especially not her grown son. But I felt powerless to stop it.

"David, they didn't fire you. You got let go. You're a very talented, hard-working individual. I'm sure if you just explain . . ." Her words were metered and even and echoed through the speakerphone into the room. Vincent's ears perked up, and he tilted his head to one side at the sound of her voice, like he did when trying to place the calls of animals through the trees.

"Ma, that's not even true. I mean, I would have gotten rid of me too, honestly. I don't even know why I am so surprised. They were paying me well, and lately I've had a hard time sticking to deadlines and staying on top of things. It's just me here, and . . ." I sighed. "It makes sense that I'm one of the positions they cut."

"Oh, honey. Don't talk like that. You are a good, solid worker. A great worker. Remember how you helped your father when he put in that new tile floor? You were such a good help then."

I was thirteen then. I remembered my dad catching Taylor and me on the back steps sharing a bag of Swedish Fish when we were supposed to be helping grout.

"Mom, I owe like a million dollars in loans. I'm drowning in loans. How am I supposed to be able to do anything with my life with so much debt?" I pressed my hand to my sweaty forehead, trying to force air into my lungs.

"Oh, honey." She sighed because she wished she had the answers. And so did I.

I had always wanted to be a writer—or more specifically, a reporter. It seemed glamorous. Important. Almost like a detective, but more expressive. A pencil tucked behind my ear, my glasses (which I didn't need yet but which I imagined one day I would) sliding down my nose as I pored over the facts of some investigative piece I had to pull together before my deadline. But it hadn't been like that. I had traded in my short-lived stint at the news station for this technical writing position because it paid so much more, and now I'd been left with nothing. Not even the surety that writing of any kind, let alone reporting, was the career path I hoped to pursue. I thought of my grandfather living in this cabin, and it started to make sense. Maybe when life hit you with too many punches it was smarter to give it all up and retreat into solitude. Smarter and safer. There was less that could go wrong when your world was shrunk to a tiny two-room cabin, on a tiny pond, with only the sounds of the peepers at night and the birds in the morning to keep you company.

That night, I opened a bottle of red wine and filled my mug to the brim. I sat and stared and drank. What the fuck was I going to do now? Would I have to leave this place? Move in with my parents and find a job back in Boston? I had really messed things up. I'd hardly paid any attention to work. I'd put in the bare minimum. What had I expected to happen?

I poured myself another glass, and another, until the room hugged in toward me from all corners. I stood and, on impulse, pulled my grandfather's box back down from the rafters. The lock was still open. I pulled back the lid and stared at the contents inside. There were a few things I hadn't noticed the first time. A dried seahorse. A large coin, too smudged and old to read the year or the country. A tiny knit cap, like the kind they might put on the head of an infant in a hospital. And those gloves, yellowed lace, small enough to belong to a girl.

I tried to imagine what I would preserve if I were to narrow my life down to a keepsake box of treasures. A photo of you from the first day we met. A screen-grab from that video taken on Newbury Street. Vincent's first puppy collar. My worn copy of *Slaughterhouse-Five*. And something from this place, from this land, from this cabin. A stone. A lure. A hand-drawn map to show me the way back to myself when I'd fallen too far off the track I expected to be on, when I'd made mistakes too big, it seemed, to recover from.

CHAPTER 28

lender, pale ribbons of gray, auburn, and yellow laced together in a tight embrace in a shadowbox on the wall of the tavern. "What do you think it's made of? You have to guess." Our tour guide's eyes widened with excitement as she smoothed the front of her bibbed brown dress and waited for a response. We stared up at the wreath.

Sanbornton Old Days, celebrated at the start of summer, honored the history of my small farm town with tours, running hourly, of the Lane Tavern, which dated back to the early 1800s. I'd always had a thing for history, and I was especially hungry for the stories now. I hoped they'd connect the dots between my grandfather, A. R., and the stories Harold had told me.

The tour guide showed us one of the first fridges ever invented and walked us through the house over wide, warped floorboards. She demonstrated how they used to put a brick into this box that looked like a toaster oven, put the box into the fire, and, once it was nice and warm, place their feet on top of it to keep them from freezing in the winter. Her black lace-up shoes clicked across the floor as she pointed to the original bar, which had a pull-down cage to protect guests from getting at the alcohol during off-hours. She told us the story of the local celebrity who invented the most popular brand of horse-drawn carriages, used all over the world back then.

"Is it made from dried flowers?" you asked, turning back to the wreath.

"It looks like bits of tree bark," I said.

The tour guide clapped her hands together and grinned. The rest of the room was bare except for a fireplace and a few paintings on the wall. The local historians had not yet been able to identify the paintings' subjects. The largest two were of the same woman, who was dressed in black and had a severe, slender nose and stony glare. Maybe a muse or a lover or a dignitary. Could this have been A. R.? The type of woman who intimidated even from a painting?

"She had to be rich, whoever she was," whispered the tour guide to me. "And admired. You needed money back then to sit for portraits—and a man to commission the work."

"Women," you said. "Nature's art pieces, made for the enjoyment and pleasure of men."

Our tour guide smirked at your comment. A middle-aged couple moved up behind us, and we all stared back at the framed wreath. Our reflections in the clear case contorted our faces into shadowy specters.

"Okay, you give up?" asked our tour guide. She stood close behind me, right by my left shoulder, close enough for me to smell her astringent breath. "It's made of hair." She gestured to her own hair—brittle brown, laced with wiry strands of gray, and twisted back into a bun. "They would cut locks of hair from their deceased loved ones. People died early and often back then." She giggled and continued in a theatrical whisper, "The women would spend hours weaving these intricate wreaths from the hair of their dead. See the colors here? All hair." She laughed again, louder this time, and tossed her head back.

You moved closer to the wreath until nearly touching the glass. "David, it's like the lock of hair. From your grandfather's box." You turned back to look at me. "What will you keep of me when I'm gone?"

Sometimes you would corner me in conversations about sentimentality and sadness, always implying that I didn't really know sadness because I hadn't lost anyone close to me. Like, real close. *Even your parents are still together*, you would say, as if my luck disgusted you. I would open my mouth to argue how ridiculous it was to compare grief like that but would stop myself because I couldn't yet imagine you gone.

"The women would cut locks of their hair to send off with their sweeties who left for war," added the tour guide. "Hair was a gift of love that could be easily shared as a symbolic token of their heart." She clasped her hands together over her chest and stared at the wreath, maybe imagining the best days of her own old love. I wondered if she had done it at any point—cut a lock and slipped it into the palm of a lover, just to get the point across.

CHAPTER 29

Harold and I strolled to the next booth at the farmer's market, and he inspected a few stalks of rhubarb as if trying to determine their authenticity. "Did you know that before Sanbornton was Sanbornton, it was called Crotchtown? Quite the name, huh!" Harold laughed. "My wife thought that was so funny. She loved details like that."

My neighbor Ricki had been the one to recommend I check out this market, which ran once a week on Tuesday afternoons from three to six in a field behind someone's house. It was a few days before the Fourth, so American flags waved from every telephone pole down Main Street's short stretch. Trucks parked on the grass. People with dogs on leashes milled about, and everyone seemed to know each other on a first-name basis. Millie sold delicate, hand-painted local landscapes. Beth sold canned jams and jellies. A younger man in a baseball hat sold handmade popsicles out of a large cooler.

I had picked Harold up from his house and driven him over to buy a few fresh fruits and veggies. He'd told me something vague on the phone the other day—"the damn doctor won't let me drive my own car anymore"—which was a relief in my book but seemed to bother Harold a lot. I wasn't sure if he had anyone else to help him run his errands, so I'd offered up my time. I needed the break from mindlessly trolling internet job boards, and I didn't exactly have anything better to do.

"So, what have you been up to there, son?" Harold asked as we left the rhubarb behind. "Catching any big ones on the pond?"

I shook my head. "Nothing much. But there's all kinds of life that has grown up since spring. I saw a couple of painted turtles, and those big tadpoles are now huge green frogs. The sound of their croaking is so loud it's incredible."

"Gotta find a lady somehow! They're just like the rest of us. Kind of like how you wear your hair up like that?"

"My hair?" I asked, reaching up to feel for anything that my hair might be doing that I wasn't aware of. He must have forgotten I'd told him that I already "had a lady."

"Oh sure, kind of longer on top and messy and pushed up. It's all about using your calling card to attract a mate."

He picked up a pie and began the same process he'd gone through with the rhubarb, pulling it close to his eyes, inspecting and turning it slightly side to side. I thought maybe he didn't have any money, so I pulled out a twenty-dollar bill and handed it to the lady.

"For the pie," I said, gesturing to the one in Harold's hands. He didn't seem to notice the transaction, so I recovered the pie as he began to set it back down on the table. He moved on to the next stall of locally produced wines. He seemed distracted, but still impeccably dressed, with neat slacks, a leather belt, and a tucked-in checkered shirt. His hair was meticulously greased and combed over. I guessed, comparatively, my hair was doing pretty crazy things, and I certainly couldn't remember the last time I'd gotten it cut.

Only then, as I followed Harold, did I remember that I shouldn't be pulling out twenties—not even for pie, not even for

Harold—because I was unemployed. Two of my other buddies back home—one was in finance and another an engineer—were going through the same thing and collecting unemployment. It sounded like they were living the life, playing video games all afternoon or hanging on the beach and getting fat off of too much beer and barbecue. Luckily, I didn't need to pay rent, but then again, my monthly loan payment was about a rent check in itself. And there were taxes to pay for the land, even here in New Hampshire where the state motto is *Live free or die*. I'd always liked the organization, the reliability of taking care of my bills each month. I'd kept folders and budgeting apps. Until I stopped receiving a paycheck.

"Harold," I said, jogging to catch up with him, the pie in one hand, "have I ever mentioned the box I found in my grandfather's cabin?"

He turned to look at me for a moment, the sun glinting off his eyes, and for a second I wasn't sure if he recognized me or not. "Oh, yes, son," he said finally. "What about this box?" He held up a bottle of honey wine, preparing for inspection.

"Well, it's like this old, locked chest. I found it in the rafters. Inside were all these letters, a pair of women's gloves, and a few other things."

He looked more excited than I anticipated. "Ooh, a treasure! I used to make my wife these treasure maps. I'd draw them out for her and hide something in the forest or in our yard or somewhere in the house, and I would have something waiting for her there. A gift or something little I picked up or found. Sometimes just a pretty rock or flowers. Every time she saw one of my maps she'd say, 'Oh, Harold,' like she was annoyed with me—every time—but I could see her smile as she followed my drawing. She loved the thrill of the hunt."

Harold laughed again, and I wondered if he wished he were dead, just so he could see his Carol again.

"So, the letters were addressed to my grandfather," I picked back up again, trying to steer Harold around to the question I really wanted to ask.

"Mr. Maloney? I remember him." Harold smiled and lowered himself into one of the Adirondack chairs set out in the center of the market. He liked to talk about the past. Those memories came to him easier.

"Did you ever know his wife? My grandmother?"

Harold wiped his heavy hand along the side of his cheek as he gazed up. "Yes, yes. I remember her. I'd see her at church on Sundays and such, but never out much more than that. She was a sickly woman, wasn't she? Died fairly young?"

"Um, I guess I don't really know. Sickly how?"

"I don't know. I heard she was sweet as pie, but died of a broken heart."

"What does that mean, died of a broken heart? Why would her heart have been broken?"

"What do you take me for? The town gossip? How would I know?" Harold laughed. "I bet Carol could have told you, though."

"Did you know anyone with the initials A. R. who used to live around here?" I knew I was reaching, but in a small town with such long roots, it seemed worth a shot.

"My, you've certainly got a lot of questions today!" He tilted his head. "Are you up to something? You know, you're not very good at hiding things. It's all over your face. I can see it. You're up to something."

I laughed and sat into the chair next to his, trying not to seem overly eager. "I'm just curious. To tell you the truth, the letters I found in the box"—I decided it would be easiest to get answers from Harold by being as direct as possible—"seem like they are between my grandfather and some other woman with the initials A. R. Like love letters. Maybe someone he met after my grandmother died."

"Really? Well, isn't that something. Certainly curious. A. R. A. R. I don't think I remember any women in the area with those initials. Because, you know, all the family names in town: the Abbotts, the Masons, the Hopkins, et cetera."

"It had to be a local woman. I'm not sure how my grandfather would have met anyone otherwise. He wasn't the traveling type . . ." I was thinking as I was talking. A flush rose to my cheeks. Harold *had* to remember.

"I really can't think of anyone. Do you know where she lived?"

"No, Harold," I said, feeling a bit exasperated despite myself. I thought of the ring and the gloves. "She must have been slender, and . . . I don't know, educated? The letter I read was in proper English; she had good grammar."

Harold just shook his head slowly. "I'm sorry, son. I wish I could be of more help. Usually I'm good at remembering the things from way back, but the initials aren't ringing a bell."

"No, I'm sorry." I reined myself in. "Of course you can't remember. That was, like, ages ago."

A black-and-white dog, a collie, trotted over to us and sniffed at the hem of Harold's pants and then did the same to me, probably picking up Vincent's scent. The summer sun was high and bright.

Harold pushed himself back up to stand. "Can't believe the Fourth is this weekend. Summer at its best!" The grass gleamed a shiny green underneath his heavy footfalls as he moved toward the parking lot. He brought his hand up to shade his eyes, scanning the lot—looking for, I presumed, his car, which he would be disappointed not to find.

CHAPTER 30

A few of my friends and their girlfriends were coming up to New Hampshire for the weekend. They were camping out and bringing a bunch of beer, burgers, and fireworks for the Fourth of July. As my savings dwindled, my most cost-effective option these days was to invite people to come to me.

I made the mistake of not telling you about this plan until a few days beforehand. I tensed every time I started to tell you because I anticipated your disapproval. The last time you'd seen any of them had been New Year's Eve, and so many times over the past few months I'd canceled on them and avoided their parties because of you. I was afraid of having to relive any part of that night. When I finally worked up the nerve to bring it up, you looked at me for a moment, your eyes pinched as if you were deciding something. "That's fine," you said, and you went back to reading your book. It was that easy.

The weather was shaping up to be one of those really hot New England weekends, the ones that make me sweat even in the shade, even with my shirt off. My friends came up the driveway in a honking caravan, peeling their sweaty bodies off hot car seats. They unloaded coolers, a beer pong table, a badminton net, a golden retriever named Yellow, and a pile of sleeping bags.

Vincent charged after Yellow, and the two of them ran immediately into the pond.

You caught my eye before stepping toward everyone out from underneath the canopy of a broad-branched sugar maple. You somehow remembered all their names: Nick, Matt, Mark, Clara, and Stephanie. You doled out hellos and made small talk about what a great weekend it was going to be. You were really trying—to be cordial, to be friendly, to be normal. Your light summer scarf perched atop your bare shoulders, only a bikini underneath. The guys stared and the girls looked wary, as girls usually were around you, especially after their last encounter. None of them knew about the New Year's accident, just your bizarre drunken behavior at the party. I realized in that moment that no one in my life knew about the accident except for you and Harold.

After they finished unloading, I went over to help Mark set up the tent. He clearly had no idea how to assemble it. I grabbed one of the ends and began fitting the poles together.

Hands on hips, Mark surveyed the property. "Dude, you're seriously living the simple life up here. Doesn't it ever get a little, I don't know . . . dull?"

"Sometimes, I guess. But it's not like I'm alone all the time. I have H—"I almost said Harold, but a relationship like that would go way over Mark's head. "Hope. You know, I keep busy."

Mark looked at me sideways. "You don't miss the city? The parties? The bars?"

I slid the longest metal pole through the center of the tent and worked it slowly out the opposite end as Mark did the same from the other corner. "Honestly? Not really. I think it's been good for me to simplify."

"So you're going to live in this shack, shit in an outhouse, and, what—farm?—up here forever?"

"I mean, my plan was to try it for a year. We'll see how it goes." As I said it, I realized for the first time that my year would be up in four months, and I couldn't imagine myself leaving. Not now. Not when my life was just shifting into gear, just readying to move forward in some—any—direction. I hadn't realized before I left my cozy life and easy Allston apartment that I wanted, or needed, some big kind of change. Something to wake me up and shake me from my average, safe existence.

Mark lowered his voice. "And things seem good"—he nodded his head in your direction—"between you two? I thought you guys were done after this winter. You stopped mentioning her at all."

"Yep, things are better now."

Mark straightened. His eyes shifted to a spot past my shoulder, somewhere in the woods.

"What is it?"

He shook his head. "Nothing. For a second, I thought I saw someone standing there. I'm hallucinating. And potentially a tiny bit stoned."

I spun around and stared through the trees, into the Patrick forest. Looking for that sign, that feeling of a nearby presence, I knew so well now.

"Should we light off some of these fireworks now?" asked Clara as she came up beside Mark. She planted a kiss on his cheek, then dug through the choose-your-own-adventure mixed bag of colored explosives the burly man behind the counter at the fireworks store had hand-selected.

The group voted to follow our original plan and go to the drive-in movie theater and fireworks show at Weirs Beach on Lake Winnipesaukee. Nick, my brother, and I used to go as kids with my grandfather, who would bring his folding chair and a cigar. He'd set up shop directly in front of the rows of cars and yell at the screen as if the movie directly interfered with his personal life. "That picture wasn't anything to write home about," he'd grumble after each one. Usually, we stayed for two.

We loaded up the back of Nick's truck with sleeping bags, a stereo, bug spray, booze, and chips. It was kind of how I'd always imagined things would be. Memories of these moments with friends and warm air and summer nights have gotten me through winters like this last one.

Weirs Beach hadn't changed since we were kids. A typical New England summer destination, the place was popular with old guys on motorcycles and families with cotton candy and pocketfuls of arcade tickets. Lake Winnipesaukee was big and clean and filled with boats and summer tourists poised for a good view of the fireworks. A small water park consisting of about five slides—another place Taylor and I always begged our grandfather to bring us to, but he said no, insisting the pools were too full of piss—loomed dark and dormant at night.

The drive-in consisted of a large, crumbling parking lot with four screens, a retro concession stand with week-old popcorn, and only an $8.50 charge for a double feature.

The first movie was about some guy the government was after because he'd figured out something they didn't want him to know, and it included a beautiful blonde he met along the way who, for some reason, joined him for his arduous escape/car chase/gun fight. We could have watched anything. You tucked yourself under my arm in the back corner of Nick's truck, surrounded by sleeping bags and pillows. It was still warm, even at that time of night. Another mosquito spun around my head with its high, incessant buzz, and I swatted at it.

"Mosquitoes have never liked me," you said. "I'm not sweet enough."

"You are plenty sweet," I said, leaning over to kiss you on the mouth.

"Stop," you laughed, pushing me back. "It's true, though, you know."

"What is?"

"Even the bugs can tell. I'm spoiled fruit."

"Bugs like spoiled fruit," I said.

You weren't smiling anymore. "There's something I have to tell you." Your eyes welled slightly, and I sat up.

"Hope, what is it?"

You opened your mouth to say more, but a bang shot off and smoke filled the sky. Our eyes turned upward. A red and blue flash exploded next. Our group cheered and raised their cups toward the brightening sky. Boom. Crash. Boom.

I caught your eyes again. "What do you have to tell me?"

"It's nothing." You just shook your head, as if releasing whatever confession had momentarily lingered there, and forced a smile onto your upturned face, which changed from red to purple to gold as I studied it. "Don't worry about it. It's nothing."

CHAPTER 31

My friends left on Sunday—a little sunburned and dehydrated, and trailing empty beer cans in their wake. Vincent sniffed at the ground as I picked up the empties and remnants of burned-out fireworks.

They all had work on Monday. You did, too. And to be honest, the silence that followed felt good. Peace was once again restored to my quiet patch of woods. I vowed to spend at least part of the day applying for jobs.

I washed the dishes accumulating around the kitchen, sorted the rest of the cans into recycling, and loaded the back of my truck with the bags of trash to be brought to the dump. It was one of the hardest things to get used to up here. No trash service. Mail was delivered to my little P.O. box at the small post office down the road. Things weren't as easily accessible as they were back in Boston. Not that I got much mail of importance. I thought of my grandfather's letters—the kind delivered by lace-clad hands. The type of mail you held on to for a lifetime and beyond because it actually meant something. Because it was something more than a credit card company trying to talk you into more debt. I tried to imagine who she could have been. A local farmer's wife? Or maybe a woman who wasn't originally from around here. Someone with status. Someone like the woman painted in the old Sanbornton tavern. The slender nose, the severe features. Or maybe someone more like you—someone who was convinced she was ruined by her own past, whatever her "mistake" was, before my grandfather ever met her.

I stopped by Harold's house unannounced because he wasn't answering his phone and I hadn't heard from him in a few days, which was abnormal because he was now in the habit of calling me daily, usually in the morning. The calls were always the same, but I looked forward to them. He would first comment on the weather, then ask if the fish were biting, and then talk about his garden or ask about mine.

I paused on his porch. The front door was slightly ajar. The painted stone animals stared at me. I called out his name. Water was running somewhere inside the house. He must be in the shower. But as I walked through the living room, I noticed the water in the kitchen sink was on: a small, sad stream trickling over a pile of dirty dishes. "Harold!"

I stopped to listen. Something was wrong.

I shut the faucet off and looked around. The counter and table were crowded with dishes, and some burnt, shriveled thing sat abandoned in a pan on the stove. I couldn't begin to guess what it had once been. This wasn't like Harold. He was tidy. He was careful. Worry rolled through my stomach and sent a prickly shot of adrenaline down to my fingertips. Had someone else been in his house? Was he hurt?

A creaking sound came from the front of the house, so I dashed through the kitchen back to the front door. I snapped open the door with a whoosh and nearly took out a blond-ponytailed woman who was standing on the front porch, looking terrified.

"What are you doing here?" I asked, my voice full of accusation, my eyebrows narrowed in anger.

"I'm sorry. I'm sorry," she gasped, catching her breath as if I'd just punched her in the stomach. "I'm Sheila! Harold's neighbor. I'm just . . . I'm just here to collect his mail for him." The food stains on her rumpled shirt and the Mickey Mouse key chain clipped to her keys gave her away as a harmless, overworked mom. Not Harold's kidnapper.

My shoulders eased down my back a bit, and I stepped onto the stoop beside her. "The water was running and the door was open . . . and I just thought . . ."

"My kids are watering the plants in his house for him. We live next door. My older daughter must have forgotten to shut things off properly. I'll have to talk to her about that." She glanced behind her toward the pale blue house neighboring Harold's. One of those red and yellow toy cars that you move by running your feet like Fred Flintstone was parked out front. Just like the one Taylor and I used to share as kids.

Her hand went to her forehead, like she was tired or hot, but she no longer looked alarmed. "You're his friend, right? David?"

"Yeah, that's me," I said.

"Thanks for all your help with Harold. I think he really appreciates the company. He's been lonely since his wife passed away a few years back."

"I haven't done much," I said.

"More than you know." She dropped her hand to her hips. "I'm sure you know he's been having some health issues. Trouble with his memory. He's in the hospital. We found him a couple days ago out in the road, really confused. He walked into a house down the street thinking it was his own. The doctors say it's dementia. They are trying to figure out what to do with him."

"Can I go see him?"

"Of course," said Sheila. She looked at me, concern lining her forehead. "He's at the Gilford Memorial Hospital."

- - -

I had accompanied you to a number of your doctor's appointments. Usually follow-ups in plastic surgery offices. You never let me come in with you, which I was glad for. The only other place worse than a hospital waiting area is the white interrogation rooms they drag you into with the tongue depressors and the cotton gowns. The prodders and pressers and cold instruments and sallow complexions.

I stood in the doorway of Harold's room. He didn't notice me at first. He stared up at the ceiling, maybe trying to look dead. Willing it to happen. His skin was pale, and the blue of his veins showed up darker under the hospital lights. My own grandfather would never have been capable of looking like this—this old, this vulnerable, and something else. Dehydrated. His hands, which lay outside of the sheet along his hips, looked flat, like the water and air had been vacuumed out of him. Like they were lying in a casket at a wake.

I stood there until a hand landed on my shoulder.

"Grandson?" a doctor behind me asked. He smiled in a stale way, like the expression had been on there too long. You would have described him as *a plastic*.

"A friend," I said.

The doctor told me Harold would need an in-home caregiver. A nursing home was an option, but an expensive one. I couldn't imagine Harold without his garden, his fishing rod, the farmer's market, and his wife's photos on each end table. How was it possible—fuck, a commonplace occurrence—that instead of getting to spend your last years, months, days on this planet someplace safe and familiar you were shipped off to board with a bunch of senile strangers drooling from their wheelchairs?

"He's able to pay for his care," the doctor continued, "but he won't tell us what he prefers. He's been pretty unresponsive. Do you know any of his living relatives?"

"No, I don't know if he even has any. He's been unresponsive?"

"Depression is a common accompaniment for some upon the diagnosis of dementia. Their remaining time is in sight, but they know their mind won't see them through to that point. It's affecting his short-term memory the most at this point, which can get dangerous."

"But Harold . . ." I searched for something to say, something to defend my friend. Nothing. So I asked, "What kind of care does he need?"

"At this point, it depends. If he wants to stay at his house, he'll need at least a regularly visiting nurse."

"Okay," I said. "But what about—"

"Oh, David!" Harold snapped to full consciousness as he finally noticed me in the doorway. He pulled the sheet up higher and looked himself over with an ashamed expression, like I'd caught him in a state of undress. I knew Harold wanted his slacks, his button-down shirt, and those brown shoes I was sure he still polished regularly.

"Hey, Harold. How are you?" I tried to sound cheerful but couldn't help feeling like a plastic myself when I did.

"Oh, son, I hate to have you see me like this . . ."

I moved to sit on the bed beside him. The gesture felt too familiar for us, but I forced myself to stay put. "You look great," I lied.

His eyes darted to the doctor, still standing in the doorway, as he tried to push himself up on the bed to lean in close to me. He lowered his voice so only I could hear him. "I've got a favor to ask you, son. Don't let them put me in one of those homes. Smother me with the pillow if you have to, but just don't let me end up there. I promised the same to Carol, but, God bless her soul, she never made it that long."

I stood up, and his old sinking face watched mine. This was one of those moments. The step-up-to-the-plate moments. You took them or you didn't. Harold waited for a confirmation. For my word.

"I'll do it," I said, making eye contact with him. Then I turned to the doctor. "I'll take care of him. At his house. During the week, Monday through Friday, whatever. I'm free. That's all he needs, right? Someone to help him with meals? To look after him? I can do that. I'll do it."

The doctor looked up at me with eyebrows raised. *Yes*, I nodded before I could stop myself. I would not run this time. I would be there to help. To take care of Harold while I still could.

I was honestly surprised that everyone also thought this was a good idea. The doctor explained they would supplement my time with Harold with a visiting nurse.

Harold insisted that I be paid as a regular home-care person would, just under the table. "While I've still got something going on up here, some sense." He said the last word angrily.

At first, I tried to resist the money. "Harold, I can't. We're friends." But my meals for the week consisted solely of brown rice and a carton of Ricki's eggs, and I was days away from calling up my father, throwing away any dignity I had left, and begging him to cover my bills until I found myself gainfully employed. Harold said he had plenty in savings. Carol had always called him cheap, but he'd known the money would come in handy one day.

Before Harold was discharged from the hospital, I stopped by his house to pick up the place. I started in on the dishes—mold growing in pans, old tomato sauce hardened to a glue-like crust on a few plates. Sheila, the neighbor, came by, and she hugged me for helping Harold. Her little daughter stood frozen in the kitchen, her gray eyes watching my every move.

"I think Maisey's got a crush," said Sheila with a smile.

"My girlfriend will be jealous," I said.

Sheila smiled politely and patted her daughter on her head. "I know he keeps some of those standing fans in his basement. Open up the windows, and I'll bring up the fans to get some air in here. I'm not sure I want to know what that smell is."

I tried to look at Harold's house with new eyes. This would be my new office, so to speak.

You had been excited about my new plan when I called you on the way back from the hospital. "This is having a purpose. This is making a difference. I can help you," you said.

I could show Harold my recent photos I'd taken in the woods. He would like that kind of thing. We could try to identify plants and rock formations together. I could write down all those stories about his wife he still remembered so clearly. I could be his stenographer, preserve the man—or the memories, at least—to make his time less lonely. The thought made me sad and heavy. It made me want to cast out and drag everyone close to me back into a place where I wouldn't end up like Harold: alone as my mind began to erase itself.

CHAPTER 32

called Harold's prescriptions into a pharmacy just outside of
Boston because I was visiting home for the day. He was set
to be released from the hospital sometime the next day. I left
Vincent at my parents' house that evening while you and I went
to see some Shakespeare play in the park on Boston Common.
The play, which I vaguely recognized from a high school English
class, involved a shipwreck and an island, some sort of beast, and a
whole lot of things we were too far away from the stage to actually
hear. It was the type of thing I went along with for the sake of
seeing that happy look you got when you planned dates. Like our
first date: 185 Oakdale Street. I would never forget that address
and how you surprised me that day, knocked me off center.

You need to get away from that cabin sometimes, you always said,
*or you'll end up mean and alone like your grandfather. Too much isola-
tion does that to a person.* And maybe spending so much time alone
had changed me. I needed little to survive, to be happy. Living in
the cabin had taught me that the quiet outdoors were powerful
enough to act as a salve on the rest of the things that were wrong
in our lives.

You packed us ham sandwiches and a thin blanket with a pat-
tern of marching elephants that looked like it was from India. I

brought a few sleeves of chocolate chip cookies from my parents' house and an unopened bottle of Prosecco I'd found in their basement. Grass stained the hem of your blue-and-white-checkered dress. Your toes pressed into the soft dirt. You held my hand when we lay back on the blanket, and we talked about maybe taking a vacation together, driving somewhere new.

The next morning, before heading back up north, I stuck my arm through one of the blood pressure machines at the local CVS while I waited for Harold's prescription to be filled, wondering what my numbers should read, thinking about how Harold's numbers said he required a whole rainbow of pills tucked inside the tiny clear plastic squares labeled *Monday* through *Sunday*.

I was already tearing my way through my second bag of ninety-nine-cent Cheetos when a finger tapped me on the shoulder. I spun around to see your mom standing behind me. I hadn't seen her in a while; her face was grim, but she looked younger than I even remembered, the smooth skin around her eyes pale and largely wrinkle-free. Maybe her new romance was doing good things for her. Her hair, lacking the telltale grays my own mother had, was twisted into a messy, fashionable bun at the top of her head. She stood under those pharmacy fluorescents in cut-off denim shorts, showing off skinny legs that reminded me of yours, but there was an anxious twitch to her as she eyed me that put me on edge.

"It's nice to see you, David. It's been a while." She said this without smiling as I tried to wipe the orange Cheetos dust from my hands onto the hem of the tattered cargo shorts I'd owned since high school.

"You too!" I said. I shook her hand, which she offered to me, limp and clammy.

"So, things are good with you?" she asked. "I heard you met Jack."

"That's right! Yeah, great new place you guys have."

"Harold. Harold Bierbaum," the pharmacist called over the counter.

"Oh, hey, that's me," I said, grateful to remove myself from the conversation.

She raised an eyebrow but nodded.

"It was great to see you . . ."

Before I finished turning away, she grabbed my arm and pulled me closer to her.

"Listen, David, you can't mess this up—do you understand? With Hope." She lowered her voice to a husky whisper. She had never said more than a few words to me before that moment, except for the curt *Hello, David*, with *David* sounding like a word she wasn't sure she liked the taste of.

The artificial sodium high from the Cheetos made my mouth chalky and dry. My heart started beating too fast. "Oh, no, I'm not going to—"

"She's had too much heartbreak for one lifetime. And combine that with her impulsiveness—well, I'm sure you know how she can be. But I can't risk losing her. Do you understand me? Not again. Last time, she was gone for two whole years in the hospital before she was well enough to return home. After what she did. After the fire . . . You have no idea what that's like, David. To see your daughter . . . to see her . . ." Her voice caught in her throat, and she blinked quickly a number of times, her face suddenly red.

"Wait." My ears began to ring so intensely I wondered for a moment if I was coming down with something. A flu. A contagion. Something I'd picked up from waiting around this pharmacy for too long. "I don't know what you're talking about," I mumbled, and yet at the same time something inside me already did. A part of me knew. I had to have known.

She looked exasperated and stepped in close enough for me to smell the mint toothpaste on her breath. She squeezed my arm again as she whispered to me, as if I was a much younger child, "*God damn it*, the fire. She lit herself on fire, David. Our whole apartment, all our belongings. Everything ruined." She looked away. Her voice softened and trailed off before regaining its usual stern composure as she turned back to face me. "I can't have that happen again. Both for her sake and mine."

Her eyes locked on me, and for a moment, my vision blurred. I swallowed hard, the pit of some old, sour fruit lodged deep in my throat. "It won't," I said, swallowing again. "I promise."

She nodded once more before releasing my arm and heading down the shampoo isle.

"Harold Bierbaum?" the woman in the white lab coat behind the counter called out again, looking in my direction. My legs, in that moment, had stopped functioning; my brain had ceased sending out the right signals because I was too occupied with puzzling out the implication of what your mother had just told me and all the things you never had.

CHAPTER 33

arold pushed a rook my way. He couldn't help the small smile that crept across his face when he made a good move. Strawberry seeds clamored over his lips and chin. I'd brought him a small container of berries I'd picked from Ricki's land. They were small but sweeter than the big, oversized grocery-store kind. I could always tell Harold's dietary proclivities by looking at the bits clinging to the space around his mouth.

Harold and I played chess often because you told me games that keep the mind exercised can be helpful for patients with dementia. Much better than plopping them in front of the TV. Apparently, his disease had not affected the chess-strategy portion of his brain yet. Or his long-term memory.

"Checkmate," he said. His cheek twitched. He worked hard to hold back a big, gloating smile. His chin's white whiskers stretched longer than his typical neat shave.

"Seriously, Harold. Couldn't you let me win? Just once?"

"I'm sorry, son, but my father raised me to be an honest man. It wouldn't be right to cheat."

"I'm sure your father was right, but you're stealing all my quarters."

We wagered Harold's quarters on the high-stakes games.

Nickels and dimes for the lower-stakes checkers. He kept the rusty can of change on his nightstand next to his bed. He waddled out with the can tucked under his arm as soon as he woke up from his nap.

I was enjoying the home-care gig more than I cared to admit. I spent a lot of time reading either to Harold or on my own as he slept. The job was like babysitting, but more fun, because I could have interesting conversations with Harold. I loved his stories of the past—what the town had been like in the fifties and sixties. We spent a week of lazy afternoons sitting in his backyard, soaking up the sun. I read these big old historical fiction books to him that his wife used to read. Stories about brave young explorers and early settlers in the colonies. His eyes watered copiously when he tried to focus on the small print himself; no prescription was strong enough to support such a vague sense of vision.

As far as I could tell, he enjoyed having me there as much as I enjoyed being there. He asked about ten times that week if the money was going to be enough. Was I eating well? Was I getting by? Did I have enough to buy something for my sweetie? Because that was how you kept them around, he told me: little, unexpected surprises.

"Did I mention my wife was a nurse, too?" Harold asked when I told him you had to work the night shift all that week.

"Yes, you did mention that," I said, thinking of you. *Hospitalized for two years.* Ever since running into your mom, I felt drained by the weight of that truth, the sick feeling that sat like a rock in my stomach when I thought of you hurting yourself like that. Had I ever really known you if I had not known this life-altering, pivotal fact? You set that fire. You lit that match. Could I be with someone who could lie about that? Or, even more pressing, be with someone who could do that to herself? I realized the answer to that question might be no. And the worst of it was my own unknown, untouchable fear of what you were capable of, what might be brewing within you like the first drops of a hurricane's rain. I wasn't prepared to take on that kind of responsibility, and yet, unknowingly, I already had. I tried to imagine Harold's wife overseeing you—the young woman with the internal scars so deep she had to test her edges, test what she could withstand, to make those scars from what those boys had done to her visible on the surface of her skin in order to share the weight. To make the inside outside. To lessen the burden.

Harold peered at the board, planning his next move. He pinched his queen with his heavy index finger and thumb, started to slide it forward, then brought it back to its original place. "There was a girl, you know."

"What girl?" I asked.

"Amelia Roberts."

At first I waited for him to continue his story or to make his move, but when I looked up, Harold was staring at me. *Amelia Roberts. A. R.*

Harold got quiet for a moment, avoiding my eyes, and then seemed to decide to follow his train of thought. "My wife became somewhat of a friend to her. She helped her out with a few things. She was one of the girls. At the hospital. You know what I mean, right? But Amelia . . ." He let out a whistle. "She was not like other girls back then!"

Harold described a young woman from a neighboring town who hung out in the local tavern, smoking and drinking with the men. She was intense and stared with eyes that made it impossible to sit still. She didn't seem to care what the rest of the town thought of her. Very intelligent. Very beautiful. Harold paused, looking pleased with himself that these memories, the oldest ones, could still be recalled on a dime.

"Do you remember anything else about her? Did she know my grandfather?"

"Oh, I wouldn't have any idea about that." Harold's eyes lifted to meet mine, and then he looked back down, shifted forward in his seat, leaned closer to the board. He was uncomfortable, was holding back. "She was a good deal younger than your grandfather. I have no idea why they would have known each other. Carol really liked her. She refused to stay in the hospital. Not all of them did. I think Carol liked her honesty. Her tendency to go against the grain. Her disinterest in a common life. You know, I think there's a baseball game on the television this afternoon." He studied the board, looking immersed, and stopped talking.

After a few moments of silence, I was afraid what he'd just said was all I would get out of him. He licked his dry lips and fingered a rook but left it on its square. I sat back in my chair.

Could Amelia Roberts really be the same A. R.? "Harold, what happened to the baby? Amelia's?"

Harold laughed. "Son, I haven't a clue. Carol said most were put up for adoption back then."

I let out a slow, unsteady breath. My hands shook a bit. My nerves felt ragged and jittery, as if I had just downed four espresso shots. This was big. Or possibly not. Amelia Roberts may not have had any connection to my grandfather. Or, possibly, the name was old news my family had known for decades and kept from Taylor and me, but the shock of realizing that so much of my own family's history lived in the layered soil of this land, somewhere beneath the surface, kicked me off balance. First Hope and the fire, and then this. It made me wonder what other things in my life I had been so naively "sure" about.

I got up, pausing our game, and checked Harold's pill container to make sure Tuesday's set had been taken, but the little crown of colorful pills sat patiently in their assigned block. I grabbed two root beers from his fridge and sat back down across from him, the pills in my other hand. I hoped I was doing this right—the pills and taking care of Harold and the house. I was just fumbling along. At least a real nurse, a friend of Sheila's, came over at night.

I handed him the pills and a root beer. He stared at the pile in his wrinkled palm. "Are you sure I should be taking all these? They get stuck in my throat, make me tired."

"I know. Kind of a pain in the ass, but they're good for you. They'll make you feel better." I sat and perched my elbows on my knees, leaned forward. Harold rested his head back in his chair and took a big gulp to force the pills down, his lips pressed in serious consideration.

"Want to read for a while?" I suggested, hoping the words on the page would calm me more than anything else.

"Always," said Harold. He lay back in his chair and closed his eyes as I read a chapter about some young American pilot in World War II. He was searching for this young French girl who had saved him and stolen his heart.

After I finished the chapter, we both remained quiet, listening to our hearts: his slow and aging, mine erratic and unsure. "You know who could clean up this chess board with the both of us? My wife, Carol. Get her out here. She'll play just one game with you and you'll see. She's a real chess player. I won the lottery with that one." He pressed both hands into the sides of his chair, lifting himself to stand, all the while calling out, "Carol! Carol!"

His old voice, croaky and loud, rang through the empty house. This was the part I didn't enjoy. "Harold? Harold."

He turned to face me, and his eyebrows lifted in surprise. "Have you seen Carol?" His bleary blue eyes welled slightly.

I looked at the old man—his arms limp by his sides, his torso lilting forward slightly, as it always did when he stood. And I surprised myself by realizing that I loved him. And because of this, I didn't have the heart to remind him of his abandonment.

"She just ran out. An errand. She'll be back soon." Carol, who took care of Amelia. Amelia, who may have loved my grandfather. "Hey, Harold, how'd you know when it was right with Carol? That she was the woman you wanted to be with?"

Harold smiled; the question seemed to calm and recenter him. He pushed his glasses up his nose. The white hair on the sides of his head and inside his ears stuck out at odd angles. Maybe that was something I should help him with, too. Grooming.

"I only felt like myself when I was around her. So I knew I had to be around her as much as possible."

CHAPTER 34

The birds started about their business loud and early that morning. The ducks, too. From the window, the sky looked warm and pale green, ready to drop buckets again. It was all too early, my limbs heavy with sleep. I tried to shake the fever of my dream from my head; my face was hot, my body slow and dumb. But it had been vivid. The longer I lived on the pond, the more vivid my dreams became.

I'd dreamed of you. It was winter. A thick blanket of ice covered the pond; everything silenced by a frozen white chill. The light caught my attention. The light from a fire. I walked out of the cabin and saw you bending down, looking at something through the ice. When you stood, I saw it. Your hair sparked and wove around your head; a trail of smoke snaked toward a gray sky. Your hair was on fire.

I still couldn't get your mother's voice out of my mind. The fire wasn't some horrible accident, some horrible act by some horrible person. It was self-inflicted. It meant hospitalization for two years. It meant that you had lied to me and you continued to do so. My mind flitted to the photo in your room of you and that girl— the nail-bitten one from the Christmas tree shop who we'd run into in December—standing in front of a brick building. I should have trusted the connection my mind made that day. A building that looked like a hospital—the type Harold's wife had worked at. And what was it that girl had said? *You'll never be normal.*

The start to the day's light began to work its way around the sheet I'd hung up to cover the front windows. "For the love of all that is good, would you please get some curtains? At the very least some blinds?" my mother had implored during her last visit. She'd promised to bring up some new stuff for the kitchen and a few pieces of "very useful" furniture she'd picked up from spring yard sales the next time she visited.

Vincent snapped his head toward the door and began to emit a low growl. The warble in his throat sounded angry, serious, which meant something was out there. He was sure of it, and by way of his superior senses, I was sure of it, too. The hairs on my arms lifted, as did Vincent's hackles. The more time the two of us spent together alone, the more in sync our primal responses were.

I'd promised Harold I would bring Vincent with me to visit that week, although the thought of my dog having his way with one of the hundred throw pillows Harold's late wife had adorned the house with made me anxious.

The last time Vincent performed this high-alert charade was because a baby calf had wandered onto my property from the nearby farm. I'd clumsily escorted the thing back underneath the barbed wire fence marking the property line in the woods as his mother—caught on the other side of the fence—mooed loudly, fearing her young calf was in danger.

The old floorboards creaked as my bare feet made their way to the door. I flung it open, and a woman stood before me.

Pale eyes hung above the half-moons of her cheekbones. Gray hair sparked like electricity around her head. Her clothes were filthy. She wore one of those old yellow rain jackets despite the weight of the overcast humidity. Her purple slivers of lips quivered. She looked wiry and thin under the oversized coat. Her feral quality was different than that of the homeless people I'd encountered in Boston. Her wolfish eyes were wild and lined with something like abandonment. The sight of her took me so much by surprise that I staggered backward into the cabin, as if I had been punched in the chest.

"Give me those letters."

Her voice—deep and cracked, as if it hadn't been used in a while—shocked the quiet of my cabin. My dry tongue stuck to the roof of my mouth as we stared at each other.

"What?" I managed to ask. Vincent crouched low beside my feet, growling, teeth bared.

Her nails were black and curled at the ends. Her shirt underneath the rain slicker, once beige, was torn and splattered with mud. I never would have thought I would be afraid of a brittle old woman, but every muscle in my body tensed.

She leaned into the doorframe. "From the chest." The woman slammed her fist into my door, and I jumped. "I want my ring back, you thief!"

At the crack of her voice on the last word, Vincent leapt at her. It was the first time I'd ever seen him on the defensive. He bared his teeth, and a sharp growl ripped through the room as he went for her arm.

She moved so quickly, in that blur of fur and limbs, that I only saw the knife—the one you'd bought me for Christmas—after she pulled it away from Vincent's shoulder. I hadn't seen her grab it from the window ledge by the door. I caught a look of astonishment in her icy eyes, equal to my own, for a brief second. Vincent let out a sharp cry and scampered behind me, whimpering loud and circling, trying to lick at the wound as his gray coat began to darken into a shocking red.

I looked back to the doorway in disbelief, but she was gone. I jumped from the landing and thought I heard a crash to the left, into the trees. I started in the direction of the sound. Vincent let out a low whine. I peered through the dense leaves, looking for a hint of something. A bit of yellow. Nothing. The woman had disappeared into the woods. I turned back to the house. A streak of blood slashed across the door.

CHAPTER 35

I leaned over into the toilet and heaved again. Tears and mucus collected in the bowl beneath me. *They see this a lot,* I reassured myself. This was an emergency animal hospital. They put out tissue boxes at every turn. At least I'd made it to the bathroom before the sob trapped in my chest erupted so violently that I started to gag.

I hadn't realized how important, how central Vincent had become in my life until this moment. What if they couldn't stop the bleeding? What if she'd hit something important with that blade? Something irreparable? I couldn't remember a time I had ever broken down like this. Not even after the accident and the depression this winter. Not over you. I had never felt such responsibility for another living thing as I did for Vincent.

The thought that she could have killed me as I slept, or Vincent as he trailed after the scent of some small animal, gripped my stomach. I would never have seen you again. Harold wouldn't have had anyone to look after him. And worst of all, Taylor would get the cabin.

I knew now that she had to be the one whose screams carried across the pond. The one who left the fingerprints in the dust. My grandfather's jacket stretched out on the picnic table. She was the ghost that had haunted me these months I'd spent alone in the cabin. The woman living across the pond.

Maybe I should have tried to reason with her. She had been shaking. She was obviously unstable, maybe ill or starving. I probably should have called the police—should do it now. But still, I didn't. And maybe I would never learn to grow in a way that made me into a man who always did the right thing—not now, or yesterday, or after hitting a man with my truck and leaving. Maybe no one, ever, grew up or changed; only the circumstances and characters around us did.

I sat on the floor of the small stall and pulled out my cell phone. I wiped my nose on my sleeve and tried to clear the grief from my voice, but it was no use. "What's wrong?" you asked before I said a word.

"I need you . . ." My voice cracked, ridiculous and pitiful. "To come here. It's Vincent. He was hurt."

They made me wait for hours. In orange plastic chairs with a coffee machine lightly humming across from me, limp packets of hot chocolate stacked beside it. And I couldn't do anything, couldn't think of anyone else I wanted to talk to but you. You said you were on your way. You'd called in sick to work. Sheila was looking after Harold. It was a Saturday.

It shouldn't be taking this long. They told me to go home, but I refused. I would wait until Vincent came home with me. This was my fault. I had been right there. I should have stopped her.

I couldn't read any of the magazine articles on "Breeding a Showstopper" or "Parenting Dalmatians." I just stared and stared and wondered what to do about that woman. She was violent, probably insane. But did anyone else know about her? Living in those woods. And what was it she said? *I want my ring back*—it sounded like a line from Gollum in *Lord of the Rings*.

I looked up from my chair, my own realization catching me off guard. The ring. The ring from the box with the initials A. R. The ring Hope wore. The ring that belonged to A. R., or Amelia Roberts, which meant . . .

I stood suddenly, and the woman at the desk looked up at my quick movement. "I'm sorry, sir, they're still not out yet." I ignored her and began to pace the hallway, running my hands through my hair. Could it be possible? That Amelia—if that was her name—my grandfather's lover from decades ago, never left? That she watched me. Watched us. What did it mean that she and my grandfather stayed together, maintained an arm's-length love through the woods? I started to hyperventilate again, my mind racing down one lane and then hopping to the next, trying to figure out who I should call, who I should share this revelation with. I sat back down, my head resting in my hands. Amelia Roberts. Out there this whole time.

"Sir?"

"Yes." I stood again, knocking over my cup of water in the process. I hastily tried to blot it up with a few of the used tissues I still had clenched in my fist.

The woman in the lab coat held out her arm and ushered me into one of the examining rooms with the steel weighing station Vincent liked to pee on. A container of dog bones sat on the counter. She motioned for me to sit, so I obeyed.

"I'm sorry for the wait," she said. "Vincent was slow to wake from the anesthesia, but he's doing very well. He's bandaged up with twelve stitches. It wasn't a very wide cut, but it went deep, so he's going to be sore and limping for a while. You're going to have to pick him up a pain prescription at our pharmacy. Was this an accident of some sort? It looks like a wound from a blade."

"Well, actually," I began . . . but I didn't have the faintest idea how to explain to this veterinarian that a crazed woman who'd visited to reclaim a ring I'd found in a locked chest in my grandfather's cabin had ended up stabbing Vincent when he lunged at her. "Hunting accident. My dad and my brother and I were out in the woods, and my brother's pretty clumsy and was turning with the knife in his hand and caught Vincent right in the shoulder."

She nodded with her eyebrows arched. Shit. It probably wasn't open hunting season on anything. Especially not dogs.

You were waiting for us at the cabin. The blood on the door had been scrubbed off. You wore your summer blue scarf piled up over a plain white tank top. Your face looked calm. This was when you were at your best, when you glowed. When others were weak. When others were in crisis. You would be the one to balance me out this time.

I tried to imagine your face younger, your cheeks fuller. The red gasoline tank in your hand. The wet carpet. The pinching smell in the air. And the match. The shot of light, the inhalation of oxygen as the flame caught and flung its lancing arms out, enveloping you.

I went over to the passenger seat and picked up Vincent to carry him into the cabin. His warm body weighed heavily in my arms. You appeared by my side, and I thought for a second I might start to cry again. Despite everything, I was so glad to see you, so glad Vincent was all right, and so sorry I'd let things go so wrong. I leaned my forehead against yours and kissed you once on the lips before carrying Vincent into the cabin. His eyes were unfocused and he was panting lightly, but he remained quiet. The pain meds seemed to be doing their job.

I laid him on the bed, and he licked my hand, sloppy and wet, before laying his head down. I had never seen him so lethargic.

"Maybe you should slip him pain meds more often," you said. You leaned against the doorframe of the cabin, your arms crossed. The dark sky behind you glowed an inky blue. There would be a full moon that night. I walked over to you, and you wrapped your arms around me; your palms warm on my back. I withdrew and pulled those hands in front of me to examine. No ring.

"What happened?" you asked.

I told you about Amelia—who I thought she was, how my father just might possibly have a sibling somewhere out there that he didn't know about, and how she must have watched us. That she knew what we found. That she wanted the ring back.

"Wow. So wait. Let me get this straight"—you pressed your palm to your forehead to focus—"you think this is the woman your grandfather had an affair with? Maybe she just saw the ring and thought it was something of value. I mean, obviously she could use the money."

You moved away from me and started to pull things out of the fridge. You had to jump up to remove the frying pan from its hook above my small stove. "You really need to call the police, David. I'm serious. You're not safe. What if she comes back and next time she attacks you?"

"Honestly, I think she was just trying to protect herself," I said. "Vincent got vicious and, like, lunged for her. I've never seen him react like that. She's old and crazy. She must have been living out there for a really long time." I thought of the yurt I found across the pond, the rusted tools. "I'm not calling the police."

The truth was that the deep thread of worry about attracting the police's attention after the accident was still there. He was still out there—the real Harold, the real person who'd fallen down

195

in the crosswalk on New Year's Eve. And I was still and would always be the one who'd hit him and left.

You put the pan on the burner and turned the knob until the blue flames caught, hissing heat through the bottom of the pan. The worn copy of *Love Poems of Rumi* you'd lent me months earlier still sat unopened on the windowsill. I wondered if you noticed this detail. If it was something that weighed negatively upon me: a typical male, unable to indulge his emotional side by connecting to a book of love poems. But could I love someone I apparently understood so little of?

You dumped a small tab of butter into the pan. A few pops of grease jumped out, and you stepped back, waving away a bit of smoke. You turned down the burner. Your specialty was fried eggs on toast for dinner.

"So, where is it?"

"Where is what?" You sighed as you pulled out two of my porcelain plates, a rim of pale blue flowers floating around each plate's perimeter. I tried to picture my grandmother standing over this sink, wondering if she should leave my grandfather, if she could, the dish momentarily slipping from her soapy fingers and banging into the bottom of the basin with a *clink*.

"You could really use a better pan. This one is all scratched up." You blew a wisp of hair out of your eye. Moonlight shone in a dusty haze through the porch screens. It would be a hot night for sleeping. The cicadas still buzzed deeply from nearby trees. "Heat bugs," Taylor and I called them as kids because their sound always thrummed on the hottest days.

"The ring. If she does come back for it, I would prefer to just hand it over. Or leave it out for her somehow."

"Jesus, David. You're not going to just give it back to her. If you're not going to call the police, don't give her a reason to come back and try to kill Vincent again—or worse, you."

"But what if that box and that ring are all she has left of my grandfather?"

You let out an exasperated sigh. "That's sentimental bullshit."

I stared at you a moment. This response for some reason shocked me almost more than the truth about the fire. It was the first time I realized, with a sadness I couldn't look straight at, that maybe you couldn't feel the things I thought you felt when we were together. You had never been who I thought you were from the beginning. That light, uncomplicated airiness from the first day had just been a high, the upside of the coin. Your jumping from the tree in the apple orchard had been an impulse, not an act of fearlessness. I had been blind to you, for some reason, unable to truly understand the complexity of those scars, from the beginning.

"Hope, why didn't you ever tell me about the hospital?" A knot deep within me worked itself loose as the words spilled out.

"My work?"

"No. The hospital you were at. For two years. That's where that girl was from, too, wasn't she? The one we ran into last winter at the tree stand. The one from your picture."

"McLeans? I've told you about that before. You just forgot."

I paused for a moment, trying to figure out what mental trick you were working. "No, Hope," I began slowly. "I did not forget. You never told me about it. You were there for two years?"

You cracked four eggs into the pan in quick succession. Pop. Pop. Pop. Pop. Hiss. "You know, after that party, all those years ago with my neighbor and his friends? It was hard to feel things. Anything, really. There was this, like, constant numbing sensation, and that was all. I just couldn't get rid of it. An absence of any feeling, real or otherwise. And eventually I started to try some of the usual sad-teenage-girl things to try to feel again. Little slices along my inner thigh. I tried starving myself, hoping that the things I noticed guys starting to notice—my tits, my hips—would disappear so I could be invisible again. That didn't seem to work, but I did learn that I had to do the wrong things in order to feel anything at all. And then one night, I was home alone, my mom was at work, and I could hear the boys downstairs laughing, the sound coming up through the floor . . ."

You swallowed here, and I thought for a moment that I might get sick again. I might have to stop you because I didn't know if there was anything more I could stand to hear.

"And there was this candle, and I thought that maybe the burn would cleanse me, make me new, like I had been before. And that maybe it was the only thing I could do to stop the sound of their laughter."

"God, I'm so sorry, Hope. That . . . just everything . . . That those guys . . . Why didn't you ever tell me all that before? I just wish I could have been there, or, I don't know . . . done something," I was stumbling, so tired, so drained, trying to find the words to express the disgust and sympathy and my inability to touch any of it within you. All of this you delivered without affectation, without any sort of emotion in your tone to convey that it was in fact you who had gone through everything you were describing.

I was sorry, Hope. So sorry. I really wished that I could have helped you back then, when you were a girl, and now, too, standing in my cabin as an adult. But there was nothing, nothing I could come up with to say or do that would make anything right.

Vincent made a small moaning sound from the bedroom. I nudged the door from the porch open a crack to look in on him. His face rested on his paws; his eyes were closed. I resisted the urge to curl up beside him on the bed, my face pressed into his warm fur, smelling his smell: animal mixed with dirt. He was always digging out there in the woods. God, I was so glad he was all right.

After a few moments of silence, I asked, "Do you regret it? The fire?"

You turned back to the pan and flipped the eggs. A yoke came loose and snaked a rivulet of bright yellow toward the edge of the skillet. You faced me, the hand holding the spatula dangling by your hip. The eggs sizzled between us. "Honestly? No. It was one of the only times I have ever felt truly powerful."

I thought of the look I'd seen in Amelia's widened, icy eyes. The flash of the blade. The red fur. Not a look of power, but fear.

CHAPTER 36

I brought Vincent with me to Harold's every day that week, and on all my errands, too. I didn't want to leave him alone. Two days after getting stitches, he didn't seem to remember he had been injured. He tried to run and jump like normal until he twitched to a stop and attempted to lick his shoulder, feeling the pull of some phantom pain.

That next weekend, Taylor joined me for a mountain bike ride through the trails in the woods. We were in the last dregs of summer now. He kept suggesting I carry Grandpa's hunting rifle with me, just in case. I had told him the whole story of the woman I now believed to be Amelia—at least, what I could make of everything I had learned so far. I also explained what I'd learned about her from Harold and every detail about her recent visit.

"You're insane," Taylor said. "You have to do something. I've been thinking, you should get the ring from Hope, show the hermit woman we have the ring, and when she goes to take it, we take care of her." His voice echoed into the open air of the porch. He always got in trouble as a kid for never following my dad's mandates to *use an inside voice*.

"Take care of her? What, am I supposed to kill our grandfather's mistress? When'd you become such a vigilante?"

"I just mean let her know she can't be coming into your house and stabbing your dog. Especially if you're not going to the police with all this."

"Easy, tough guy. And for the record, it wasn't like she intended to stab Vincent. She just got scared and reacted in self-defense."

"Why are you defending her?" asked Taylor.

"I don't know," I said. "Because someone has to."

One time when Taylor and I were young, a group of neighborhood kids chased a huge skunk into our yard during a spring afternoon. They trapped it back there, taunting it, throwing rocks at it. Taylor was terrified of getting sprayed, but we stood on our porch and watched. The skunk bled as it hobbled over the grass, trying to find a place of respite. My friends beckoned for me to join them—to pick up my rock, to take aim—but I couldn't. It had the same aura of terror and sadness as Amelia, a quality that I couldn't play villain to.

"But how can you even sleep knowing she could be creeping in the woods around the cabin?"

"Taylor, has mom got you watching the *Twilight* movies again? She's not going to do anything to me."

"But how do you know that?" he nearly whined.

"I can just . . . tell. She looked as shocked as I was after hurting Vincent. I really don't think that was her intention. She just wanted her ring back."

"Well, fine. Just forget it," said Taylor, in that tone that made it impossible to not see him as a little kid sitting on our steps, with sirens whirring in the background.

"Are you still seeing that guy you met online?" I asked. "The one with the blue hair?"

"Don't try to change the subject," he said.

- - -

Although the temperatures remained in the high seventies, a crisp, lingering breeze replaced the mugginess of summer. Taylor and I brought the bikes down the road behind the farm where the trails pick up. The trails snake for hundreds of miles, all the way up to the Canadian border, through open fields and past lakes, massive stretches of mud, and forests that still managed to feel wild, untamed, and remote.

The mud spray covering the backs of our legs and riding up our shirts began to dry and harden as we sat to rest and catch our breath. On a boulder surrounded by golden pine needles, we squeezed water into our mouths from the bottles we'd carried with us and wished we brought something more to sustain our growing appetites.

Taylor leaned over, assessing the damage to his skinned knee and the back of his arm from an earlier crash. Smarter riders would have been prepared with provisions or maybe a first aid kit, but we were just getting our feet wet, feeling the ache in our lungs and the scream of our quads that reminded us we were alive as we pedaled over rocks and deeper into the woods.

A rustle of leaves sounded in the bushes next to us. We turned as a trio of pheasants erupted into a panicked flight over our heads. The birds quickly settled in some low bushes across from us, calm again. I leaned my back against the rough bark of the tree behind me.

"Can I ask you something?" Taylor asked. His lips pressed together in a tight line. "Are you going to stay with her? Hope?" His eyes were serious, his face red and sweaty.

"I don't know." I looked down at my hands. "She's been through a lot. I don't want to be just another person on the list of people who have let her down."

She lit herself on fire, David.

I pulled my bike back upright and straddled the seat, preparing to take off on our last stretch of downhill before we made it back to the main road. "Why don't you forget about my love life and focus on trying to keep up," I called over my shoulder as I whizzed past the peeling whites of birches and the towering authority of the pines and splashed through one of the last puddles on our trail back home.

SECOND FALL

CHAPTER 37

On Wednesday, Harold called me Jeffrey.

"Harold, who is Jeffrey?"

"Oh, Jeffrey, you scoundrel. Keep your hands to yourself, do you hear? I always knew you had a thing for my Carol." He smiled when he said it, but then a scowl—foreign to Harold's usual demeanor—overtook him. "I really can't stand for this in my house, Jeffrey. I'm going to have to ask you to leave."

These interactions made me crazy. His condition was deteriorating so quickly, I could barely keep up. He became as frustrating as a child looped into an incessant game of copycat. He took off in other worlds and other decades, and I was left in his dirty kitchen that smelled vaguely of cat litter, trying to clean up after him, trying to play nurse, trying to play Jeffrey. Lately, right around the end of the day, at dinner, he would become excessively agitated. He would see people and things invisible to my eye.

I kept trying to prop Harold up at the dinner table that night, and he kept sliding sideways, as if the chair beneath him were melting.

"Harold, you have to sit up." I held his shoulders and tried to right him.

"Get your fucking hands off me, Jeffrey!"

I turned, shocked. It was the first time I'd ever heard Harold swear like that. He was a good Catholic man, through and through. "Harold! It's me, David!" I tried to raise my voice to help him recognize me, but tonight, I couldn't reach him.

It was already dark outside. The days had grown remarkably shorter; soon, the clocks would be turned back.

"You can't make me sit here," said Harold. "Who do you think you are? I'm a prisoner in my own home! Somebody help!"

I tried to prop him up a fourth time. His arms weighed as much as downed tree limbs, and his heavy torso lilted this way and that.

Eventually, he settled down and made his way through dinner, with me having to mop up most of his meal from the table and his face. When he finished eating, I helped him to the bathroom and closed the door behind him.

After twenty minutes had passed, I stood outside the door and knocked. "Harold?"

No answer.

"You okay in there?" I started to panic. I knocked again, harder, louder. "Harold?"

I heard him moan, and I flung open the door.

He looked up at me from the bathroom floor with watery eyes. His eyebrows lifted in alarm, confusion. He may not have recognized me. His pants were bunched around his ankles, and shit coated his bare white thighs, the small blue tiles on the floor, and the neat khaki slacks he'd taught me how to iron just so.

"Hey, hey, hey," I cooed. He looked so helpless it made me want to bolt from the room, from his house, forever. I was in way over my head. I ignored the rising feeling in my throat, grabbed behind his arms, and braced my feet against the floor. "Okay, I'm going to help lift you, and then we will get you cleaned up."

He startled and flinched at my touch. "Where's Carol?"

"Oh," I grunted, trying to lift him. His dead weight hung heavy in my arms. There was no push-off on his part. Just resistance. "I'm sure she's around here somewhere."

The smell hit me, and my stomach turned. I tried not to look at the brown mess, at Harold's old, naked body, his skin looking like the belly of a cat, all stretched downward. As if sensing my gaze, he humbly admitted, "I didn't make it."

"I see that, buddy. No big deal. I just need you to help me out a little bit here." He felt like he weighed four hundred pounds. "On the count of three, we're going to lift together, and I'll sit you back on this toilet thingy."

The hospital had delivered a special high chair that fit over the toilet with side handles and a cushy, elevated seat so he wouldn't have to bend down so far. Clearly, it wasn't enough.

"Okay, ready, Harold? Count of three. One, two . . ."

I had dragged Harold a foot off the ground when he started yelling, "Oh, no. Oh, no. Oh, no." He leaned back, and I was afraid he would fall into the shower and hit his head. My back groaned. His arms flailed until he reached for me, his hands covered in shit, smearing it across my shirt as he slumped back onto the cool tiles.

"Damn it, Harold!" I panted and tore my shirt off over my head, trying to ignore my gag reflexes. "What the hell am I supposed to do now?" I turned away, pacing down the hall and back to him. "I can't even lift you! How am I supposed to handle all this? You're not even helping! The least you could do is try—"

The noise stopped me. Harold's chin slumped to his chest. The soft flap of his hair, not in its usual, careful hold, flopped over his forehead. He whimpered softly. I dropped to my knees as my heart exploded into a pile of shit messier than the one I knelt in.

"God, Harold. I'm so sorry."

"If only Carol were still around," he said softly. "She'd know what to do."

By the time the night nurse arrived, Harold and I were in his room, trying to get him changed. Nearly an impossible task. I managed to get both his feet into one leg of his pajama bottoms. The old white T-shirt with the antiqued armpits covered his drooping chest. The whole time, Harold grumbled nonsensically to himself. I was so frustrated, so exhausted, it took every last bit of willpower and patience I could muster to not get up and leave the room, leave Harold, leave the house, and hide in the comfort of my cabin, never to return. But I couldn't do that. I wouldn't do that to him. Not now.

She wore those floral scrubs nurses wear even though she wasn't in a hospital. Chunky white shoes adorned her feet, and a stethoscope hung from her neck as if a doctor might call on her at any moment.

She shook her head when she found us in the bedroom. "This isn't enough." She shook her head again. "He needs better care. He needs to be in a home."

I sighed and sat back, letting her take over the reins and finish his dressing. "Well, this is all we can afford right now." I didn't know if this was true, but getting sent to a home was the last thing Harold wanted.

"That's right," Harold chimed in.

"His condition seems to be worsening quickly. I think he should be admitted to the hospital. At least to get reevaluated."

"I'm not going anywhere!" Harold shouted. "Not without my Carol! I'm not going anywhere without her." He turned to me. "Right, David? Don't let them take me anywhere without Carol. I know you'll look out for me."

I knew then that he would never get any better. I hadn't let myself think it before. Harold would never again sit in my canoe. We would never share tea and the newspaper at Starbucks. His old car would never make its slow roll down my drive. It took everything I had left not to let Harold or the nurse see my eyes well as I nodded my head *yes* and turned to leave the room.

CHAPTER 38

I squeezed the phone between my shoulder and my ear as I swore under my breath and tried to flip my now-burning bacon. My mom's overly patient tone—not to mention her habit of calling far too early and too often—could drive me crazy sometimes. Usually, she called with nothing specific to say; she just liked to hear I was still breathing. Today, far from appreciative, I found her care grating. After my night with Harold, I had barely slept, and I felt cranky, unmoored.

"Did you talk to your father?" She said *father* in a singsong way that made it clear she was trying to sound casual when she was obviously excited about something.

"About what, Mom?"

"You mean he didn't call you? I've asked him to call you a hundred times! Uncle Bill's work—the advertising agency—is hiring a copywriter. Isn't that great news? He's trying to get you an interview for today or tomorrow."

"Today or tomorrow? I can't do that! I've got Harold." A flash of the shit-streaked bathroom filled my vision, and a new job at a shiny desk didn't sound so bad. "Could I work from home at this position?"

"Well, honey. That's the thing. You see . . ." I could almost hear my mother shifting from foot to foot. "They need someone local. You would have to move back home. But Bill says the position pays very well! Wouldn't that be great? You've been saying how you want to be able to save up more money and start writing again, and you could be closer to . . . Hope."

"But I don't want to leave the cabin. The land. Everything up here." Just the thought of doing it—abandoning Harold, the pond, and the solitude—seized my heart in something of a panic attack.

"But, honey, it's already been about a year! It's time to get serious again. You have so many opportunities at your fingertips, and you don't even realize it. So many more options than I had at your age. It might be the perfect time to move back."

"But I want to save money so I can work on the cabin. Maybe put in a real kitchen." I looked through the screen over the water just as a great blue heron sailed to the south end of the pond. The leaves were in their full change. Red and orange and yellow, so beautiful it took everything I had to ever leave my patch of land. To do anything other than sit and stare and empty my mind.

"Well, honey. The cabin will still be there. But you know you need a job. A real job. And you're such a talented writer and worked so hard to get to where you were."

"Mom, I got fired from my last job."

"You didn't get fired sweetie, you got laid off. There's a big difference."

I dropped the blackened pieces of bacon onto the plate and covered them with a paper towel. Neighbor Ricki had sold me the bacon, fresh from some fattened pig, and I had found a way to ruin it.

"So, what do you say, can you get ready and drive to Boston? Bill's boss said he would love to meet with you."

"I'm sure he said that."

"He did! Will you just go on the interview at least? For me?" That was my mother's final pitch to drive something home—the softening of her voice, asking if we could do it *for her*, and then, if we ever dared say no to that, she would put Dad on the phone.

I did have the day off from Harold tomorrow because they'd taken him in to be reevaluated. I knew I wouldn't be able to handle him much longer. "Okay, fine. I'll do the interview. But I'm not wearing a tie."

"Oh, great, honey! That's great news. But maybe you should bring a tie just in case."

CHAPTER 39

The advertising agency stood smack in the middle of downtown Boston's financial district. Suits whizzed past at alarming speeds until 5:00 p.m., when the perpetually drunk students of Boston's many local colleges miraculously replaced them.

Uncle Bill was waiting for me in the lobby with a coffee for each of us. Dress shoes made smart smacking sounds on the marble floors. The whir of the revolving glass door hummed behind me. I suddenly felt underdressed and underprepared, despite the fact that I'd opted to wear one of Dad's ties after all, an olive-and-black number that was too long for either of us.

Uncle Bill slapped me on the back, making the coffee he'd just handed me slosh over the edge of the cup. Bill took up so much more space than my mother that it was hard to tell they were related. His voice boomed through the lobby as we moved toward the row of bronzed elevators, and he swiped some key-pass thing. "A great company. Seriously, Dave. And they told me you're basically a shoo-in. I talked with the head of HR and the director of marketing. Told them all about you. Very excited to meet you."

I shrank further inside my slightly wrinkled button-down shirt. I didn't like being talked up. I preferred to start with a clean slate so I didn't have to live up to anyone's expectations. The director was going to take one look at me and realize I was just a kid. A phony who'd just crawled out of the woods, who couldn't take care of his friend when he needed him, and who couldn't hold down a "serious, well-paid" job as a copywriter to save his life.

By the time I reached the director's office, I had completely convinced myself I was a total fraud and should probably head to the nearest McDonald's to try and get a job there. Bill sat me down in a leather chair across from the director's desk and told me to wait. He slapped me on the back again, and this time the coffee—of which I had yet to take a sip—sloshed onto my pants.

I rubbed at the wet spot by my crotch, hoping it wasn't too visible. My hands were sweating. I put down the silly briefcase thing my dad had lent me, inside of which my mom had placed perfectly printed copies of my résumé (on heavy-stock résumé paper) and an additional note: *Good luck on your interview, honey! I am so lucky to have such a smart, talented son! I know you'll get the job! Love, Mom.* It was much like the notes she used to leave in my Batman lunchbox as a kid.

I felt I shouldn't be in this office with the chrome pencil holder and the clean Mac computers. I wasn't cut out for this. I missed Vincent. I missed Harold. I missed the freedom of my New Hampshire square of land.

I waited a few more minutes, seriously considering getting up, tossing my coffee, and scramming down those bronzed elevators back to the marbled lobby. This wasn't for me. I wasn't a suit-wearing, corporate type. I knew that. Didn't I? I'd thought the interview would be a welcome break, a change of venue, an opportunity to check out future opportunities. But now all I felt was guilt. I should be with Harold. I should be at the hospital. Harold was alone, without a single friend in the world save myself, and here I was, sipping on overpriced coffee in a fancy leather chair, preparing to sell myself to some corporate suit.

"David, my man, I've heard so much about you." The director clapped me on the back and took a seat across from me, behind his desk. He leaned back in his wheelie chair and smiled. This man was Bill, just in a much smaller package. I could see why the two got along so well. "Call me Matt."

"It's nice to meet you, sir. I have a copy of my résumé here . . ."

He waved a hand at me. "Put that away. Just talk to me for a bit. How's that?"

"Um, sure," I said, sitting back in my chair, trying to affect his breezy demeanor.

"Great, that's great. So, your uncle tells me you're a pretty talented writer. Is that right?"

"Um, yes, well, I do what I can, you know. I really enjoyed my past experience, and as you'll see on my résumé—"

"Couldn't have liked your last job too much if you're not still there, am I right?"

"I guess so."

Matt tilted his head back and laughed. "It's so true. That's great. I like an honest man. Not so easy to find these days. Not to mention it's common for young people like yourself to switch careers every few years. But I'm hoping we'll change that." He smiled. "So, I'm not sure how much Bill told you about the company and the position, but you would be working within our marketing department with the design team, creating ad copy for some of our biggest Boston clients. You'll put in a lot of hours here. As the saying goes, we all work hard, but we play hard, too." Matt winked at me like we were on the same page.

I simply nodded, my lips pressed together tight.

"So, I hear you've been working a few odd jobs up north. Your uncle told me. But now I want to tell you a little story. When I was about your age, a little older, I had these 'grand plans' of starting my own company, and I floundered around in my parents' basement—no money, no girlfriend, trying to make something of myself, you know? Hard to believe when you look at me now, right? But then a door opened, an opportunity came through, and I realized, *Why try to reinvent the wheel?* As they say. And that's how I got here today, realizing I can do better work for someone else."

I nodded again and smiled, not sure what type of response he expected. Matt shook his head. "Enough about me! Let me introduce you to the rest of our team."

For the next thirty minutes, Mark dragged me around through the maze of cubicles where the creative team and marketing people and business folks did their best to look friendly and shake my hand when I offered it. I was shown the bathrooms and kitchen, which boasted cereal dispensers and a fully stocked fridge of cold beverages. *We've got corporate yoga on Wednesdays and happy hour at the local pub every other Thursday. Summer Fridays and team meetings every Monday.* I nodded and pretended to jot down notes in the little pad I carried with me and smiled when appropriate, but the whole time I thought of Harold. Of his face looking up at me from that disgusting, shit-covered bathroom floor. A question— *What am I going to do?*—buzzed incessantly behind my eyes as Matt paraded me through the building, showing me what could be my future.

CHAPTER 40

turned down the radio—a guy with a soft, feathery voice singing about a girl just out of reach—and with one finger loosened the noose around my neck. I couldn't stop sweating even though it was early October and shouldn't be nearly this hot. I tried to imagine having to wear a suit every day, all year long, and shuddered, hoping my mother couldn't hear my apprehension through the phone.

"You got the job! Oh my goodness, that is such good news."

"Yeah, they kind of just offered it to me on the spot."

"Are you serious? That is incredible. They must have been overwhelmed by your talent."

"I'm sure that was it, Mom."

"Well, come home then! We have to celebrate! And, goodness, I'll need to start making up your room like you had it. Although I'm not sure how much I like the idea of Vincent sleeping upstairs. He'll track mud through the whole house!"

"Mom. Please. Don't get ahead of yourself. I haven't made the decision to leave New Hampshire yet. Or figured out what I'll do about Harold."

"I know, I know, sweetie. But that would be quite the commute!"

"I'm stopping by Hope's now to tell her the news."

I didn't find it necessary to tell my mom I hadn't yet accepted the position. I'd told them I needed a few days to think it over. "Smart man!" Matt had said. "That's a good sign. Thinking things through before making a decision. I like that."

Although we hadn't seen each other in nearly two weeks, I had explained to you how bad things had gotten with Harold recently, and I wanted your opinion on this new job. You knew far more about the prognosis for patients like Harold than I did. Maybe the best thing would be for me to take it. I'd been turned off while I was talking to Matt during the entire interview, but now that I was out of there I could think more rationally. Maybe I was closing myself down to a new opportunity because it meant change. But I did need some sort of change. I couldn't live off Harold's allowance forever, and as much as I hated to admit it, he needed a professional to take care of him now. I didn't know what I was doing. And eventually, I needed to get my career back on track.

I took a right when I was supposed to take a left on the way to your house. I was distracted. When I finally pulled down the drive, the house seemed older than I remembered it. The windows were small and dirty, and the front door hung heavy from its hinges at an angle. Not a huge stretch for you to think it was haunted.

I parked my truck and sat for a minute. Maybe if I took the job and had more money again, you and I could do things. Go away on a vacation. Get beyond the details of your past that haunted us both now. You'd never liked the idea of me living in New Hampshire anyway. I could save up the extra money from my new salary and really fix up the cabin nice so you'd love staying there.

I would take the job, I finally decided, if it would make things better between us. I needed you, and this could help us change into a couple who were better for each other.

I got out of the truck without bothering to lock it and walked up to the porch. I imagined your surprised smile at seeing me. I knocked on the door, but it swung open under the weight of my hand. "Hope?" I called out, but your bedroom was tucked away in the back corner of the house. You probably couldn't hear me. If anyone was home at all. I never remembered your nursing schedule, but I was pretty sure you'd said you were off today. It annoyed you when I forgot things like that. You lost patience with me, took it as a sign that I didn't really love you.

The lights were off, but the sun outside sent wavy patterns through the dusty windows. The home now held a feminine neatness to it.

I would leave a note for you. You would think that was thoughtful. I thought I heard a low humming sound, and I stopped moving. "Hello?"

I walked through the living room. The fireplace was now filled with unlit candles. Definitely your touch. I walked through the kitchen toward your bedroom, an afterthought addition that looked disconnected from the rest of the home. Your door was shut, but light streamed from underneath. The large windows in your room faced the afternoon sun. I wished you were home so I could hug you and hear you squeak with excitement over the new job. Over me coming home. Sort of. I would leave the note.

I turned the knob and opened your bedroom door. At first, it was too bright to see. Light bounced off each speck of dust, blinding me. Or maybe that was what I wished for. Blindness. Wished, in that instant, I didn't see what I saw. I wished it had been an illusion, a trick of the heat and the sun and the mirror and my mind looking for something that wasn't there. But there you were. Laid out on your unmade bed. Head back. Eyes closed. Clothes off.

And there was Jack—your stepdad, more or less—shirtless, his hairy back facing me, kissing his way up your pale inner thigh.

I thought maybe you called my name as I stumbled back through the house, knocking over an end table with a small pile of antique postcards, tripping on the living room rug and sending myself sprawling onto the front porch. I ran to my truck, dove inside, and slammed the door shut behind me. My hands shook as I tried, again and again, to get the key to fit in the ignition. I had to get out of there. Now. Now. Now. This couldn't be right. I was wrong. It couldn't have been you. There was no scarf. It was your bedroom, but certainly not you. It couldn't have been. It wasn't you.

If only it hadn't been for those unmistakable scars, that red hair, maybe I could have believed it. If it wasn't for the fact that your eyes had met mine for a split second, maybe I could have convinced myself otherwise. But no. That was impossible now. It was done. You had warned me, anyway. You had said, *I have to do the wrong things to feel.*

I hadn't understood, and I didn't now, either. Not really. But I did know one thing: we were over now in a way that no new puppy or apology or career change would ever fix.

CHAPTER 41

I sped up Route 93 North from Massachusetts into New Hampshire, the foliage increasing in vibrancy and color variability with each mile. The sun was bright and sharp. I kept rubbing my eyes, trying to clear my bleary vision. I sprayed my windshield with fluid over and over. Everything was too bright, turned up too high, as if in a dream. My heart raced, and I pressed down harder on the accelerator.

I remembered Vincent just then. *Shit*. I'd left him at my parent's house. It hadn't occurred to me to stop back there before fleeing back up to New Hampshire. But I had to escape. How could I face anyone after what I had just seen? After that image of you and . . . I couldn't think it. My stomach turned, and for a moment I thought I might get sick.

I don't think I will ever understand how you could have done something like that to me. With that kind of man. And to your own mother, no less.

My cell phone buzzed, and I glanced at it. You were calling. I pressed *ignore*. You called three more times, and each time I declined the call, swearing to myself that I would delete the voicemails and the photos and the messages and any other scrap or trace of you I could find. I would hit the delete button on a relationship that had crashed its way through two falls, one snowy intersection, and a million other mistakes, big and small, along the way.

The phone vibrated once more. "Jesus Christ," I muttered. I reached down to silence the call, but this time it wasn't you. It was Sheila, Harold's neighbor.

I slowed my racing truck somewhat closer to the speed limit and answered the call, switching it to speaker, flicking my eyes between the road and the phone. I moved into the middle lane. "Sheila? What is it? Is Harold okay?"

"Hi, David. Where are you? The nurse told me you were visiting your parents."

"No, no. I'm actually on my way back to New Hampshire. What's going on? Is he okay?"

"He's okay right now, but David, he's still in the hospital. Last night—"

"I'm on my way there now," I interrupted, and I ended the call before she could finish.

The fluorescent lights of the hospital and its waxy floors made me even queasier as I skidded up to the nurse's station. A big black-and-white clock ticked on the wall behind the desk.

"Where is he?" My words came out in a rush.

"Where is who, sir?"

"Harold Bierbaum. He was admitted yesterday for a reevaluation." I leaned my elbows on the counter.

"Are you family? Visiting hours now are for family only . . ."

"Yes, um, I'm his grandson."

The woman looked skeptical, but she took my name and typed Harold's into the system. "Okay, Bierbaum. Oh, actually, he's in X-rays right now. You're going to have to wait in the waiting room. It shouldn't take too long."

"X-rays for what?"

"During the night, he fell trying to get out of bed, so they are scanning his hip."

"You let him fall? Is he okay?"

It was my fault. I shouldn't have left him.

A few of the other nurses, all of whom had dark circles under their eyes and weary expressions on their faces, turned their attention to me as I raised my voice. This was not a group of people who had patience for raised voices or accusations.

"I didn't let him fall, *sir*. I wasn't even here. X-rays are down on the second floor. You can wait for him in the lobby there."

My sneakers squeaked as I skidded down the halls. White and green, white and green—the alternating linoleum squares and the uniform eggshell walls made it nearly impossible to find the right direction. Elevator Bank 1 did not bring you to the same place as Elevator Bank 2. *Check at the reception desk, sir. Check with the other reception desk, sir. Just down the hall, sir. You can take that flight of stairs, sir. Have a seat, sir. It will be a few more minutes, sir.*

I picked up the nearest magazine, something about gardening, or tools, or parenting. I had spent too much time waiting in rooms like this, in uncomfortable chairs like these. How many sick people's hands had picked up these same magazines? I wondered which one it would be—parenting or gardening—that would pass on the one virus I would never recover from. But right then I didn't even care. I hoped I got something. Something to end the dark thing lurking inside of me.

I pulled my phone from out of my pocket and stared at the screen. Twelve missed calls from you. I considered switching the thing off, but no. I had to end this now. I started to type. *Please stop calling me. There is nothing to say. You are fucking crazy. I wish I believed you when you told me you were ruined. We are done, Hope. GOOD-BYE.* I stared at the text for a beat and pressed *send*. My heart raced. I stuck the phone back in my pocket and leaned into the chair, trying to bring my breath back to normal.

I was sure of it in my bones. We were over. I didn't want to leave a window cracked for a possible reconciliation. There was no coming back from this, no unseeing what I saw. The angle of your thighs. Your underwear on the floor. I was willing to forgive you for a hundred million other things, but you couldn't convince me I was the one overreacting this time. You were good at that, twisting things so I couldn't remember where I stood in the first place.

I knew with a strong finality that I would never reach out to you. Never convince myself it was worth trying to get back to how things were between us when we were first together. I had mistaken my constant anxiety around you for some sort of lust, some desperate love that could only be satisfied by being near you.

I had to let you, let it, our relationship, go for good.

I watched the TV in the far corner for a few minutes. Dr. Phil on silent.

"Excuse me, sir. Have you been helped?" asked a woman with blue scrubs and a badge.

"This is where they take X-rays, right?"

"Yes, that's correct. Do you have an appointment?"

"No, I'm just waiting for a friend. Harold Bierbaum. They told me he would be in here."

"Oh, yes. Bierbaum. Actually, they just wheeled him into surgery."

"Surgery! Are you sure? Harold Bierbaum? Why is he in surgery? I was told I could find him down here."

"I'm sorry, sir. You just missed him. Try the fifth floor. You can check in with reception. You might be able to catch him before he goes in."

I looked around me, over my shoulder. Looking for something, someone, to explain to me clearly what was happening.

"Sir, are you okay?" she asked.

How had things gotten like this so fast? How had everything become so fucked up all at once? I needed someone, a familiar face, something, to help ground me. My eyes wouldn't focus.

"Sir, fifth floor," the woman repeated. She wore a soft look of sympathy.

I sort of nodded, and I staggered down the hall. I might never find the right elevator bank. I might die in this dreary, whitewashed hospital before I ever found the fifth floor—or was it the sixth?—before I ever found Harold. They would find me shriveled up in some stairwell. Heart attack. I had been feeling a pain, hadn't I? Some sort of deep, internal thing, like something had crawled inside me and was punching from the inside out. A terrible Hope thing. A thing sprouted from you lying naked on your bed. The back of that man's head. Your beautiful closed eyes. And all that sunlight.

I leaned against the wall, suddenly dizzy. When I recovered, I found the nearest stairwell and sprinted up the stairs, taking them two, three at a time—until I tripped. Even then I kept going, and I used every last bit of air and energy and strength and will in my body to find the door with a little 5 next to it.

I pushed through it. "Harold Bierbaum!" I yelled.

"Excuse me?" said the woman sitting at the desk.

I looked around. Was this the same floor I started on?

"Harold Bierbaum," I repeated.

"They just took him in to prep for surgery."

Resting my elbows on the counter again, I tried to catch my breath. My eyes watered, and my stomach cramped. "Can I see him?"

They must have noticed my disheveled hair and how I looked like I'd just had the wind knocked out of me—a feeling I now feared would never go away. When I was a kid, a rung splintered beneath me as I was climbing across the wooden jungle gym our father had built for us, and I fell to the ground, stomach first. The feeling I'd had on impact was largely the same feeling I had now.

"Sure," she said, "you have a few minutes to see him before they take him in. Follow me."

When I finally found Harold, I was shocked at how much he had aged since I last saw him, which wasn't more than forty-eight hours ago. His cheeks had sunk and his jaw hung slack, as if it had come unhinged in the fall. At first, I wondered if maybe that was it. He'd broken his jaw. But the nurse shook her head and confirmed. It was his hip. He was on pain medication now. Probably sleeping.

This was my fault for giving up on him so quick. As soon as things got challenging, I drove straight home. Didn't blink. Even interviewed for a new job! And maybe he knew. Maybe he could sense I had thrown in the towel, so he had, too. And maybe my last job had sensed that same thing. And maybe so had you. That I was in over my head. And you would have been right. I was in way over my head—but that wasn't a good enough reason to run home. And for what? To work with Matt in that shiny office, to wear a tie and say things like "my man" while clapping other men on the back? Or to know you were fucking your stepdad? The same slimy, denim-clad man I once stood in your kitchen with as he told me ghost stories about philandering farmhands?

My eyes stung as I watched the ragged rise and fall of Harold's chest. My friend, my poor, good friend, looked so helpless, so sad. "Harold," I said. My voice came out hinged and creaking like an old door.

Harold let out a sigh, and his head slowly rolled in my direction. "David?" He recognized me. A small miracle.

"Hey, buddy. How are you? I'm so sorry I wasn't here last

night. I went . . . home. I went on this interview. But I'm not taking it. I'm sticking with you. I'm going to help you recover from this hip thing. I hear you're getting a new one. You'll be good as gold before you know it!" It was a phrase he liked to use. *With a little super glue, these glasses will be as good as gold! I'll just wash off this [insert dropped food item] and it will be as good as gold!*

I thought of Carol's rock paintings. All those small, lonely animals waiting on cool stones throughout Harold's house. As if Harold thought of the animals too, he added, "And Carol . . ."

"Don't you worry about Carol," I said.

He coughed, opening and closing his mouth a few times, looking like a bass out of water.

"It's okay, Harold. Just rest." I laid a hand on his arm. He blinked his eyes open with deliberate effort, forcing himself to focus, to stay awake, conscious. My eyes started to well. He was so different from the Harold I'd first met the previous winter. There was so much less . . . life . . . in him.

A tube snaked into his hand, and a heart rate monitor was clipped onto his index finger. His cracked lips moved up into a small smile. I sat in the chair next to his bed and held his hand, soft as a dinner roll, and gave it a slight squeeze.

"I need you to do me a favor." His voice dropped to something of a hoarse whisper. "Go catch yourself a fish. A big one. And when you're done, come back, and I'll be out of here. Don't wait around for me."

I smiled, but the weight of my own sadness left me helpless, scrubbed clean so there weren't any grooves to sink into and hide away from the realities of this small hospital room. The reality of poor Harold's mind and body giving up on him, and the reality of a love for you I would have to give up on myself.

CHAPTER 42

You left me twenty-four messages on my phone over the course of twenty-four hours. I deleted each one without listening. Sometimes now I wonder what you could have said in all those voicemails and if maybe I should have listened. Were they apologies? Explanations? Or were you angry? I wondered if maybe there was something you had told me earlier—some clue of what you were going through, as to why you had fucked things up so completely in this way—that I had neglected to pay attention to. Maybe there was something I could have done to avoid things getting to this place.

But there was no going back now.

I deleted your phone number and every picture of you—and there were a lot—I had saved on my phone. I blocked you on social media and threw out the things in the cabin that reminded me of you: the lunar calendar you'd hung up, the book of love poems, a small painted canvas of the pond, and even the scarf you'd made me.

It would be for good this time.

I tried sitting on the pond in my canoe like Harold asked, but I was too restless, too useless bobbing on top of the water like a washed-up log. Instead, I set to chopping the tree that had dropped across the drive after the high winds the night before—remnants from a hurricane that had circled its way up the coast. The geese over the pond honked loudly, flapping against the water, announcing the start of their southerly migration.

The horse whinnied from the other side of the pond, and I straightened. The hairs on the back of my neck prickled, and I knew there was something else I was avoiding. There was too much that I had shielded my eyes from, too many realities I had skirted because I'd been afraid of the truth.

With the wind still whipping through the trees, I dropped the axe and made my way purposefully through the woods, crossing the stream, hugging the edge of the pond, until I spotted the clearing. Amelia's clearing. I wasn't thinking about what I would say or what she might do; I was on autopilot, crunching over the dried leaves, snapping the twigs that reached their bony fingers my way. Ready to face fate head-on.

This time I noticed a part of land in the back that had been cleared for a garden and was surrounded by chicken wire, and a dirty glass structure stood beyond that—something like a greenhouse. Behind that was the horse, tied to a tree. It whinnied, that familiar sound I'd heard all year, its nostrils flaring and lips shuddering. Another chorus of geese squawked a blue streak as they crosshatched the pond.

I hadn't dared venture into this part of the woods since the first day I came across it. A small fire burned in the front yard, the air heavy with charred leaves.

There was movement beyond the door, a slight creaking with the wind. Amelia stepped out from her yurt cautiously, one foot then the next, knees bent low like an animal on the defensive. I held up my hands, showing I meant no harm, no retaliation. I stayed where I was, sure any sudden movement might spook her into reacting. She held a broom in front of her chest as if in protection, but she kept walking toward me until we were only a yard apart. We stood there looking at one another for a few odd moments as she took all of me in. I felt exposed under her icy gaze. A black void in her mouth had replaced her teeth. The wrinkled skin of her face, tan and tired, sagged under the weight of her years. It was hard to tell how old she really was.

"Amelia," I said.

At the sound of her name, she straightened. She was taller than I'd realized—at least five foot ten.

How long had it been since she'd last heard someone speak her name?

"You don't look like him." The words scraped up from her throat, sounding cracked with rust. She looked at me for a second more, coughed to clear her throat, and started sweeping the hard-packed dirt walkway we stood on that led to her yurt, as if I had interrupted her chores.

"Like who?"

"Theo."

I wondered if she had been the one to find him, slumped over a tree stump, clutching his chest. A failed heart. What would she have done? Who would she have been able to go to for help?

She gazed down at the dry earth and took in a gulp of air before continuing. "I didn't realize. I didn't know you were . . . his grandson." Her voice gathered strength and momentum as the words lay one on top of the other like the careful stones of the property walls snaking through these woods we both loved. She stopped sweeping and stood to her full height once again. She was a commanding woman—the type who must have silenced a room back in her day.

"Would that have mattered?"

"Well, yes." Her mouth opened as if she were about to explain further, but she stopped herself. She stepped closer to me, and my heart rate accelerated.

"Because you had an affair with him?" My intention was to catch her off guard with my bluntness, with the shock of what I already knew, but instead she smiled a bit, as if in on some mischievous secret.

"If that's what you want to call it."

"What else could you call it?"

"Love," she said flatly. Her eyes filled, not with emotion, but with the sting of cold air on the irises. Facing me, this close up, was the shock, I realized. Her knuckles around the broom handle were white with effort. "Theo was a good man. He was strong. He had his own code and didn't let others tell him how to live."

"I'll say. He seemed perfectly okay cheating on my grandmother."

Her eyes blinked slowly, each lid moving with effort. "He never left her, even when they hadn't loved each other for years. Even when he loved me. They lost a bit of their love with each baby that never was." Her words were defiant, but her chin trembled. I was afraid she was going to cry. Water dripping from a long-dried well. I thought about putting a hand on her thin, bony shoulder, but as if the mere thought of such a gesture bothered her, she flinched, shifting her feet in the dirt.

Time slowed to the breakdown of this interaction, syllable by syllable. It was a conversation I would never forget: the way the fall air felt on my neck, the thick black under her cracked fingernails, and how those expressive eyes devoured me.

"You almost killed my dog," I said.

"An accident," she said. "I was afraid you would wreck Theodore's land. Cut the trees or build some big house. Sell the land and kick me out. I couldn't let that happen. I've been looking after it since he left. I wouldn't have anywhere to go. I saw you had my things Theo had saved, those letters, and, well, I didn't want to lose what I had left of us. Like I said, I didn't know you were . . ."

Amelia trailed off and cleared her throat again, coughed once, and continued sweeping.

Her unwavering simplicity and earnestness in her devotion to my grandfather nearly broke my heart. Since he *left*. As if still, even now, she held onto hope of his return. Maybe we never *have* another person, despite the rings or the promises or the shared lives. We only have the memories of their warm skin against our own, the rhythmic rise and fall of their chest as they slept, and the things they touched and left behind.

"And you've been out here, this whole time?" I asked.

My eyes scanned the woods, and I instinctively looked back toward my cabin. It wasn't entirely visible from her property, mirrored across the pond. I could make out the peak of my roof, the black poke of the chimney against the trees. I wondered if they used smoke signals or birdcalls or flashes of light across the water to communicate with one another in secret.

"Theo saved me when my family didn't want me. My town didn't want me. My friends wouldn't look at me. You couldn't even say the word *pregnant* back then. I had nowhere to go. And when the baby came along . . . well, it was a blessing for all three of us." Something in her face changed, but she never let go of her broom.

"What do you mean, all three of you?"

Amelia stared into my face, as if deciding something. A desperation etched around her eyes now. As if what she was going to say had some bearing on me. On her. On my ability to understand. She wiped her mouth, stared down at the filthy and withered bristles of her old broom. She took a deep breath.

"Theo's wife couldn't have children. A handful of pregnancies, but none of them stuck. She was getting too old, so we made a deal. A pact."

Now she really had my attention. I took a step closer, and her spine stiffened. "Amelia, what do you mean? What kind of deal?"

If she had any eyelashes, they would have fluttered; she looked almost girlish for a moment, the memory taking her back. "I would have been institutionalized. Locked up for who knows how long. Theo knew I wouldn't do well caged up. I am a wolf. Wild. Always have been. Some of those girls never wanted to go back to the real world after the shame, but it didn't suit me. Theo's wife wanted a baby. So we made a plan: she could raise the baby as her own, but I could stay nearby so Theo and I didn't have to be apart. Theo helped me build my own place out here." She waved her arms to indicate the expanse of her small arrangement. "That way, I could still be a part of Patrick's life, too. From a distance."

"I don't understand." My head spun as I tried to arrange the things I knew to be true to fit this new version of reality, this new version of my family's past. "Patrick?"

All at once, I remembered the trees—the Patrick trees, the name etched across the trunks in the land by my house. She had been the one, writing and rewriting her loss into the skins of those trees, like you had written yours into the soft skin of your inner thighs and, later, with a flame, across your cheek and neck.

"Patrick," Amelia repeated, "is your father. The name *I* gave him. The name no one else knows. It's the only part of him I got to keep." She nodded as if backing herself up, her eyes locked on mine. "You couldn't imagine. *I* couldn't imagine. The pain. Of giving up your baby. It was the hardest thing I ever did. But your grandfather, he took care of me. He never let go of his end of the bargain. That's more than can be said for most of the men who got their girls into trouble back then. The stories I heard in that hospital . . ."

I remembered what Harold said about Carol working in the institution, the pregnant girls. My head spun. "But my father's name is Frank."

It was such a dumb thing to say, but Amelia simply nodded

again. A small smile on her lips. She liked seeing the shock as I registered what she was actually trying to tell me. I raked my hands through my hair and spun around a few times muttering, "Holy fuck holy fuck holy fuck."

This woman's DNA, her genes, were running through my own veins.

"Certainly got a mouth like your grandfather," muttered Amelia. When I turned back to her, my jaw tense, she seemed to have lightened. "After the incident with your dog, when you didn't call the police, I figured it out. Who you were. I figured you must have known. I've been waiting for you since then. I knew you'd come."

I surveyed the clearing, her woodpile stacked neat and high by the tree line. The fire pit in the front yard. The pile of rusting tools—a trowel, a rake, an axe—leaning against the side of the yurt. "You lived here while he—they—lived there? As a family?" I gestured back toward my land. I had to get this right. To understand things exactly as they had been.

Her lips coiled back like two worms left in the sun. She was not the sentimental type. Decades of solitude had stripped her of that, of the flowery love language we read in that letter. "That's right. It wasn't easy, seeing them with him, with my Patrick. They let me hold him, nurse him those first three days at the hospital, but then that was it. I kept my word. I never met him after that. I watched him grow, sure, but from a distance. That was part of the deal. He was not to know about me. It may not seem like it, but Theo saved me. I wouldn't have made a good mother anyway. Especially not at that age. I was tough then. A rebellious child myself." Her voice was softer now, her eyes downcast, as if seeing grumpy old Theo's face in the dirt beneath her feet. "Even though she got the baby, your grandmother still died of a broken heart because she never really had Theo. And I was to blame. Well, Theo and me. That's why he was so unhappy

236

all those years. Don't you see? Having to live two lies. Two lives, really."

I collapsed into one of the rusted folding chairs by the fire. This was all too much. It was surreal. "But you . . ." I said, looking back up at her. "You're a lot younger than him."

"Twenty-two years."

The wind picked up again, and I thought I felt it. That instant and almost imperceptible shift in the air that hints at things to come. That hints of winter. I looked back up at Amelia's face and tried to search for signs of my father written there. His light eyes and heavy eyebrows.

After a few moments of silence, Amelia spoke again: "I know your girlfriend stole my ring, by the way."

I couldn't help myself: I laughed at this—rested my face in my hands and laughed and laughed until the laughter had the potential to turn into tears, not caring if they did. "She's not my girlfriend," I said when I finally stopped, catching my breath.

Amelia nodded solemnly, as if she understood the whole thing between you and me. She took a step closer, brushing her free hand against the front of her smock. "I'm glad it's you, who moved into Theo's home. I imagine it was Theo's way of making sure someone was still here to look after me. He was always tough, but he loved you all more than you knew."

"This is so crazy," I said, standing again, turning, pacing, running my hands through my hair over and over. "This is all too crazy."

Amelia grabbed my arm to hold me still, and the surprising strength running from her fingers stopped me. "That's just it," she said. "It wasn't crazy. It was love. I loved him. And that baby. But I had to let it go. I had to settle for this—for a front-row seat to watch the life I wished I was living."

She took a sharp breath in then, as if something ancient had become dislodged and she was trying to hold it back. I could see she needed me to understand, to believe she wasn't crazy. These were necessary sacrifices women had to make—giving up babies, shunning society, starting fires, even cooking up earthworms for their dutiful husbands. Because of the pressures that were put upon them. And the things that were taken away. And the unwanted weight they were forced to carry.

Amelia looked off into the trees, maybe to a spot where my grandfather's ghost hovered—wondering, I would assume, why the hell people were still talking about him and dredging up his old personal business all these years later. And I wondered how he could have done that to my grandmother and to this woman. To have left her out here, never telling a soul.

"And he loved me, too," said Amelia, sounding surer of herself this time.

Amelia was the product of a time when sexuality was repressed; when divorce, especially among the Irish Catholic, was unheard of; and when my grandfather, a sour, blistery man, loved an untouchable woman through the trees for so many years. Had she been out there when Taylor and I slung our makeshift rods into the pond? Or when we bathed in it, naked and soapy, the water up to our small waists, because grandfather thought indoor showers were for sissies?

"I'm sorry," she said. "I never meant to hurt anyone." Her voice was quiet now, but she still made direct eye contact with me. Her eyes were softer though, their yellowy whites red-rimmed. She took a step closer, still holding my arm, searching my face, maybe looking for him there. "Will you come again?"

I forced myself not to turn away, not to flinch at the musty smell of her clothes or to match her move toward me with a step back, because I knew I would. I would come again.

CHAPTER 43

The next morning, I got to the hospital as early as they allowed. I paced the hallway downstairs, drinking a too-hot cup of cafeteria coffee, the caffeine making my nerves worse off. A different woman, hair stiff with hairspray, manned the desk. She pressed a receiver to her ear, and I tried to peek through the squares of glass in each of the doors as I waited, looking for Harold. I hoped he wasn't in pain. I hoped the surgery had gone well. I hoped he wasn't calling for Carol. I hoped he remembered who I was again, like yesterday. His eyes had looked tired, and his slightly garbled words had tumbled through the pain medication over his lips, landing somewhere on his chest, but he'd remembered me.

"Can I help you?" the woman finally asked when she set down the receiver.

"I'm here to see Harold Bierbaum."

Something about the way she paused and the way the other nurse behind her stopped talking when I said Harold's name gave me that weird feeling. A twitch in my neck, like I'd entered some version of the movie *Groundhog Day*, doomed to repeat a single trying day over and over.

The woman typed a few more things into her computer. "I'm sorry . . ." she began.

"Listen," I said. "Just tell me where he is. Yesterday, the woman here sent me around the entire hospital trying to find him. I almost missed him before he went in for surgery. If you don't know where he is, do you know who would?"

Something about the woman's shoulders—the way they sort of slumped as I spoke—made me freeze. That screwdriver, the one stuck in my gut and endlessly twisting since I last saw you, had returned. "Oh," I said.

"I'm sorry," she repeated. Her next words, the useless stream of syllables, were words I didn't want to hear. Words I couldn't hear. "Are you family? Let me call the doctor, and he'll come out and talk to you."

Her mouth moved, but I couldn't connect to what she was saying. She pressed the phone receiver back up to her ear, her eyes on me, waiting for a reaction. A woman and her son passed me in the hallway. I stared at them staring at me. A man with a chain around his neck and huge white shoes came out of one of the rooms. I looked up at the clock and back down at all those white and green squares checkering the floors.

A continuous beep chirped in the distance. A hand pressed on my shoulder. A man about my height with white and black hair like a skunk and frameless glasses perched on his nose stood to my right, holding a clipboard. I looked back to the woman at the desk, and she nodded, her eyes filled with recognition and sympathy. She understood what came next.

"Are you a relative of Harold Bierbaum?" repeated the doctor.

"Yes," I lied. I didn't have time to explain to him how I'd picked up Harold at a local Starbuck's after mistaking him for an old man I'd run down with my truck and how the hours, the days, I'd spent with Harold over the past six months—talking, playing games, fishing, and sharing meals—had made us something like family.

"During surgery, Harold suffered a pulmonary embolism,

which led to a massive stroke. And, well, he didn't make it out of surgery. I'm sorry."

I couldn't tell if the man's hand was still on my shoulder or if only the imprint, the energy, of the hand remained.

"I will get someone to speak to you regarding final arrangements. Take a seat here for a moment. Would you like us to notify anyone else of Harold's passing?"

"No," I said after a long beat as I lowered myself into one of the chairs in the waiting area. "It's just me."

The doctor nodded. He had done this before, too. I'd seen it on TV shows and movies, just never this close up. "Would you like to see him one last time?"

No, I didn't want to see him. I wanted to get out of there as fast as possible. I wanted this in the past. And worst of all, I wanted to answer one of your calls. I wanted so desperately for you to be there. To be my Hope again—those small arms circling my waist, those untouchable scars, that crazy tangle of red hair splayed across my chest. I wanted you back. So much so, I thought I might break from the weight of it. And the worst part of it was, in that moment, I wasn't sure whom I missed more: you, or Harold, or that lost version of myself.

When my own grandfather died, I had felt the twinge of something, that strange force of life when you realize a familiar and constant entity has been suddenly removed. This was followed by a brief adjustment period, and then something like relief settled in its place, for Taylor and me at least, because we no longer had to suffer through the weekends where Grandpa would abash us with reasons why we were not man enough. Man enough for what? We'd never figured it out. As far as I could tell, it was Amelia and her lost child and you and your lost innocence and my grandmother and her lost marriage and Harold's wife who cared for all those lost girls in the old hospitals—it was you and them who were the strong ones, if being "man enough" was equated to strength. You were the ones who had suffered and survived the circumstances and the truths the world had delivered to you in the best way you could, however imperfect that looked. You were the ones who'd been forced to carry the weight of our mistakes.

Sitting in that waiting room, the heavy, resounding question of *What do I do now?* rendered me immobile. I thought to cry, but instead I felt filled with a total and complete exhaustion. I wanted to leave the hospital and sleep for three days straight. To ignore all the responsibilities, decisions, and mess that had filtered down to my shoulders as of late.

And then there was Harold. This sweet man, this friend of mine, who had come to rely on me. And now he was irrevocably gone, and his house and all those painted stones—what would come of all the things he'd left behind? I'd never done this before. Sat up front in the passenger seat of someone else's death.

"Sir? Thank you for waiting. I'm so sorry for your loss," said a voice as I forced my head out of my hands.

CHAPTER 44

The funeral was small. A couple of old-timers I had never met before peppered the pews. Sheila sat with her daughters and husband next to me up front. My mother had offered to make the drive north for the funeral, but I'd told her to stay home.

The church was New England quaint, but just like any church I'd visited in the past, it made my knees ache, and I felt dizzy shifting on the hard wooden bench. The priest had asked beforehand about the eulogy, and I figured that although I had not in fact hit Harold with my truck, I still owed him that much—to speak on his behalf—for being my friend, one of my only friends, up here in New Hampshire.

As I walked to the altar, I couldn't stop the undeniably selfish questions from rising within me: *What about me? What will I do now?* I stood at the podium, a small microphone leaning my way. I hated speaking before crowds, although I couldn't remember if I had ever actually done it before. The paper I held was crinkled and creased from my sweaty palms. I looked up and realized from the expressions on the faces before me that I'd stood in silence looking at my hands for a beat too long.

The crowd shifted. There was no casket. Harold had been

cremated, as had his wife. I imagined him saying, *No sense taking up extra space on this earth after I'm gone.*

"Most of you do not know me and may even be wondering why I'm up here right now," I began. "Admittedly, I didn't know Harold for that long. We met this past year. But at the same time, within this year, he became my best friend. I may not have known Harold when he was growing up, or as a young man my age, but I got to know the man he had become. Generous, caring, dedicated. It didn't matter how long we had to sit together on the water, he was determined to at least get some sort of fish on his line. More often than not, it was a clump of weeds."

This released a few chuckles from the crowd, and the vise around my throat eased slightly.

"Harold loved his wife, Carol, more than anything. And although I never met the woman, I heard her come alive through his stories each and every day. Harold also loved pie. And all food in general."

Another few laughs. Sheila tucked Maisey's head against her shoulder.

"There was never a meal he ate where he didn't express his humblest appreciation for the food before him. As far as I could tell, he lived the rest of his life like that as well—with the utmost gratitude for whatever he encountered. And now, I'm expressing my sincerest gratitude for having ever met a man—and a true friend—like Harold. Thank you."

Beads of sweat coalesced at my hairline, and the vise around my throat constricted once more as I made my way back to my seat. My eyes watered despite myself. This was silly, crying at my old friend's funeral. Wasn't it? But Harold wouldn't have judged me. He wouldn't have cared. He would have been happy to see me—his glasses sliding down his big nose, those wisps of gray hair circling his crown.

Sheila placed a hand over mine when I took my seat beside her. "Harold would have loved that," she whispered.

Her daughter turned her head up to me, still snug underneath her mother's arm, entirely unaware of what we were doing. Of what it all meant. I wished we could switch places. I wished I could be the one tucked warm and snug and unaware underneath someone's arm. In a lot of ways, that had been me up until this past year—so blindly dumb to the real world, until, for better or for much worse, I met you. And Harold. And Amelia. And with the taste of those names in my mouth, the tears came for real.

CHAPTER 45

Taylor met me at the cabin. He brought Vincent, who had been at my parents' house since my interview, with him. Much to the disappointment of my parents, I'd turned down the job. I wasn't sure what, exactly, I'd do next. But I knew I wasn't ready to leave New Hampshire and the fledgling adult life I'd created for myself here. And, as it turned out, Harold had left me some money—the remainder of the account he had been paying my "salary" from. It wasn't much, but it was enough to give me some time.

Taylor came prepped with loads of items from my mom: dinners in careful, reheatable containers; the odd decorative adornment for the cabin; and jumbo packets of toilet paper and paper towels I didn't have any room for. She kept asking to come up, but I kept saying no. I wasn't in the right mindset for dealing with my mom yet. I was still too close to it all to have the conversations she would want to have.

I collapsed onto the tree stump next to my brother's—one of two my grandfather had cut down and carved into pond-side seats at the water's edge.

"I'm sorry about Harold," said Taylor. "I know you two were tight."

"Yeah," I said. I rested my elbows on my knees and looked out at the water. "I just can't believe it all happened so fast. That everything can change so quick, you know?"

I didn't have to look at Taylor to know he was nodding in agreement. Despite our age difference, we always shared an understanding of each other that didn't need to be expressed through words. I guessed that was the primary benefit of growing up with a sibling.

"Hey, do you think the rods we made from sticks are still underneath the cabin somewhere?" he asked.

"I don't know where else they would be. Although, now I'm afraid to look. Who knows what else I'll find under there. A locked box of ladies' underwear? It's weird to think we knew so little of his real life, you know? The real Theo."

I had explained—in every excruciating detail—my interaction with Amelia and everything I'd learned. That she had been living in our reflection across the pond this entire time. That he had kept her there. And about Dad.

"And you're sure that she's, you know, our grandmother? How are you going to tell Dad? Do you think he knows?"

I took a sip of my beer, let the fizz numb my mouth and throat for a brief, satisfying moment. "I have no idea. But the way he always was with Grandpa, he must have known or suspected something. He never even got out of the car when he would drop us off, remember? You'll have to meet her. Amelia."

Taylor puffed air out through his lips. "Talk about skeletons in the closet. And I thought it was a big deal when I came out to Mom and Dad. If only I had known about all this drama!" Taylor took off his knit hat, scratched at his scalp, and pulled it back down. "I wonder if Dad knew her. Like, did she come around? Or did he ever run into her in the woods? Jesus, do you think he knows she's still right here? Alive? His own mother?" He paused, looking over the water, tucking his elbows in closer toward his ribs, probably feeling the thing I'd felt so many times over the past year. That maybe someone was out there now, watching me at that very moment.

"I think I'm going to write it in a letter and give it to him," I said, "explaining everything I know, and then he can deal with it how he likes."

"Yeah, direct confrontation is probably not the way to go with Dad."

Our father didn't like to be caught unawares. He liked to ruminate on his own before acting. We'd learned early it was always better to issue Dad a warning, gentle hints, about a potential shock—a bad grade on a report card, say—instead of springing the surprise on him when the thing showed up in the mail.

A chill folded itself into the night sky. Taylor picked up two more logs and tossed them on the fire. We usually argued over who could build a bigger fire, a more successful flame, trying to balance the logs in just the right way. But Harold's death and the knowledge of our grandmother sobered our usual competitiveness.

"And Hope?" asked Taylor.

I shook my head. I wasn't ready to talk about you with anyone. Not yet. Maybe not ever. You had taught me things about myself I hoped to never have to learn a second time. Taylor knew me well enough to notice this wasn't a button to press, a wound to prod with a joke.

"Does it feel like, you know, home, at this point?" he asked instead. "Being up here, I mean, after all those years of this being Grandpa's?"

"Yeah, I think so."

"But will you really stay up here by yourself? It's not like there's much to do. Not much in the way of nightlife or a dating scene."

"It's not all about getting wasted."

"Speak for yourself," said Taylor.

I zipped up my fleece-lined jacket. "Hey, thanks for coming up last minute." I tossed him another beer from the cooler. "After the funeral and everything, I needed to see . . . someone."

"No problem." He zipped his jacket up higher, too, as if warding out that possible future. Of living or dying alone, and not knowing which was worse. He threaded the worm on the end of his hook and cast the line into the black water. Taylor was never in competition with himself. Never trying to prove something. To win. To get that big fish. He was relaxed, and I tried to be the same way as his red-and-white bobber bounced on top of the water.

We cast lines out for Grandpa, for tradition, and that wild ability for each of us, at any point, to change from the person we were yesterday into something new.

A breeze rustled the leaves that were beginning to fall, showing their true colors. The big frogs finished their croaking for the season. The crickets died down. It was nearly silent. And yet, was that the sound of footsteps crushing branches and dead leaves? Was there a whinnying of a horse in the distance? Was that slight movement her?

"Did you try that peanut brittle Mom made?" Taylor asked. "It was nearly impossible for me not to eat it on the way up. In fact, you owe me—"

"I have to tell you something about Hope," I blurted. The words rushed out of me; I went against my brain, my initial reaction to stay quiet. I've always been good at secrets, but never with my brother. That screwdriver-in-my-stomach thing happened, and I waited to hear my own words of what happened with you, of how things ended, spoken out loud for the first time.

"What about her? Have you talked to her at all since you sent her the breakup text? Classy move, by the way."

For a second, I paused again, but it was too pressing—no,

crushing—not to get it out. Not to tell someone. "Hope and her mom's boyfriend. I . . . I saw them. Together."

It was the first time I'd let myself acknowledge it out loud. Hearing the words come out of my mouth made the whole fucked-up thing that much more real. But not saying it trapped the black, oily confession, the shame, somewhere in my throat, searing my lungs.

Taylor's face remained blank for a moment, and then his eyes widened. "Wait . . . Are you serious? Where'd you run into them?"

"I ran into them in her bedroom. In a compromising position."

Taylor tried to fight the corners of a smile from lifting, but he couldn't help himself. A laugh burst through the hand covering his mouth. "That is so. Messed. Up. No wonder you broke up with her over text!" He bent in half, tears piling in the corner of his eyes, his laugh on mute, which meant he was near hysterics. It was a laugh that always made me smile, and even now, seeing his response, it all felt lighter somehow. "Holy shit. That is the worst thing I've ever heard," he managed to get out. "Wow, your life sucks."

"Yup." I laughed with him, despite myself. "I can't even wrap my head around it. I don't *want* to wrap my head around it."

"I think it's for the best."

"Now you say that?" I said, trying to sound mad, but I laughed, too, with relief.

Taylor bent at the waist again, mumbling "oh my god" in between laughs. My abs were starting to hurt.

"No, seriously, that is the worst thing I have ever heard."

I punched him in the arm, and we laughed until our sides ached.

The sun had nearly set. The mosquitoes were gone until next spring.

"Hey," said Taylor, sitting up, suddenly serious. His eyes watched the water. "I think you've got something."

250

CHAPTER 46

My mother twisted her napkin in one direction and then the other. Over and over. There was a lot to worry about, being the mother of two sons. She worried about things like *What will the neighbors think?* And *Is the grass at an appropriate length?* And *Will my eldest end up being a forest-dwelling hillbilly forever?*

I'd invited my family to stay at the cabin that night, all four of us. I wasn't sure where they would all fit, but it seemed like the thing you were supposed to offer as an adult. They'd made the hour-or-so drive up for my annual birthday dinner. My mom had picked this little inn-type place that served red wine and lots of duck and lamb and dishes with things like lentils and fennel.

We sat on red benches in the restaurant, which had been converted from a 1700s farmhouse. The ceilings were low and the room was warm, sleepy.

"Mom, aren't you glad you have at least one successful son?" asked Taylor.

"This is only your first real job. Give it a few months," I said. Taylor had landed a job working in finance somewhere in Boston. He already had a crush on his boss. But Taylor had a natural tendency to get bored easily, to distract quickly. I didn't give him long before he began looking elsewhere, both romantically and career-wise.

"But, honey, why would you turn down that great job offer working with Uncle Bill?" my mom asked. "I mean, it just seems crazy to me. Don't you want to make a living to support yourself, and someday to support your own family?"

I sighed and rested my head in my hand.

"Honey, you're getting a little ahead of yourself," said my dad. "He better not be supporting a family anytime soon. Wear a condom, son. You too, Taylor."

"Oh, Frank! Stop!" said my mom, covering her mouth with a napkin.

"I just realized it isn't for me," I said. "I'm picking up a few freelance gigs. I think I'm going to try to do that full-time. Start my own freelance writing business. Plus, my neighbor Ricki is starting this farm-to-table restaurant I'm going to help her with."

"Are you sure you know how to do that?" asked Mom.

"I'm not full yet. Are we getting dessert?" asked Taylor.

"Of course he knows how to do it. He's my son," said Dad.

"Whose son?" asked Taylor, who had had too much wine.

"What's that supposed to mean?" asked Dad, dropping his fork.

"Mom, can I eat the rest of your lamb?" I asked, already reaching across the table and cutting the line of questioning short.

They made up excuses about why they couldn't stay—a house to clean, a comfortable bed to sleep in, weights to lift—so I returned home alone that night, a little more buzzed off the wine from dinner than I cared to admit. Before I left, I handed Dad the blank envelope with my letter inside. I would let him deal with it how he wanted.

"What's this?" he asked. "Finally reimbursing me for the thousands of dollars I wasted on tuition for that useless degree of yours?"

"No, Dad," I said. "Just read it."

"It just kills me to think how lonely you must be up there," my mother whispered to me through her wine tears as she hugged me good-bye. "That's why I wanted you to take that job. That's all I care about. You know that, right? I just want you to be happy."

It did feel different living in the cabin without you visiting or Harold to care for, but I would figure something out.

As I drove home I thought about how my grandfather, philanderer though he may have been, left me the cabin and the land for a reason. He must have believed I could handle it. That living up in those woods would somehow be good for me. And over the past year, it had become real, less of a temporary experiment and more of a home. A life.

I turned on my blinker as I approached my long drive, always wary of the cars that coasted over the hill, way over the speed limit, through the unlit streets in that area. The night was dark. No moon. I felt at peace. Happy, even, after a night with my family, for the first time in a while. I rolled down the window, listening for the last peepers croaking for the season.

It was then I smelled the smoke.

Or saw the flickering orange across the smooth water of the pond.

It was then I let out something like a scream before I started to move, jumped out of the truck and left the driver's side door hanging open wide and broke into a run to try and save my home.

After what felt like days had passed and the last fire truck pulled away, I sat alone with the wet, smoldering remains of the cabin. All my things, my grandfather's—gone. Vincent panted beside me. At least I still had him.

Arson. I waited for the word. I was sure I could already hear it hanging in the tree branches, snagged, waiting for one of the firemen to pull it down and turn it over to me. I gritted my teeth and waited. I was already blaming you, and it felt so good to do so, to pin the end of this all on you. I was so sure. This was your thing, wasn't it? This was how you would get back at me for the humiliation of finding you out, of ending things once and for all. I hated you then. So I waited to hear it. And I waited some more. But it never came.

Creosote build-up in the stovepipe. Burning soft wood like pine had caused sap to build up over the years, and it had just caught fire. An accident. That was it.

I talked to the police and my parents and my neighbor Ricki, and after the deep, shocking sadness of what I lost—and I stupidly thought there could be nothing else for me to lose—had blanketed my adrenaline and all had fallen quiet, I noticed it. Something on the picnic table. Something where nothing should have been.

At first, I thought it was an animal. A curled, shimmering, red thing. A chipmunk. Something Vincent had caught and killed. To be that still, it must be dead. I stood and moved closer. Vincent sat patiently, wagging his tail.

No. Not an animal. An animal skin, or some kind of fur. A fox tail? I stared at those deep, warm tones, and suddenly I stood very straight.

This *was* from you. That much I could be sure of. But instead of the act of vicious retaliation I had been so prepared for, my muscles tensed and ready for the fight, the blow, this was a sacrifice, an offering of our love lost. Lifting it slowly from the table, I recognized it finally for what it was: a foot of red hair, all of it, tied up with a small yellow ribbon. Your apology. Your good-bye.

CHAPTER 47

Starting from scratch would be good.
I kept telling myself this. I had been gutted and cleared out, and all that was left was a level piece of earth, a flat surface. But a workable surface, a place where things could grow. I would put Harold's money toward rebuilding. I set up a tent, and although I woke to frost, we would work until we could, my father said. Until the snow stopped us. I had already dug the holes for the footings of the new cabin. My cabin. We'd worked on some plans and researched the types and traditions of log cabins, and I'd settled on something modest, but maybe a little more livable than the old cabin.

Today, once Taylor and my father arrived, we would pour the concrete and lay the foundation. They'd both taken off ten days from work. Taylor would probably be fired for it, but he'd insisted. A shipment of wood was scheduled for delivery that afternoon. My father had also said, in a serious voice he almost never used, that *We had to talk. The three of us.* So he had read my letter. And by the lack of surprise in his voice, he must have known all along. There had been a muffled cough on his end of the line, the emotion tangling his typically sarcastic lilt. *She's still alive? Still out there? You're sure?* he'd asked. *I'm sure*, I'd said. He'd gone silent for so long I thought we'd lost connection.

Dad, are you still there?

Pause.

I'm still here, he said.

The maple-red and howling-yellow hues of my surroundings reflected in the water that flattened black beneath me. Together, Vincent and I bobbed over the still pond. I wouldn't be catching anything today. It was not what I was there for.

I'd started writing that morning in the cold shadow of my tent. I wasn't sure exactly what at first, but I surprised myself by writing this to you, *my* version of the events of our relationship. Because I did love you, Hope, probably still do, and I'm sorry. For the things I did and the things that happened to you in the past, and the things neither of us could control. I wanted to blame you; I wanted to call you crazy, to hold you responsible; but none of that was true. What's true is that we were forced into these boxes in our lives, forced behind our fences from an early age—from society, from the ones we love—without out even realizing it.

From the water, I tried to imagine what it had been like from her side of the pond. What years of almost-total solitude, preceded by decades of being cast as second-string in her relationship with my grandfather and the decision to sacrifice her own son to the care of another woman because she had no other choice, because it was the best option presented to her at the time, had been like. Or maybe I had it all wrong. Maybe this was the life she'd chosen—one of nature and solitude and survival.

The box—painted to look like a stout, boxy cow with big, doe eyes—sat between my knees. One of Carol's originals. I had a few of them dotting my own property now. For the new cabin.

A green toad doorstop. A blue jay to perch in the rafters of the new porch.

The smell of wet, burned things was strong on the water. Vincent watched me curiously. He didn't usually come out with me on the canoe—too likely to take off after a loon and tip the thing—but I needed a witness.

I wasn't sure of the best way to do this. I checked the direction the wind was blowing. The box lay heavy in my lap, all of Harold crammed inside those small four walls. I opened the top and faced west. There wasn't a single ripple on the water. A calm settled over the pond. The plastic bag inside the box was open. I took a deep breath and tipped it upside down over the water, and the gray ash and bits of bone trailed out with a soft hiss. They snaked in a slow current toward the tree line until every last bit of Harold disappeared below the surface.

He was finally sleeping with the fishes and, in Harold's case, this was a very good thing. I closed the box and placed it back down into the bottom of the canoe. Vincent whimpered, and I scratched the fur behind his ear. He licked my hand and his ears perked up, on high alert, his gaze steady toward the shore.

Amelia let herself be seen this time, leaning against an old birch. I could have sworn I saw the light of her piercing blue eyes all the way from my spot on the water. My grandmother. The hermit. The crazy lady who was not crazy, just isolated. Just afraid. Just a product of a doomed love and poverty and unfortunate circumstances. She had been watching me, must have known I was saying good-bye to someone. And maybe she sympathized, living in these woods all these years, trying to say good-bye to a man and a child she could never truly have. She continued to stare, and I began to turn away—but then I stopped, looked straight back at her, and lifted my hand in a little wave. Maybe soon, she would speak with her only son. Maybe they would meet and stand face-to-face and feel the thread that had grown between them decades before. She stood straighter, away from the tree. For a moment we both froze. Then her reluctant hand lifted into the air and she gave a small salute in my direction.

CHAPTER 48

The view was clear and cold. The remaining leaves hung on by their last breath. Mount Washington and Lake Winnipesaukee in the distance. Vincent, stronger than the bumbling puppy of last spring, moved ahead with far more energy and vibrancy than me.

"Dude, I heard Hope was, like, committed or something," Mark had said when I saw him last.

"That's not true. You don't even know anyone who knows her."

"No, seriously, I do. You know Clara's friend's cousin, Melinda? She worked with her at the hospital or something."

"She wasn't committed."

"Seriously. You escaped a sinking ship by breaking up with that one. She was one crazy bitch."

"Mark," I'd said sharply, "shut up. You don't know what you're talking about."

He had held up his hands in defense and tilted his head to eye me sideways, but he could tell I was serious.

As much as I couldn't bring myself to reach out to you because it had to be the end, it curdled my stomach to hear anyone speak ill of the girl I'd loved through two falls. But it was enough. Eventually, I had to let you go. I knew this, as you did, even though parts of me that didn't like to think rationally disagreed with a screaming fury. Because Mark was right about one thing: You were not someone to attach myself to. I couldn't hold on to someone who destroyed good things because she was fighting to make the pain she felt inside, that old scar tissue, alive and bleating on the outside. It wasn't good for either one of us.

I had learned from you that sometimes in life you need to raze the forest, cut the line, clear the air in order to rebuild and grow stronger. We both needed to let go of the past to move forward. Something Amelia was never able to do.

There are things I never got to say to you. Things like *I'm sorry* and *I love you* and *good-bye.* So this is it, Hope; this is my stack of letters. This is our story. You can lock them away in a box somewhere or not, but I at least wanted you to know how it looked from my perspective. And I didn't want either of us to forget.

The leaf-peeper crowds had cleared from the trails. A man and his son scrambled up the rock face ahead of me, where the granite gets smooth and at times slippery on the final ascent to the top. Another middle-aged woman—thin and fit, with tanned runner's muscles—stretched at the summit.

The rocks on the trail were wet and shiny. I took another photo. An orange-spotted salamander crossed my path. A real tiny one, the kind my brother and I would catch and collect and forget to feed as kids, until one day, a month or a year later, they were tiny salamander skeletons and we watched as Dad dumped our tank of bones behind the pool in the backyard.

An American flag and a small, three-sided, roofless fort sat on top of the summit. Vincent and I climbed into the fort to get out of the wind. The walls were only as high as my shoulders.

The rocky summit expanded into a view of the other presidential mountains. Vincent slurped the water I poured into his collapsible bowl as I pulled out a ham sandwich for myself. A few of the guys were coming up later that day to spend the night, to drink, to help with the building, and to pull out their musty tents one more time before it was too cold to do so. I needed space and fresh air before being social, so I'd chosen to move. To hike.

I leaned against the cool wall of the fort, open on one side to the mountaintop.

"Dad, do you think humans will ever learn how to fly?" the boy asked his father. They sat together on the edge of the summit, gazing over the lakes. A protective hand rested on the boy's back.

"The way things are going, you never know."

Vincent whined, and I poured more water from my bottle into his bowl. I closed my eyes, for a moment hearing nothing. Only the breeze scraping across the top of the mountain, a few birds overhead, and the great, deep silence underneath it.

Vincent pulled on his leash, ready to move. I was packing my things back into my bag when my fingers grazed the knife-edge of a folded slip of paper, poking out from the inner pocket. I pulled the paper out. It was folded neatly in half and had been torn from a notebook or journal; I wondered how long ago it was hidden there. I imagined your small, girlish hands separating the page, scribbling your note, and tucking it away for me to read at some other time in some other place. Your final words.

Vincent tugged at his leash, looping the end closest to his collar into his mouth. I took a deep breath and opened the paper.

In your loopy handwriting, a poem. One that reminded me of those early, irreplaceable mornings in the cabin. This was a letter I would save and tuck into a box with a careful lock and hide away for months, and years, and maybe even decades.

To love the leaf after it has fallen
what a chore to heave upon any heart
yet we do so today and tomorrow and the next
because what that weight
has to teach us
is infinite.

With Love,

Hope

ABOUT THE AUTHOR

Christine Meade is a freelance writer, a book editor, and a writing teacher. She holds an MFA in creative writing from the California College of the Arts. A native New Englander, she currently lives and writes near Boston, MA.

SELECTED TITLES FROM SHE WRITES PRESS

She Writes Press is an independent publishing company
founded to serve women writers everywhere.
Visit us at www.shewritespress.com.

Fire & Water by Betsy Graziani Fasbinder. $16.95, 978-1-938314-14-8. Kate Murphy has always played by the rules—but when she meets charismatic artist Jake Bloom, she's forced to navigate the treacherous territory of passionate love, friendship, and

The Rooms Are Filled by Jessica Null Vealitzek. $16.95, 978-1-938314-58-2. The coming-of-age story of two outcasts—a nine-year-old boy who just lost his father, and a closeted young woman—brought together by circumstance.

family devotion.

Arboria Park by Kate Tyler Wall. $16.95, 978-1631521676. Stacy Halloran's life has always been centered on her beloved neighborhood, a 1950s-era housing development called Arboria Park—so when a massive highway project threaten the Park in the 2000s, she steps up to the task of trying to save it.

Beautiful Garbage by Jill DiDonato. $16.95, 978-1-938314-01-8. Talented but troubled young artist Jodi Plum leaves suburbia for the excitement of the city—and is soon swept up in the sexual politics and downtown art scene of 1980s New York.

Love is a Rebellious Bird by Elayne Klasson. $16.95, 978-1-63152-604-6. From childhood all the way through to old age, Judith adores Elliot Pine—a beautiful, charismatic and wildly successful man—and is bound to him by both tragedy and friendship. He defines the terms of their relationship; he holds the power. Until finally, in old age, the power shifts.

How to Grow an Addict by J.A. Wright. $16.95, 978-1-63152-991-7. Raised by an abusive father, a detached mother, and a loving aunt and uncle, Randall Grange is built for addiction. By twenty-three, she knows that together, pills and booze have the power to cure just about any problem she could possibly have . . . right?

CPSIA information can be obtained
at www.ICGtesting.com
Printed in the USA
FSHW021732241019
63289FS